PRAISE FOR *LABYRINTH LOST*

A Bustle Best Book
A NPR Top YA Book
A *Paste* magazine Best Book
A School Library Journal Popular Pick
A Barnes & Noble Teen Best Queer-YA-Fantasy Selection
A Tor.com Best YA SFF Selection
A New York Public Library Best Book for Teens
A Chicago Public Library Best of the Best Book
A Los Angeles Public Library Best Teen Book

"A richly Latin American, giddily exciting novel."

—*New York Times*

"The best new series of the year."

—*Paste* magazine

★ "This work is a magical journey from start to finish…"

—*School Library Journal*, Starred Review

"Zoraida Córdova's stunning storytelling and wondrous world-building make this one to remember, and bonus: there's a multicultural, bisexual love triangle to give you the swoons."

—Bustle.com

"Córdova's magic-infused, delightfully dark story introduces readers to an engrossing, Latin American–inspired fantasy setting and an irresistible heroine."

—*Publishers Weekly*

"*Labyrinth Lost* is more like reading *Paradise Found*. Zoraida Córdova brings us a new generation of witches, enchanting and complex. Every page is filled with magic."

—Danielle Paige, *New York Times* bestselling author of *Dorothy Must Die*

"Dark enchantment in a witchy coming-of-age tale… *Labyrinth Lost* brings a new perspective to the fantasy genre."

—*BookPage*

"Córdova's rich exploration of Latin American culture, her healthy portrayal of bisexuality, and her unique voice allow this novel to stand out among its many peers."

—*RT Book Reviews*

"Alex is a necessary heroine, and this dark fantasy nicely paves the way for a sequel."

—*Booklist*

"A brilliant brown-girl-in-Brooklyn update on *Alice in Wonderland* and *Dante's Inferno*. Very creepy, very magical, very necessary."

—Daniel Jóse Older, *New York* Times bestselling author of *Shadowshaper*

"A magical story of love, family, and finding yourself. Enchanting from start to finish."

—Amy Tintera, author of *Ruined*

"Córdova's prose enchants. *Labyrinth Lost* is pure magic."

—Melissa Grey, author of *The Girl at Midnight*

"Magical and empowering, *Labyrinth Lost* is an incredible heroine's journey filled with mythos come to life, but at its heart, honors the importance of love and family."

—Cindy Pon, author of *Serpentine* and *Silver Phoenix*

"A thrilling, imaginative journey through a bittersweet bruja wonderland. I can't wait for the next Brooklyn Brujas adventure."

—Jessica Spotswood, author of *Wild Swans* and the Cahill Witch Chronicles

"An inspired tale of family, magic, and one powerful girl's quest to save them both."

—Gretchen McNeil, author of *Ten* and the Don't Get Mad series

"Córdova's world will leave you breathless, and her magic will ignite an envy so green you'll wish you were born a bruja. An un-putdownable book."

—Dhonielle Clayton, author of *The Belles* and *Shiny Broken Pieces*

LABYRINTH
LOST

ALSO BY ZORAIDA CÓRDOVA

The Brooklyn Brujas series
Labyrinth Lost
Bruja Born

The Vicious Deep series
The Vicious Deep
The Savage Blue
The Vast and Brutal Sea

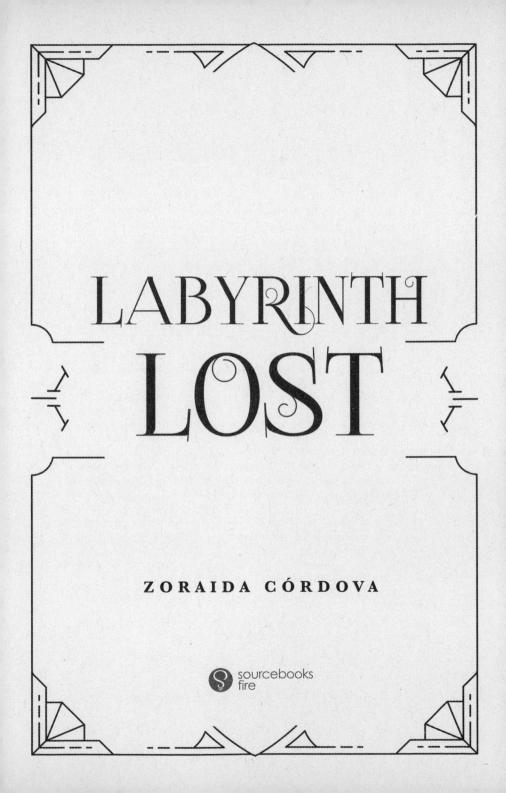

LABYRINTH LOST

ZORAIDA CÓRDOVA

sourcebooks
fire

Published by Sourcebooks Fire, an imprint of Sourcebooks, Inc.
P.O. Box 4410, Naperville, Illinois 60567-4410
(630) 961-3900
Fax: (630) 961-2168
sourcebooks.com

Library of Congress Cataloging-in-Publication data is on file with the publisher.

Printed and bound in the United States of America.
VP 10 9 8 7 6 5 4 3

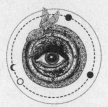

For Adriana and Ginelle Medina,
my favorite brujitas.

Mar del Fin

Bone Valle

The Labyrinth

The Poison
Garden

All roads lead to the labyrinth.
Home of the Devourer, Mother of
Wretched Beasts, Destroyer of Los
Lagos, and Enemy to all the Gods.

Look twice.

Trust no one.
Not even yourself.

STAY OUT.

Los Lagos

Bone Valle

Laguna Roja

Las Peñas

Wastelands del Este
(Forest of Lights)

Meadow del Sol

Caves of Night

River Luxaria
(Lover's Lament)

Selva of Ashes

PART I

THE
BRUJA

1

Follow our voices, sister.

Tell us the secret of your death.

—RESURRECTION CANTO,
BOOK OF CANTOS

The second time I saw my dead aunt Rosaria, she was dancing.

Earlier that day, my mom had warned me, pressing a long, red fingernail on the tip of my nose, "Alejandra, don't go downstairs when the Circle arrives."

But I was seven and asked too many questions. Every Sunday, cars piled up in our driveway, down the street, and around the corner of our old, narrow house in Sunset Park, Brooklyn. Mom's Circle usually brought cellophane-wrapped dishes and jars of dirt and tubs of brackish water that made the Hudson River look clean. This time, they carried something more.

When my sisters started snoring, I threw off my covers and crept down the stairs. The floorboards were uneven and creaky, but I was good at not being seen. Fuzzy, yellow streetlight shone through our attic window and followed me down every flight until I reached the basement.

A soft hum made its way through the thin walls. I remember thinking I should listen to my mom's warning and go back upstairs. But our house had been restless all week, and Lula, Rose, and I were shoved into the attic, out of the way while the grown-ups prepared the funeral. I wanted out. I wanted to see.

The night was moonless and cold one week after the Witch's New Year, when Aunt Rosaria died of a sickness that made her skin yellow like hundred-year-old paper and her nails turn black as coal. We tried to make her beautiful again. My sisters and I spent all day weaving good luck charms from peonies, corn husks, and string—one loop over, under, two loops over, under. Not even the morticians, the Magos de Muerte, could fix her once-lovely face.

Aunt Rosaria was dead. I was there when we mourned her. I was there when we buried her. Then, I watched my father and two others shoulder a dirty cloth bundle into the house, and I knew I couldn't stay in bed, no matter what my mother said.

So I opened the basement door.

Red light bathed the steep stairs. I leaned my head toward the light, toward the beating sound of drums and sharp plucks of fat, nylon guitar strings.

A soft mew followed by whiskers against my arm made my heart jump to the back of my rib cage. I bit my tongue to stop the scream. It was just my cat, Miluna. She stared at me with her white, glowing eyes and hissed a warning, as if telling me to turn back. But Aunt Rosaria was my godmother, my family, my friend. And I wanted to see her again.

"Sh!" I brushed the cat's head back.

Miluna nudged my leg, then ran away as the singing started.

I took my first step down, into the warm, red light. Raspy voices called out to our gods, the Deos, asking for blessings beyond the veil of our worlds. Their melody pulled me step by step until I was crouched at the bottom of the landing.

They were dancing.

Brujas and brujos were dressed in mourning white, their faces painted in the aspects of the dead, white clay and black coal to trace the bones. They danced in two circles—the outer ring going clockwise, the inner counterclockwise—hands clasped tight, voices vibrating to the pulsing drums.

And in the middle was Aunt Rosaria.

Her body jerked upward. Her black hair pooled in the air like she was suspended in water. There was still dirt on her skin. The white skirt we buried her in billowed around her slender legs. Black smoke slithered out of her open mouth. It weaved in and out of the circle—one loop over, under, two loops over, under. It tugged Aunt Rosaria higher and higher, matching the rhythm of the canto.

Then, the black smoke perked up and changed its target. It could smell me. I tried to backpedal, but the tiles were slick, and I slid toward the circle. My head smacked the tiles. Pain splintered my skull, and a broken scream lodged in my throat.

The music stopped. Heavy, tired breaths filled the silence of the pulsing red dark. The enchantment was broken. Aunt Rosaria's reanimated corpse turned to me. Her body purged black smoke, lowering her back to the ground. Her ankles cracked where the bone was brittle, but still she took a step. Her dead eyes gaped at me. Her wrinkled mouth growled my name: *Alejandra*.

She took another step. Her ankle turned and broke at the joint, sending her flying forward. She landed on top of me. The rot of her skin filled my nose, and grave dirt fell into my eyes.

Tongues clucked against crooked teeth. The voices of the circle hissed, "What's the girl doing out of bed?"

There was the scent of extinguished candles and melting wax. Decay and perfume oil smothered me until they pulled the body away.

My mother jerked me up by the ear, pulling me up two flights of stairs until I was back in my bed, the scream stuck in my throat like a stone.

"*Never*," she said. "You hear me, Alejandra? Never break a Circle."

I lay still. So still that after a while, she brushed my hair, thinking I had fallen asleep.

I wasn't. How could I ever sleep again? Blood and rot and smoke and whispers filled my head.

"One day you'll learn," she whispered.

Then she went back down the street-lit stairs, down into the warm red light and to Aunt Rosaria's body. My mother clapped her hands, drums beat, strings plucked, and she said, "Again."

2

La Ola, Divina Madre of the Seas,

carry this prayer to your shores.

—REZO DE LA OLA,
BOOK OF CANTOS

When I wake from the memory, I can still smell the dead. My heart races, and a deep chill makes me shiver from head to toe. I remind myself that day happened nearly nine years ago, that I'm safe in my room, and it's seven in the morning, and today is just another day.

That's when I notice Rose, my little sister, standing over me.

"You were dreaming about Aunt Ro again," she says in that way of hers. It's almost impossible to lie to Rose. Not just because of her gifts, but also because she speaks with a quiet steel and those big, unwavering, brown eyes. She's never the first one to look away. "Weren't you?"

"Freak." I put my hand on the side of her face and push her away. "Stay out of my head."

"It's not my fault," she says, then mutters, "*stank breath.*"

I reach behind me to shut the window I cracked open when it was too hot in the middle of the night. It's freezing for October, but a good excuse to bring out my favorite sweater.

Rose walks over to my altar, tucked away in the farthest corner of my attic bedroom, and pokes around my stuff. I rub the crud from my eyes and flick it at her.

"Don't you have your own room now?" I ask.

My mom went into a redecorating fit over the summer when she suddenly realized our house hadn't changed in six years. That it was too big and too empty and too *something*. Plus, three teenage girls fighting over one room was giving her gray hair.

"I could hear your dreams," Rose says. "It gives me a headache."

Rose, the youngest of us three, came into her powers much too early. Right now it's small stuff like dream walking and spirit impressions, but psychic abilities are a rare gift for any bruja to have. We've never had the Sight in our family. Not that Mom's ever heard of, at least.

"I can't control my dreams," I say.

"I know. But I woke up with a weird feeling this time." She shrugs, runs her index finger across the thick layer of dust that cakes my altar. Out of all the brujas in this house, I'm not winning any awards for altar maintenance. A small, white candle is burned to the stub, and the pink roses I bought over the summer have shriveled to dust. There are two photos—one of my mom, Lula, Rose, and me at the beach, and one of my Birth Rites ceremony with Aunt Rosaria.

"Lula said to wake you up," Rose says, rubbing the altar dust between her fingers. "We have to make the ambrosia before we leave for school. You also might want to clean your altar before the canto tonight."

"Sure, sure," I say dismissively. I busy myself in my closet, searching for my favorite sweater. I try to push back the swirl of anxiety that surges from my belly to my heart. "We both know she's wasting her time, right? We've done three spells already and none of them have worked."

"Maybe this one will," Rose says. "Besides, you know Lula won't rest until she gets what she wants."

Funny how no one asks what *I* want.

Rose starts to leave, then stops at my door. She lifts her chin in the direction of the mess in my closet. "Lula was already here looking for something to wear, in case you were wondering."

"Of course she was." I roll my eyes and mentally curse my older sister. When I get to the bathroom, it's locked. Now I have to wait for Lula to fluff her dark curls to perfection, then pick out all of her blackheads.

I bang on the door. "How many times do I have to tell you not to go in my room?"

There's the click of the blow dryer shutting off. "Did you say something?"

"Come on. Hurry up!"

"Well, your fat ass should have gotten out of bed earlier! Chop, chop, brujita! We have a canto to prepare for."

I bang my fist on the door again. "Your ass is fatter than mine!"

"I'm hungry," Rose says.

I jump. Knowing how our floor creaks, I have no idea how she walks so quietly. "I hate when you sneak up behind me."

"I wasn't sneaking," she mutters.

I want to get mad. Why can't Lula be the one to make breakfast for a change? I just want a nice, hot shower to clear my head. I want to go through the motions of the day and pretend like we're one normal, functional family. I look at Rose's sweet face and resign myself to the burden of being the middle child.

"Come," I tell Rose. I bang the bathroom door one last time. "And you better put my sweater back where you found it!"

In the kitchen, I grab all the ingredients I need while Rose sits at the table.

"Mom says if you guys keep fighting she's going to take your voices with a Silencing Canto."

"Then it's a good thing she already left," I mutter.

There's a cereal bowl and spoon on the drying rack and a green votive candle next to my mom's favorite good luck rooster. The candle makes the room smell like a forest, and it's the only indication that my mom was here.

Since it's a Monday morning, my mom's already on a train into Manhattan, where she works at a gynecologist's office. My mom, whose magical hands have safely delivered more babies than the freshly med-schooled doctors she files papers for, is a receptionist. That's my mother's calling: bringing souls into this world. Calling or no calling, a bruja's got to pay the bills.

When I try to flip my first pancake, it sticks on the pan. My calling is not making pancakes. Unless it's making bad pancakes, in which case, I'm on the right track.

Rose is already dressed and sitting at the kitchen table. "I want that one."

"The burned one?" I flip it onto a blue plate and set it in front of her.

"It tastes good with syrup and butter."

"You're so odd."

"That's why you love me."

"Who told you that?" I say, adding a smile and a wink.

Rose pulls her staticky, brown hair into a ponytail, but no matter how much we spray it or cover it in gel, little strands threaten to fly away. It comes with her powers—something about being extra charged with other worlds—but it sucks when you're a poor girl from Brooklyn going to a super-ritzy junior high in Manhattan. Rose even gets a proper uniform. Lula and I never got uniforms. Then again, Rose is a genius, even compared to us. Lula barely passes, and even though I'm at the top of my class, I still got left back a year after—well, after my dad. I have high hopes for Rose to do more with herself. When I went to sleep, she was still awake and reading a textbook that is as incomprehensible to me as our family Book of Cantos.

Just then, Lula comes bouncing down the steps, a pop song belting out of her perfectly glossy, pink mouth. Her curls bounce as if her enthusiasm reaches right to her hair follicles. Her honey-brown skin looks gold in the soft morning light. Her gray eyes are filled with mischief just waiting to get out. Her smile is so bright and dazzling that I forget I'm mad at her for hogging the bathroom. Then I see she's wearing my favorite sweater. It's the color of eggnog and so soft it feels like wearing a cloud.

"I want funny shapes." She pecks a kiss on my cheek.

"*You're* a funny shape," I tell her.

I make Lula's pancakes, this time too mushy in the center. I throw the plate in front of her and leave a stack for myself.

"I thought you were starting on the ambrosia," Lula says, annoyed.

She has zero right to be annoyed right now.

"Someone has to feed Rose," I say matter-of-factly.

Lula shakes her head. "Ma works really hard. You know that."

"I didn't say she doesn't work hard," I say defensively.

"Whatever, let's just get this done before Maks gets here." Lula walks down the hall to the closet where we keep our family altar and grabs our Book of Cantos. It has every spell, prayer, and piece of information that our ancestors have collected from the beginning of our family line. Even when the Book falls apart after a few decades, it gets mended, and we just keep adding to it.

"Yeah, wouldn't want to keep Captain Hair Gel waiting," I say.

Rose snickers but quiets down with a stern look from Lula.

"You can walk to school if you hate him so much." Lula sucks her teeth and purses her lips. Maks, Lula's boyfriend, drives us to school every day. He wears too much cologne, and I'm pretty sure his rock-solid hair is a soccer violation, but as long as he keeps saving goals, no one seems to mind.

Lula slams the Book on kitchen table and flips through the pages. I wonder what it's like in other households during breakfast. Do their condiment shelves share space with jars of consecrated cemetery dirt and blue chicken feet? Do their mothers pray to ancient gods before they leave for work every morning? Do they keep the index finger bones of their ancestors in red velvet pouches to ward off thieves?

I already know the answer is no. This is my world. Sometimes I wish it weren't.

Lula rinses the metal bowl I used to make the pancake batter and sets it beside the Book.

"Can I help?" Rose asks.

"It's okay, Rosie," Lula says. "We got this."

Rose nods once but stays put to watch.

"Alex," Lula says, "boil pink rose petals in water, and I'll get started on the base."

I do as I'm told even though I know my sister's efforts are wasted. But that's a secret I'm keeping to myself for now.

Lula empties a container of agave syrup into the bowl followed by raspberry jam and half a can of sweetened milk. When she's done whipping it into fluffy peaks, she moves onto the next item of the canto. She takes a white taper candle and a peacock feather. With the hard tip of the feather, she carves our intention into the wax. "Wake Alejandra Mortiz's power."

This is Lula's fourth attempt to "wake" my power. Ambrosia is the food of the Deos, and Lula seems to think it'll be a nice incentive to get them to give us answers. I doubt the gods are interested in bribes made of sugar, but she'll try anything. Lula believes in ways that I don't.

"There," Lula says. "Now when we get home from school, we have to light the candle at sunset and do the chanting half of the canto."

"I'm not sure about this, Lula," I say. "Maybe we should save the spells for a day I'm not so busy."

Lula reaches over and slaps the back of my head. "Spells are for *witches. Brujas* do cantos."

"Semantics," I say. "All brujas are witches but not all witches are brujas."

"You're impossible," Lula mutters, returning the Book to the family altar.

The kitchen fills with the sweet, rose-scented smoke. I turn off the burner and drain the rosewater into a mason jar. While Lula isn't looking, Rose sticks her finger in the ambrosia. I bite my lips to keep from laughing.

"You always claim to be so busy," Lula says, tracing her shimmering nail across the page. "It's just school, Alex. This is your life."

"You're starting to sound too much like Mom."

"And you don't sound like her at all."

"You never want to listen to me. I have a really long day. First period gym, then student council, then class, then the paper. I have to use my lunch period to finish the reading on *Romeo and Juliet*. I have indoor track practice and lab and—"

"Oh my goddess, please stop. No wonder your magic is blocked. You've got a broomstick up your butt."

"My magic isn't *blocked*." I bite my tongue.

Lula shrugs and taps the metal whisk against the bowl to get rid of the excess ambrosia. Then she separates it into two clean mason jars. "I don't know why you're more worried about school than your powers. You're going to overthink yourself to death."

You don't understand, I want to say but don't. Lula isn't the one who got left back a year because she was too afraid to leave her room and missed too much school. Lula isn't the one who's seen or done the things I have.

"I know it seems scary," Lula says, reaching over and tucking my hair behind my ear. "But this is important. Waking your magic could really bring us together. We all know that ever since what happened to Dad, Ma hasn't been the same. All we need is a little push and you'll see. You can't have your Deathday until your powers show. You're going to be sixteen in less than two weeks. It's the perfect time. I know the other cantos didn't work, but that's why we're going to try again."

Deathday: a bruja's coming-of-age ceremony. While some girls are having their bat mitzvahs, sweet sixteens, or quinceañeras, brujas get their Deathday. There's no cut-off age, but puberty is when our magic develops. Sometimes, like with Rose, when you're born with powers, the family chooses to wait a little while for them to mature. Over the years, modern brujas like to have Deathdays line up with birthdays to have even bigger celebrations. Nothing says "happy birthday" like summoning the spirits of your dead relatives.

Lula ignores my worry and keeps trying to convince me she's right. "Remember my Deathday? Papa Philomeno himself appeared. And he's been dead for like a hundred years. I went from healing paper cuts to mending your ankle that time you fell from the tree. Magic is in our blood. We come from a long line of powerful brujas."

"A long line of *dead* brujas, you mean," I say. Why do I bother? Lula doesn't want to hear the bad parts. She just wants to concentrate on the power instead of the consequences.

"You say that now. Magic transforms you. You'll see."

I breathe deep, like there isn't enough air in the whole world. I brush my messy hair out of my face. It's easy for Lula to talk about power. She sees magic as something to be revered. All I can think of is the blood and rot and smoke and whispers of my dreams. All

I can think about is the terrible thing I did. The secrets I keep from my family every day.

Lula's phone chimes three times. Maks must be outside.

"Trust me on this," Lula says. "And hurry up and get dressed. Maks is here."

I start to head back up the stairs when I hear Lula shout, "Rose! That's an offering!"

Rose is licking the excess ambrosia from the whisk, a guilty smile spreading to her round cheeks. "What? The ambrosia's a metaphor for our divine offering. It's not like the Deos are going to eat *all* of it."

Lula looks up at the ceiling and asks, "What did I do in my last life to deserve you two?"

"You were a pirate queen who stole a treasure from Cortés and then ended up deserting your crew to man-hungry sharks," Rose tells her. "We're your punishment for every lifetime to come."

Lula rolls her eyes. "Seems excessive."

I leave them and run upstairs to get dressed.

I can't believe I let Lula talk me into doing another canto. I still haven't learned how to say no to her. I'd like to meet someone who can. I know if I'm not careful, I'm going to get caught. The cantos she picks are harmless really, unless you account for attracting ants because of the ambrosia. Maybe I can stay late after school and come home after sunset. She'll be mad, but she's always mad at me for something.

I get a tight feeling in my chest and brace myself against the wall. Something feels different today. Even Rose felt it.

I can hear Lula shout and Maks press down on his horn. A cold breeze blows through the window and knocks a photo off my altar. It's a picture of Aunt Rosaria. In it, Aunt Ro is alive and smiling. Her dress is as blue as the summer sky and in her arms is a crying baby. It was a few days after I was born, and my parents chose her as the godmother for my Birth Rites. It's how I want to think of her. Not dead. Not rotting. I put the picture back in place beside my turquoise prex—a bruja's rosary—and a candle that's been burned to a tiny stub and not replaced for months.

Something inside of me aches. "I miss you. Mom's getting crazier every day without you."

I put on jeans and a plain gray T-shirt and fasten my watch. I gather my hair in a long ponytail. I stare at myself in the mirror. Sometimes I'm afraid I'm going to wake up and my magic is going to show. It shows on Lula. It makes her radiant, breathtaking. She walks with her head tilted to the sky, and a knowing smirk on her face because she can feel heads turning.

I'm not jealous or anything. Lula's the beauty in the family, and I'm okay with that. Rose is the special one, and I'm okay with that too. I'm not sure what I am yet, but I'm certain I wasn't born to be a bruja.

I grab my backpack and double-check that everything I need is in there. Another breeze knocks Aunt Ro's photo from my altar again, kicking up the dust. I'll have to clean it when I get home. Rose's altar has a picture of our father and a statue of La Estrella, Lady of Hope and All the World's Brightness. Lula's altar is the only clean part of her bedroom. It's a shrine to La Ola, Lady of the Seas and Changing Tides. Lula's got a prex made of every kind of stone, and she has all kinds of feathers and candles for all the moon cycles. She mostly chants her rezos for good grades and for Maks to stop a lot of goals.

I don't ask for anything. Not anymore.

I place a candle on top of Aunt Ro's photo, so it can't be blown off again. Then I go to shut the window but find it isn't open.

A third breeze.

I feel something inside of me stir, and I have to hold my breath to reel it back in. It's my guilt. The thing I've kept hidden from my family—the thing that makes me a liar every single day. I know the reason Lula's canto to bring forth my powers didn't work. Lula thinks my powers are sleeping.

She's wrong.

I can feel the secrets pushing against my veins, and in turn, I push right back—hiding them deep inside, where I hope one day even I won't be able to find them.

Hear me, La Mama, ruler of the sun,

levanta a la bruja, her power undone.

—WAKING CANTO,
BOOK OF CANTOS

Y ou okay?" Lula turns in the passenger seat of Maks's
car.

I nod. If I tell Lula that a photo of our dead aunt
jumped off my altar by an invisible force, she'd just make us go
investigate, light some sage, and then we'd really be late for school.
Priorities. Plus, we'd have to come up with some elaborate lie for
Maks. Or maybe not.

"Hey, gorgeous." Maks turns to Lula. "I like your new sweater."

I hit my head against the window in the backseat. Lula takes in
his compliment with kissy noises, then holds his free hand as he
pulls out of the driveway. We wave good-bye to Rose as she boards
her bus to school.

Maks is okay. Though, he is superclueless. He's been dating my
sister for a year, and when he drops her off at her Circle meetings,

he just thinks she's doing yoga. If he had any sense, he'd *feel* how amazing my sister is, that he's not worthy of her.

Lula fawns over him—his dark hair, his new shirt, the irreverent shape of his earlobes. My own sister! I miss the days when we were kids, before magic became our sole focus, before my dad vanished and took away my mother's happiness, before Lula discovered she liked kissing beautiful boys because she was beautiful too.

"Someone has a b-day coming up," Maks says. His bright-blue eyes find mine in the rearview mirror.

"They do say the whole word now," I say. His smile is contagious. "You're not texting."

He laughs, making a sharp turn at the light. Who gave this boy his license?

"Alex!" Lula snaps.

Lula thinks I'm too cold. I like to think I'm the right amount of cold. That way, no one can hurt me. If Lula were more like me, she wouldn't have such a large collection of heartbreaks.

I just have the two.

Then Maks slams on the brakes. Tires screech and Lula screams. My head slams into the back of the driver's seat. Pain flares down my neck. Car horns blare and people shout. There's the smack of hands on the bright red of Maks's car and pain pulsing through my skull.

I hear my name called from a distance. A woman's voice I haven't heard in a long, long time.

"Alex, look at me," Lula says, louder than the voice in my head.

My head feels heavy when I lean back. I squint against the pain behind my eyes. Maks is already out the door. Cool fall air carries impossible smells: deep-red blood and the smoke of just-blown-out candles from my nightmare.

At the crosswalk, Maks shoves someone. The guy we almost hit is hidden under a blue hoodie. He points a finger in Maks's face. Maks puffs up his chest, but the guy in the hoodie is bigger, more muscular, and doesn't look like someone easily intimidated.

Lula climbs into the backseat and holds up my chin.

"Focus on me," she says, snapping her finger in front of my face.

I blink a few times, then settle my eyes on her gray ones. "My neck hurts."

In seconds, she goes from my unruly sister to the healer she was born to be. Mom says Lula's power comes from the goodness of wanting to do good. Lula presses a hand on my neck. Her warmth spreads through me like sunshine. I see her and me—the thing that links us together—beyond this world and into the next.

And then my vision is clear and she says, "Better?"

Better than ever. I feel like I've been hit with adrenaline. Until I see Lula's face. "Oh, Lula…"

A bruise blooms on her smooth forehead. She presses her hand on it. "Recoil. You know that. It's fine."

"It's *not* fine." I hate the recoil, the unyielding give-and-take of the universe. My sister can heal, but it comes at a price. Mom tells her to save it. Nicks and scratches heal easy enough. But Lula doesn't listen.

"Let me worry about me."

"But look at you!" I try to take her face in my hands, but she pulls away from me. The green spot on her forehead is darkening.

"This is what we do, Ale." *Ah-ley*. My family nickname. "I

know sometimes it's scary. But we can't just turn our backs on who we are."

I scoff. "Right, and end up like Aunt Ro and Mama Juanita and Dad. Our lives are cursed. Magic is the problem."

Lula looks down at her lap. "Don't say things like that."

"Who else is going to say it?"

If I were braver, I would tell Lula the truth. Maybe they aren't cursed, but I am. I'm the reason our lives changed—the reason Dad left us. Instead, I look out the window, where Maks and the blue-hooded boy are still fighting. Lula hops back to the front seat and presses down on the horn.

"Maks!" she shouts. "Come on. Alex is fine. We're late."

Maks slams his door shut. His face is red from screaming. The impatient traffic jam starts to drive around us.

The guy we almost hit gives us the middle finger, then keeps crossing the street as the pedestrian light turns white. I watch him as he walks. He rubs the long string of blue beads around his neck, an odd length for a rosary. Then I lose him in a crowd of pedestrians.

Maks takes Lula's face in his hands. "Baby, you're hurt. I'm so sorry."

He kisses her forehead, and I count the seconds before he lets go. One…six…ten…

I tap the back of his seat. "You guys know I'm still back here, right?"

He turns to me and winks. "Want one too?"

"I'll pass. Can you park without killing us?"

Lula's back to sister-mode. Her resting witch face silences me.

Maks smirks, but the humor is gone. "Buckle up."

And I do something I haven't done in years. I whisper a little prayer.

4

The encantrix walks alone,

her power too great.

Her madness, even greater.

—THE CREATION OF WITCHES,
ANTONIETTA MORTIZ DE LA PAZ

At the steps of Thorne Hill High, Lula pulls me into a hug.

"I'm *fine*," I groan.

"Wait for me after school. We have to—"

"Sunset," I say quickly. I wish she wouldn't talk about bruja things in public. "I know. I got it."

She kisses my cheek, and I grumble because her lip gloss is so sticky it only comes off with soap. I leave her and Maks to loiter with the soccer team and race up the steps. The school's tall gothic spires cast pointed shadows across the hordes of students hanging out front. I check my watch. I have two and a half minutes to make it to the girls' locker room and then first period gym. At my locker, I quickly change into my uniform. I throw on my hoodie because it's cold.

A sharp pain pulls from my belly button so hard I drop onto one knee.

"Are you okay?" a girl asks.

"Cramps," I lie, trying to breathe through the pain. I feel a shortness of breath as my heart races. *Get a grip, Alex.*

The girl raises her eyebrows, like she's positive I should be studied by NASA, and walks away.

Today is not off to a good start. I shut my locker harder than I intended. Static pricks my fingertips like needles and leaves burn marks on the metal door. The slam echoes through the changing room, turning heads in my direction. I bend my head down and concentrate on tying my shoelaces. Girls around me snicker on their way out. Their whispers echo against the metal doors and sharp acoustics of the locker room.

"That girl is so creepy. Her whole family is so weird."

"My mom says *her* mom smells like garlic. She's like a voodoo priestess or something."

"Did you know her slutty sister is dating the goalie?"

I let go of a shaky breath. A new pain pulls at my chest. I'm used to people thinking I'm weird. Despite my best efforts at not being seen, something always calls attention. When I was a kid, my mom used to put good luck charms in my backpack without telling me, so they'd fall out at school and scare the other kids. No one likes a real rabbit's paw strung with smelly incense pouches and seashells that jingle with every step. Even now, I keep to myself, except when I'm busy making lab-partner situations awkward. I don't care when people say things about me. I've learned to take it. But I really hate it when they say things about my family. I ball my hands into fists and pull back the anger itching at my fingertips.

I exit the locker room and search the stairwell for the single familiar face that cheers me up.

"*Today*, loser," a boy says behind me. Then, when I don't speed up to his liking, he huffs and puffs and shoves me aside. He beats me to the next landing—Ivan Stoliyov, suspended for punching people and throwing a desk chair at Principal Quinn's head. He reminds me of a blond troll. I'm mentally putting him in check with a witty remark that'll never actually leave my lips when I, very gracefully, trip up the steps.

"You are *extra* coordinated today," Rishi says.

From down here, all I can see are her purple boots, two inches of lime-green socks, and the start of a galaxy printed on metallic leggings. On top of that, she wears her standard-issue red Thorne Hill gym shorts and the black-and-red gym shirt. Somehow, she manages to make it look beautiful. Rishi Persaud usually stands at five foot four, but her chunky boots give her an extra five inches to put us at eye level.

"I like your outfit," I say. I want to say something more. Something that conveys how relieved I am to see her face or that I missed her over the weekend or that I might be falling apart at the seams because I can't handle family and school and my nightmares.

Instead, all I do is dust off my jeans and bask in her calming presence. Rishi has that effect on me. She's so wonderfully bright, like when you stare at the sun and when you look away you have that spot in your line of vision. That's how Rishi makes me feel. She's about the only person in school who isn't weirded out by me, and I don't want to do anything to mess it up.

"I felt extra spacey this morning," she says, and points at her leggings. Planets and supernovas stretch around her thighs and calves.

"Funny."

"You're a mess." She bends down. Her multicolored bracelets jingle as she ties the laces to my sneaker.

"I can do that myself, thanks."

"Clearly not today." She stands back up. "What would you do without me?"

I smirk. Shake my head. She hooks her arm with mine and pulls me along, exiting the stairwell.

We walk into the gym where kids run around playing basketball and girls who don't want to sweat sit up high on the bleachers.

"Want to come out today? There's a show in Williamsburg. It's kind of a scene, but I think we'll survive."

I want to say yes. I want to be the girl who goes to concerts and hangs out after school and everyone laughs at her jokes because she's effortlessly funny and look at her hair it's so shiny... I want to be that girl.

Instead, I'm the girl with a jar of sugar and an impending magic spell waiting for her at sunset.

"I can't. I have boring family stuff."

Rishi makes a face. In the two years we've been friends, I've never let her into my house. She's picked me up, but the farthest she's ever got is the front porch. It's not like there's a sign that says, "Welcome to Bruja Land! Don't. Touch. Anything." It's that I'd be too embarrassed.

"Your life would be way more exciting if you spent more time with me," she says, dodging a stray volleyball.

I wipe my suddenly sweaty palms on my gym shorts. I look at Rishi again. Her hands are decorated with the burned-amber swirls of henna from her cousin's wedding this past weekend. She smiles like there's sunshine inside her and walks like she's ready to fly. I wish I had a fraction of that. Sometimes when I'm with her long enough, I forget about all the things I can't tell her—the fear, the cantos, the ghosts. I forget and let myself just be.

The right corner of her lips tugs upward, revealing a tiny dimple. The crystal of her nose ring twinkles with the same brightness in her rich-brown eyes. When she looks at me, I feel like she's seeing right through me. Like she knows I'm hiding a big part of myself.

"What?" My stomach flutters and I fidget with the hem of my uniform shirt.

"There's something you're not telling me."

My cheeks burn. There are lots of things I'm not telling lots of people. Rishi. My sisters. My mother. Even myself. Sometimes I'm afraid I've put on so many masks that one day I won't be able to recognize who I am. Still, I smirk to play it off because I can't think of any other way to be.

"I didn't finish reading *Romeo and Juliet*," I say.

"Alex, you know I'm totally psychic. You won't be able to hide from me much longer."

That makes me smile. "Of course you are."

"Speaking of psychics," she says, "they're supposed to have a bunch at the Ghoul Ball next weekend. Do you have a costume yet?"

"Can't I just go as a really stressed-out high school sophomore?"

"Alex, you are not allowed to bail on me. If you're not having a birthday party, then we will celebrate early with a thousand strangers."

"I'll be there." Damn, my guilt is at an all-time high today. First my family. Now Rishi. Since I can't invite her to my house, I lied and told her there'd be no birthday party at all.

"Want to walk around the track?" Rishi starts to stretch. The gym teacher isn't here yet, as evident by most of my classmates sitting around on their phones and a handful of guys failing to slam-dunk basketballs.

I start to follow Rishi out of the gym when I hear, "Duck, you freak!"

I don't generally answer to "freak," but I want to see the source.

When I turn around, Ivan is holding a volleyball over his head. He throws it as hard as he can in our direction. I hold my arms up as a shield, but it wasn't meant for me. The ball slams into Rishi's face. Her head snaps back and the force of it knocks her on the floor.

Ivan holds his belly and laughs. Some kids laugh with him. Others are too embarrassed for Rishi to say anything, so they look away.

"Dick!" Rishi shouts at him. A tiny trickle of blood starts to flow from her nose.

"Are you okay?" I ask, even though it's a stupid thing to ask. Of course she's not okay. She wipes the blood away with the back of her hand, but it starts to gush down her face. I unzip my hoodie and press the fabric to her nose.

Anger flashes through me. I feel a tick in my neck and an itch in my palms. I turn around to face Ivan. He picks up another ball and gets in my space. I feel his energy, dark and hateful, brush

27

against my own. Then, his eyes flash red for a second. I step back. Something is wrong. The feeling twists in my gut.

"You got a problem?" Ivan asks. "Want to get messed up like your little girlfriend?" He slams the ball into my shoulder.

"*Stop*," I shout. My hands are shaking.

"Make me." He won't back down.

I take a step toward him, but Rishi stops me.

"Alex," Rishi says. Angry tears spill from the corners of her eyes. "Help me up."

She holds out her hand. It's covered in blood. Ivan moves to grab my wrist, but I push him as hard as I can. I feel my head spin at the sight of Rishi's blood. I shut my eyes to make the dizziness go away, but I see the warm, red light of my dream again. The rotten stench of dead flesh fills the air. Then, I hear the last words my dad ever spoke to me. "*Sh, my darling. Everything will be okay.*" He lied. Nothing would ever be okay—not truly.

I close my eyes. *Remember to breath. Remember to pull the tide back. Remember to keep it buried.* But there's something else there, struggling to break free again. Just like last time. Dread digs into my chest and won't let go. I feel a swell in my heart, and when I look down at my hands, they're covered in blood. The wind is knocked out of my lungs. Something breaks inside of me and I can't hold on anymore.

My magic slips.

My ears pop and adrenaline rushes through my veins. I wait for something to shatter or move, but instead, Ivan falls on his hands and knees, choking. The head of a black snake slithers from his mouth, flicking a bright-red tongue.

Ivan makes a final, terrible gagging noise, and then the whole snake is out. It slithers across the waxed gym floor between feet that run for the exits. Piercing screams fill the air as Ivan shivers and collapses. The snake grows bigger by the second, like it feeds off the people screaming. When there's no one left in the gym but the three of us, the snake darts for Rishi.

"No!" I shout.

The snake freezes, turns its head in my direction. That red tongue flicks at me. It nods. It *knows* me. Then, the snake slithers out the door and into the halls.

"Alex." Someone calls my name. I turn around but no one is there.

"Who's there?" I whisper. The temperature in the room drops.

"We need to go!" Rishi holds her bloody hand out for me to take.

But there's that voice again. I fall backward onto the gym floor. I can hear the rush of waves, the crackle of static. Rishi tries to help me stand. I stare at her fingers. Pink nails. Brown henna. But then she's gone as Aunt Rosaria appears between us.

"Alex, what's wrong?" Rishi shouts.

I crawl backward, my insides clenching and twisting painfully. *Recoil.* My skin burns from the inside like there's fire in my veins. Aunt Rosaria's open lips are a black hole, but the sound is lost. She grabs her throat with one hand and points at me with the other, a long, accusatory finger. I hold up my arms to shield myself from her. My magic slips defensively. The blast sets off the sprinkler systems. It shudders the windowpanes. It fills the air with the howling winds of a storm. Magic flares in my veins, and I panic, pulling it back like a lifeline that is slipping from my fingers. Aunt Rosaria starts to fade into the shadows, my name the last word on her cold, dead lips.

5

The Deos created the brujos and brujas.

Bless our kind, vessels of their Eternal Gifts.

—FROM THE JOURNAL OF
PHILOMENO DE LAS ROSAS

I run all the way home. The last thing I heard before I took off was Rishi and Lula looking for me in the throng of students. I went out the side door and bolted down the street. I realize running from this is like trying to outrun the sun. Sometimes I feel like all I want to do is run. Sometimes I wonder what it would be like if I never stopped.

When I get to my street, I slow down. Sweat drips from my temples and down my nose. My muscles burn down to the core. I run into my house. I press my head against the kitchen door until I stop shaking. I practice my breaths like Mrs. Castellano, my guidance counselor, once told me, "If you hold your breath, Alejandra, your panic attacks will get worse. Breathe and you will see how much easier it is to make sense of your emotions."

She was wrong then and she's wrong now. There is not enough

air in the world to calm me down. So I do the only thing that makes me feel better—I clean. I attack the dishes with soap and a sponge. I run the soapy dishes under water. I place them on the drying rack so hard I break one. I grip the sink and try to rationalize today's events.

I couldn't have done that to Ivan. It had to be Aunt Ro's ghost. But why would she do that? Why would she point at me? Aunt Rosaria hasn't shown herself to any family member since her death. Not even on the night of the Waking Canto. My mother's circle blamed me. I broke the enchantment with my midnight appearance. They would never find the true reason for my aunt's death. They're afraid she's lost to the realms beyond the veil. But if she's lost, why appear to me when I didn't even summon her?

The back door slams shut.

"Why didn't you wait for me?" Lula asks. She drops her backpack and stares at me. Her face is a mixture of awe and glee.

She knows.

"Too many people," I say, turning up the water even though it's already sloshing over the sink and onto the floor. She lets me wallow in my guilty silence. "What happened to Ivan?"

She walks across the kitchen and leans against the wall beside me. Her cool, gray eyes watch as I scrub away the remnants of chicken parm from two nights ago.

"Oh, he's fine. Animal control had the snake cornered, and then it did the most curious thing."

"What?"

"It vanished into smoke. *Poof.*"

I chance a glance at Lula. Her curls are wild and her pouty lips glisten pink. Then I look at myself in the mirror on the kitchen wall: tangled, sweaty hair; bags from sleepless nights under my big, brown eyes; the sickly green pallor to my tan skin.

Lula lets out an excited squeal and hugs me. She bounces up and down, then leaves a sticky kiss on my cheek.

"How did you do it?" she asks.

I shake my head. I rinse the plate in my hands. I grab for another glass to clean. I breathe. And breathe. And breathe. And Lula bounces around me, doing a bruja dance of joy.

"Do you know what this means?"

"Rose gets to eat all the ambrosia?"

"Smart-ass. This means the three of us finally have our powers!" If she had peacock feathers, they'd be proudly displayed. "This is huge! Think of the things we could do. Why aren't you more excited?"

"Because I made a snake come out of a boy's throat!"

"You *conjured*, Ale! I mean, he'll probably have nightmares for a few nights, but the snake disappeared when you did. What did he do to you?"

He broke Rishi's nose. He attacked me. He had the same red eyes Miluna had on the day...

"I wonder the extent of your powers." She keeps going, pacing around the kitchen table. "Maybe you'll learn to heal, like Ma and me. Pa could control weather a little. Do you remember? Before his disappearance—"

"Dad *left*," I shout. The glass cracks in my hand. "He *left* us."

Lula stops her frantic pacing. I stare at myself in mirror again. *You are* not *a bruja. You are a girl who needs to get far, far away, where the blood dreams can't follow.*

"You don't know that," Lula says. Her bottom lip trembles and her stormy-gray eyes are glossy with tears.

But I do know that. I was there.

Everyone has a theory of why Patricio Mortiz, benevolent brujo and loving family man, disappeared without a trace. Some think my father was taken by the kind of people who still hunt people like us. But there was no struggle or ransom note. I know in my heart that he left because of the magic inside me. No matter how much I try to forget, the memory floats on the surface of my mind.

It was an accident. Back then, I repeated that like a mantra.

I was ten years old and suffered from nightmares and paralyzing headaches. No one could figure out what was wrong with me. My parents' Circle came over one day and bathed me in seawater and rubbed ashes on my face to scare away the ghosts. But it wasn't ghosts. It was something inside that wanted to rip me in half to set itself free.

One day, the pain was so bad I stopped going to school. I was alone in the house. Something woke me, a voice calling from the shadows. Claws scratched against the wooden floor. Miluna prowled toward me, her paws trailing ragged, black shadows. Her normally green eyes were red as rubies, and her pearly white teeth were bared and covered in yellow froth.

It was an accident. I repeat it still.

Miluna attacked me. I raised my hands in defense, and the magic coiled in my heart was unleashed. I saw ribbons of red and flesh. Then, I remember darkness and, for the first time in a long time, relief. I woke to my father shouting my name. "Alejandra, Alejandra, are you okay?" He picked me up and carried me to the couch. My body shook with recoil. My veins buzzed with freed magic.

I cried and screamed and my father held me tighter. He brushed my hair back and kissed away the tears on my cheeks. He cleaned the blood on my hands and face.

"Everything will be okay," he said, but I could see the fear darkening his gray eyes. I will always remember the way he looked at me, as if he didn't know who I was. "Miluna was possessed. She didn't know it was you. There are bad things in this world, Alejandra. They hurt people like us. I'll take care of it. I promise. It'll be our secret, but you can't tell a soul. Do you swear it?"

"I swear it," I cried. I clung to him, but he pulled away. Wouldn't look into my eyes.

"Sh, my darling. Everything will be okay."

He ran outside. From my window, I could see him digging a small grave. I told myself my dad would make things right.

When I woke up again, he was gone, and I knew it was because of me. My own father was afraid of me. I pulled my magic deep inside and kept it there. Our secret.

Now, in our kitchen, Lula gasps. My whole body tenses with magic.

"Alejandra," my mom says.

I hadn't even heard her come in. The door is wide-open, letting in the cold.

My mom presses her hands against her mouth. "Oh, my sweet girl."

When I look up, I see what I've done. Everything—the dishes and the beads of water and soap on them, the flower pots, the jars of pickled chicken feet and frog eyes. The vials of cooking spices, the chairs, the frames on the walls, the fruits, and the collection of good luck roosters on the kitchen sill. Even the ends of Lula's hair.

All of it. All of it is floating around me.

In a heartbeat, my mom drops her shopping bags. The air is thick, like a steam room. Then she puts her hands on my face. "Mi'jita," she says. *My little daughter.* "Don't worry. Everything will be okay."

I've heard that before, and I know it isn't true. Then, like the fall of our tears, everything I've done comes crashing to the ground.

Father, my father, my light through the dark,
my soul and my hope and my path to embark.

—REZO DE EL PAPA,
BOOK OF CANTOS

SOMETHING IS WRONG AND YOU'D BETTER TEXT ME.
NO CALL ME.
SILENCE WILL GET YOU NOWHERE.
IF YOU DON'T CALL ME, I'M COMING OVER AND YOU
  BETTER LET ME IN.
…ARE YOU OKAY? I HAVE ALL THE WORRIES.

All texts from Rishi over the last two days.

For the first time in six years, I skip school. My mom is so busy planning my Deathday ceremony that she *lets* me. Rishi stopped by this morning and Lula took my homework from her but said I was sick and sleeping. Sometimes I want to tell Rishi the truth. I wonder if she'd be surprised or scared or even believe me. Rishi likes her days with a side of weird. Lula reminds me we're discouraged from revealing ourselves. Otherwise, she'd tell Maks in a heartbeat. Our uncle Harry married a human who died when she tried using his Book of Cantos to make herself younger.

I'm in the car with my family, I start to type. We're getting supplies for my magical birthday ceremony. BTW, I'm a witch.

Then I delete it and retype. I'll explain. I promise.

Lula turns around in the front seat. She tries to grab my phone, but I yank it away. "Is that Rishi?"

"Why?"

"Just kidding. Who else would it be?"

"Lula," my mom warns. "Be nice."

"I'm just saying."

"Better than the whole swim team having my number," I hiss so just Lula can hear me. If looks could kill, I'd be dead for three lifetimes.

"Too bad you can't invite her," Lula says, "so at least you'd have one friend there."

I sink in the backseat and watch the Brooklyn brownstones pass by. A few blocks later, we get to a row of shops that look so old a really good East River gust could cave them in. At a red light, my mom dabs her lipstick on, then rubs her lips together to smooth it out. The plum color brings out the beautiful gold undertones in her brown skin, the freckles around her cheeks that look like constellations. She closes the visor, caps the lipstick, and hands it to Lula. She copies Ma's exact lipstick application. Lula's wild curls are extra scrunched and smell like rose oil. Her skin shines from her homemade coconut milk and brown sugar scrub. I think I still have eye crud in my eyes from this morning.

"Oh, relax," Lula tells me. "I'm just playing."

She keeps the visor down, so I can see her resting witch face. She's mad that I levitated the whole kitchen because she's always wanted a physical power. She wouldn't even help me clean up after. Rose nudges my arm and gives me one of her calming, close-lipped smiles. Fine, I'll play along for Rose.

Mom parallel parks in front of Miss Trix, a rundown shop located on the only undeveloped street of Park Slope. A wind chime made of mismatched shells greets us in the funky-smelling botanica. Normally, buildings have vines crawling on the outside brick. Here, the vines have made their way into the shop, as if they're eating the store from the inside out.

Mountains of books balance in precarious stacks, because Deos forbid you need the book all the way at the bottom. The windows are caked with dust, and spiders have erected a web metropolis on every available corner. There's a giant caiman bolted to the ceiling, like it's swimming in the middle of a swamp. It's yellow eyes look so alive, even though Lady swears it's as dead as her first husband.

I turn around and come face-to-face with the pickle wall. Rose picks up a jar of human eyes, each one with a different color iris. A blue one moves around of its own volition.

"I don't like him," she whispers, setting the jar back on the shelf.

"What's not to like?" I ask.

Lady, the storeowner, Alta Bruja of the Greater New York area, and my aunt by marriage, greets us with a smile.

Her dark laugh makes me think of cigarettes being crushed into an ashtray. "Don't mind the eyes, Rosie. They can't hurt anyone from in there."

The fringe on her clothes bounces when she waves. Her black lipstick makes her mouth look like a bruised plum. She stands behind the register, a rickety, black metal thing with large, white buttons for the numbers. It probably survived the Coney Island fire of 1911.

Lady has always been an enigma to the younger generation of brujas. Only the Viejos know her real name. After her second husband died trying to make the journey back to Cuba, she married an aunt on my dad's side. She became part of our community and teaches the younger brujas everything, from our history to magic realms to cantos. Lula and her Circle have a bet about how old Lady really is. They've guessed everything from thirty to ninety-one. When we were little, I had a theory she was a vampire, but Lady likes browning under the sun like Sunday bacon.

"Alejandra, come here." Lady refuses to call me Alex. She says the Deos don't take kindly to false names. I just hate the way some people say "Alejandra." It's like trying to say it right makes their tongue have a seizure.

I try to blend into the corner of dusty books, but when I don't move, Lady makes a beeline for me. She grabs my hand and spins me in place. Then she traces the map of lines on the palm of my hand. She grabs my chin, and one of her long, black nails digs into my skin. I try to pull back, but she holds on harder. Her dark eyes widen.

"You have it." Her deep voice is soft as smoke. "It" makes me think I've been diagnosed with some incurable plague. "An encantrix, like Mama Juanita. The highest blessing of the Deos."

"What?" I shake my head. I can't be an encantrix.

Lady turns to my mother. "Carmen, did you know?"

"It's been two generations since one appeared in the family," Mom says. "I thought the gift was lost. Mama Juanita—she could do everything. Command the elements. Heal the sick. Speak to the dead. She wrote her own cantos. And she made the best sopa de pollo in all of Brooklyn."

"Didn't she get struck by lightning?" I ask, moving from denial and on to panic.

Lady waves her hand in the air, dispelling my worries. No big deal. It's only *lightning*.

"How do you know that's what I am? I just made a few things float." I also made a snake of smoke come out of a boy's throat... I also killed Miluna. I made my father leave us. That's not a blessing. That's a curse.

"You're a late bloomer, mi'jita," my mom says.

"Our magic isn't as strong as it was when we were free to practice." Lady crosses her arms over her chest, and her long, fringe shawl dances around her. "Nowadays, some brujas are lucky if they can make a pencil float, even with years of practice. Some can only see the future in two-minute intervals. Some can only heal shallow cuts. The gifts of the Deos get weaker with each generation. That's why you are so very curious. What you did—what your mama told me—that's physical. That takes *power*. Only an encantrix has that kind of power. You might be a great one."

A feather falls from somewhere and brushes my skin. I take a step back, knocking against an armoire. The knob digs into my spine. I try to turn around to hold the structure steady, but a small, bleached skull falls off and smashes on the ground.

"Encantrix or not, you'd better clean that up," Lady says. She points to the black velvet curtain that leads to the back of the store. Lula scoffs and tries on a prex made of sparkling crystals, and Rose mutters something to the mounted head of a jackalope. My mom goes over the list of things we need for my ceremony with Lady.

I rush to the back, where she keeps the cleaning supplies. There's a door painted dark purple. At eye level is an etching of a golden sun and silver moon for La Mama and El Papa. The sun is crowned by the sideways crescent of the moon. It's the same moon I wear as a necklace, a gift from my father. I trace the painted symbols on the door. Directly below the sun is a gnarly-looking tree with thin, stringy leaves.

"Encantrix." I sound the word out.

The seashell wind chime snaps me out of my thoughts. I grab a broom and dustpan and head back out to clean up the mess I made. Some of the bone dust gets up in my nose and makes me sneeze.

"Gross," I mutter, dumping the contents in the garbage can near the register.

"Gross yourself," he says.

A guy, possibly around Lula's age but trying to look older, stands on the other side of the counter. He's got brilliant diamond stud earrings and a fresh, buzzed haircut like the boys around the block. I find myself staring. His hands are covered in tattoos, like he dipped his arms in solid ink up to his wrists. From there, the ink continues in swirling lines, like jellyfish tendrils drifting on the sea of his light-brown skin.

Thick, dark lashes fringe his eyes, which can't decide between green and blue. When he sees me, he smiles, revealing a tiny dimple, like a comma at the edge of his mouth. He licks the cold off his full lips. Touches his necklace. Blue beads like a long rosary. A prex.

My face burns when I realize this is the same guy we almost ran over the other day.

He grabs a few things on the way to the counter. I should probably go to my mother, but I don't want to deal with Deathday things. So I stay put and try to ignore the guy's presence, even though he seems to take up the whole room with the way he walks right up to me. He sets a red votive candle, some dove feathers, and a jar of tongues on the counter. The tongues swim in the murky, green liquid like they're mocking me. I flick the bell at the register to let Lady know she's got a customer.

"I'll be right there," Lady shouts from the front of the shop.

I put the broom and dustpan in the back. When I return, he's still standing there. Again, he smiles when he looks at me.

"What?" I ask. I wonder if he's aware of how his stare makes me want to turn around and run.

"You look familiar."

"I just have that kind of face."

"No, you don't," he says, smirking. "I *remember* you. Red Civic. Riding with that pretty boy that wore too much cologne."

"Sorry about that."

"You weren't the one driving." He crosses his arms over his chest, making his muscles more pronounced. It makes his tattoo appear like it's moving. The ends of the inky tendrils stop at the finest points.

"My eyes are up here," he says, making a *V* with his middle and index finger and points them at his eyes.

I've never seen a boy with such strange-colored eyes, let alone a permanent wrinkle between his brows, like he spends more time frowning than anything else. I ring Lady's bell a few more times.

"Deathday shopping?" he says, smirking. "You look excited."

"How'd you know?" I ask, matching his sarcasm.

"Overheard your mom. I'm Nova, in case you were wondering."

"I wasn't." The pads of my hands itch. It's like the magic I've tried to push back so long has gotten a little bit of freedom and now it wants more. It coils inside me at the base of my belly and spreads. I take a deep, calming breath and push it back. "Shouldn't you be out jaywalking?"

He laughs, then leans close to me, so I can see the dip between his brows is not a frown mark but a thin scar. And it's not just there. He's got three more matching nicks, one on each cheek and the last on his chin, like the cardinal points of a compass.

"Most girls get pumped for their Deathday."

"Yeah, *you* know what a bruja wants."

"Not really. I just guess until I get it right." His smile falters, but not for long. "It's okay to be scared. You just have to do your part and welcome your dead. It's tradition."

"It's not fair," I say. I don't know why I say it. It just came out. He's a stranger. But sometimes it's easier to confide in strangers than the people who love us. "It feels like I don't have a choice in my life."

"You could always not do it."

I can't really tell if he's joking, but I can't deny the little spark of hope that fills my heart. Every bruja and brujo I know has had their Deathday.

"How?" I hope I don't sound too eager.

He shrugs. "I'm sure you're not the first witch in history to fear her own strength. Sorry to break it to you, brujita." *Little bruja.*

"Didn't you hear? I'm superspecial. I'm an encantrix." Why did I admit to that? A second ago I wanted to deny it.

His eyes brighten with surprise, then appraisal. "Good for you."

"I'm not sure 'good' is what I was going for."

"Well, you only get one Deathday."

"Except the actual day we die."

He chuckles, and it makes his face look softer. "That's a little morbid, even for me."

I rest my hands on the cool glass. He leans closer to me. His eyes are bluer now. Smoke from the sage bundle burning in the corner descends around us. "I think it's sweet that you're nervous."

"That doesn't answer my question. How?"

"Well, I usually charge for my wisdom." He raps his knuckles on the countertop.

I doubt he's the kind of person who would give me a straight answer. I think he likes to hear himself be charming and clever. Then again, I don't really know what kind of person he is at all. But I can't exactly ask my mother or sisters or my best friend, so a stranger is going to have to do.

"Look," he says, "if there are cantos for raising the dead and making it rain, then there should be something for stopping your Deathday. That is what you're talking about, right? I mean, I wouldn't do it because you don't know what the recoil might be or the effects it could have. *You* shouldn't do it because you don't seem like you know the first thing about performing a canto and might set your house on fire. No offense."

"How is that not offensive?" I'm filled with the urge to turn him into a slug. Then I lose my spark when I realize he's right. I wouldn't even know where to begin.

What *do* I want? To stop my Deathday? That's only half the problem. I'd still have this magic inside me. Magic killed my aunt Rosaria and Mama Juanita. My magic killed Miluna and set my father running. I could've hurt Rishi the other day. It destroys. I wonder...

"I'm saying. Just 'cause you can doesn't mean that you should."

"You don't know my reasons."

He grins slyly. "I don't have to. If you want to compare the monsters in our closets, I'd win by a landslide. Besides, I don't care what you do. I just figured I'd give you a little warning."

"Why?"

His blue-green eyes flick from my lips to my clavicle. "I'm a nice guy."

I snicker. "Okay. Where would you start?"

Nova looks over his shoulder where Lady and my mother are comparing the benefits of different bushels of sage. My sisters are in a corner giggling probably because this is the longest I've voluntarily talked to a boy my own age.

Nova leans in closer to me. I look at the in-between colors of his eyes—they're like the shades of Caribbean seas—and hate that someone so cocky is so pretty.

"Listen, Ladybird," he says, "the ceremony happens whether you want it to or not. But if you reject your blessing, it'll have an effect on your power. The whole point is that the ceremony makes your power stronger but easier to contain."

"If I wanted a lesson on spells, I'd talk to Lady."

He makes a face. "Spells are for—"

"Witches, I know the drill."

Nova laughs and raises his hands. "Fine. Every Book of Cantos has something to block negative forces. My grandmother uses them on her bakery, so she doesn't get bad reviews. You can probably use the same to block the blessing of your ancestors. But you'd be foolish to try. You don't know what could happen."

"What if—" I bite my tongue. Nervous sweat accumulates between my shoulder blades. "What if I wanted to get rid of it?"

"I already told you it's too late to stop the party without getting your moms pissed."

"No," I whisper. "Get rid of the magic."

"Oh. Damn." Nova stares at me. I hate that it makes me feel exposed, judged even. I can practically feel his thoughts racing. Would he tell Lady? Perhaps I'm not special in feeling this way, like I'm in a body that doesn't fit quite right, but saying the words aloud makes me realize that, maybe, I can change my fate.

Nova raises an eyebrow and shakes his head. A fat vein in his throat jerks when he tenses. I decide I don't care what he thinks of me. He doesn't exactly look like a saint.

He rings the bell on the counter and says, "Then I don't think I'm the person who can help you."

Finally, Lady makes her way to us with my mom. I get shooed away from the register.

"What are you planning, Trouble?" Lady asks Nova.

47

For a moment, I'm afraid he's going to rat me out. Nova winks at me and that dimple appears, like we weren't just discussing a bruja's greatest family betrayal. I go stand beside my mother. She looks at Nova, trying to place him. Surely all the brujos and brujas in the tristate area know each other. She tells me all the time that there are so few of us left and our connections matter.

"Look at that face," she whispers to me, like we're schoolgirls.

"*Ma.*"

Nova smiles—no sarcastic laugh, no mocking twitch of the lips. Just a smile. His dark hair is shaved short, so all you focus on are his cheekbones and lips and lashes.

I take the list from my mom's hand. Everything is crossed out except for one: blood of the guide. I shut my eyes and think of Lula's Deathday. We strung white fairy lights in the yard and spent all night hot-gluing sparkles on her midnight-blue dress. I glued my fingers so many times that they were raw and bloody. I probably bled as much for her Deathday as the sacrificial dove. If I think on it, I can see Lula's slender hands holding the dove, red dots smattered all over her perfectly calm face.

Lady punches numbers into the register. "Love canto? Finally met one you couldn't charm with your pretty green eyes."

In this light, they're more blue than green. But I don't tell her that.

"Nah, Lady," he says. "Ain't never had no trouble with love."

"That's a double negative," I say.

Lady's grave laugh fills the store. Then she says, "Twenty-five dollars."

"You raised the price on liar tongues? What the hell, Lady?"

He takes out crumpled-up bills from his pocket and smooths them out like each dead president just insulted his mother.

Lady shrugs. "You think rent here's getting any cheaper? You want to do your love canto or don't you?"

"It's not a love canto!" He pushes the money toward her, a sudden jerk going through his body. He glances at me, then gives me his back. Beneath the close crop of his hair is a crescent moon tattoo, El Papa's symbol, right behind his ear.

"Just put the rest on my bill," my mom says.

"Five bucks," Lady tells my mother, shoving his candle and tongues and feathers into a black plastic bag. "What do you say, Nova?"

Nova looks to the floor for one, two, three, before facing my mother and saying a somber, "Thank you, Ms…"

"Carmen," she says.

"Nova Santiago."

"You're a bleeding heart," I tell my mom.

My mom is always the lady who gives a dollar to the young, homeless kids on the street. She always says, "If it were you, I'd want someone to help you too." This is different. So he's not doing a love canto. He could be doing a canto to make someone lose their voice. Who needs *liar tongue* for any kind of good magic?

"Santiago?" Mom asks. "Are you Angela's grandson?"

"Yes, ma'am." Nova nods, losing the confident posture from before. "Angela the Great." He says her name like he doesn't think she's great at all, like he doesn't understand why people call her that. My mom doesn't seem to catch that, but I do.

"I ordered some of her sweets for Alejandra's Deathday next week," Mom continues.

"Alejandra," he says, and I realize I never told him my name.

"Alex," I correct him.

"I work at the bakery," he tells me. "I'll probably be the one delivering them."

"Oh, you'll have to stay!" Mom says.

I tug on my mom's sleeve, but she slaps my hand away.

"Alex doesn't have many friends." The traitor who birthed me pleads my case. "It'll be nice to have some young blood."

I want to cut off my head and add it to the mounted wall. They can label it "Head of a Friendless Girl."

"It's okay if you're busy," I say. What's more embarrassing than your mother trying to recruit friends for you?

"It's okay," Nova says, walking toward us on his way out. "I'll probably be out on deliveries. But I got you, Ms. Carmen. I'll have Angela throw in some extra goodies just for ya'll."

My magic swirls at the base of my stomach and I yell at myself internally to quell it. He takes my mom's hand and thanks her once again. Then he stops right in front of me. The studs in his ears twinkle like faraway stars. He lowers his face, and I don't know if he's going to hug me or kiss me on the cheek good-bye, but either way, I feel like a deer in headlights when he smiles. It seems sincere. Although, what do I know about boys?

He whispers, "I'm sure you'll look beautiful surrounded by your dead."

Seashells chime when he leaves.

I look around the store to see if that was weird for anyone else, but Mom and Lady are already deep in conversation. Rose is still chatting with the mounted jackalope. Lula's on the phone, probably with Maks.

My mom pays for our ceremonial supplies. The blood of the guide we have to get somewhere else.

I think of Nova saying, *You'd be foolish to try.*

Except, I'd be foolish not to. Nova is wrong. It's not like getting my period or having a growth spurt. It's a choice, like my dad leaving, like Mom raising three girls by herself, like me studying hard to get far, far away. It hits me like a cold wave. I can choose to not have a Deathday. Can't I?

As we leave Miss Trix and drive to the exotic pet store, I repeat his words over and over. My mom picks out a parakeet with powder-blue feathers and a yellow part in the center shaped like a heart. I rest her cage on my lap on the way home. She flutters restlessly the entire time. A part of me wants to open the cage, roll down the window, set her free. But I don't. I hold the cage tighter.

For the longest time I feared this magic would get loose, and now it has. Everyone keeps telling me that this is a normal part of being a bruja. That I can't stop this from happening.

And for the first time, I wonder: What if I can?

7

Protect me from the living,

protect me from the dead.

—REZO DE EL GUARDIA,
PROTECTOR OF ALL LIVING THINGS

My answers are going to be in the Book of Cantos. As much as I hate to admit it, Nova is right. If there are hexes that give unfaithful lovers groin gangrene and potions that melt warts in the blink of an eye, then there has to be something to get rid of my powers. What will my family say? Lula and my mom, they don't see themselves the way I do. They see themselves as beings of a higher calling. Chosen. All I see is their bruises from the recoil. It has to end somewhere, and it has to end with me.

Rose watches me curiously on the ride home. I wonder if she can see my intent. But as Mom drives down the Brooklyn streets, Rose shakes her head and keeps watching the night fall.

"Alejandra, are you even listening?" Lula says.

"*What?*" I ask.

"I'm just *saying* how cute it is to see you flirting."

I scoff. "I wasn't flirting."

"It's okay, mi'jita," my mom says. She turns on her signal and makes the right onto our street. "You don't have to be embarrassed. He seems like a perfectly nice young brujo."

There's no use arguing with them. I lean my head against the cool glass window. It helps the throbbing pain that starts at my temples and travels down my neck.

"Why is it so dark out?" Lula asks. "It's not even five."

Then Lula shouts as a dark shape slams into her side of the car. My mom swerves to the left, narrowly missing two cars at the intersection. Rose knocks into me, and I hold her in case it happens again.

"What the hell was that?" I shout.

"I don't know." Mom white-knuckles the wheel. She turns back, but the street is empty. We make a hard left into our driveway, crashing into the garbage bins. She shuts off the engine; her keys rattle in her hands. The streetlights down the block explode one by one. Long shadows move across the quiet neighborhood houses.

"Control yourself, *Encantrix*." But even as Lula says it, she knows I'm not doing this.

"It isn't me!"

"Get in the house," my mom shouts at us. She opens the glove compartment and riffles through the junk until she finds a flashlight.

The street is so quiet all you can hear is our heavy breathing and quick steps. Rose grabs Lula's hand and I grab Rose's. We start to run up the narrow driveway to get to the kitchen entrance. I hold out my hand for my mom, but she's still standing at the car, shining

53

a flashlight at the side where we were hit. I let go of Rose and go back to my mom.

"I said get in the house!" She starts to push me away, but I've already seen it. The car is dented. A black substance, like moss, covers the damage.

"What is that?" I ask.

Something lands on top of the car. In the dark, I can't see its face, but I can hear the scratch of metal and snap of teeth. The smell of a thousand corpses lives in its mouth. It breathes me in, like a hound on a scent.

The outdoor lights turn on. Lula and Rose are banging on the windows, screaming for us to run inside. The creature hisses at the flash of light and jumps back into the shadow before I can see the rest of it. My mom grabs my wrist and pulls me all the way into the house. We slam the door and bolt it shut.

"What's happening?" Lula shouts, pacing circles in the kitchen.

Rose presses her head against the wall beside the sink, rubbing her temples over and over. "We have to go."

I turn to my mom. "What is that thing?"

She doesn't answer me. Her dark eyes are fixed on the door lock as she mumbles a prayer to La Mama.

"Mom!" I've never shouted at my mother. Not ever. But I have to so she'll snap out of it.

"I think it's a maloscuro. They're shadow demons." She squeezes the bridge of her nose, like she's trying to remember more details but fails. "I need the Book."

"It's right here," Lula says, flipping through the Book of Cantos. "Maloscuro. Once they were brujos who broke the

Mortal Laws of the Deos. El Papa broke them until they were nothing but charred skin and bone. Yet he didn't let them die. They lived, dragging themselves on hunched backs and broken limbs, holding on to shadows. A circle of brujas banished them to Los Lagos, where they could no longer harm the mortal realm. They're attracted to great power. Light can ward them off but…"

"But?"

Lula look up at me from the page. "It cuts off."

"These were the things Uncle Julio warned were under our beds?" I ask. "How sweet."

"That's not funny," Lula snaps. She slams the Book shut and points at the door. "That thing is still out there. We have to do something! We can't just sit around."

I've never seen Lula so afraid.

"My Circle blessed this house," my mom says, wiping her brow with the back of her trembling hand. "It can't enter here. We can wait it out till sunrise."

"Alex, use your power," Lula tells me.

"I don't know how!" There's a tight pain in my belly and a greater pain in my chest.

The house rattles as a force slams into the structure. Picture frames and dishes shatter as they fall to the floor.

"Lula!" my mom shouts. "Get the candles and Papa Philomeno's finger bone. Alex, bring me the sage. Rose—Rose?"

Rose slides down to the ground. She shuts her eyes and throws her glasses across the floor. A bloody tear runs down her cheek. My mom bends down to brush Rose's matted hair back. Rose's hands are spread out at her sides. Her eyes widen and dilate, until there is only black. A strangled cry comes from my little sister.

"Alex, the sage!"

I run into the storage closet and grab a sage stick. Then I remember. I rip open the box with my father's things. I dig through old clothes and papers until I find it. A mace. The handle is made of wood and steel. The spikes are consecrated silver metal.

When I run back to the kitchen, Rose begins to speak.

"Rosie?" I edge closer to her.

Her eyes settle on me. She trembles with the spirit that's taken over her body. The lights blow out all around us, and my little sister points to me and says in a stranger's voice, "It's you. I've found you."

"What does that mean?" Lula asks my mom.

I start to reach for Rose, but the kitchen window shatters as the maloscuro breaks through, the force of it knocking me on my back. Its sinewy body separates the three of us from Rose. The creature turns its head to me. Tar-black skin that looks hard to the touch covers long limbs that end in claws. It slinks forward on all fours, leaving black marks on the tiles. The face is the worst. Even with its wide mouth distorted by curved teeth and a crooked nose that sniffs for my scent, I can still see where it was human once.

When we were children, they would scare us to sleep with stories of the maloscuros under the bed. But we aren't like normal families. Our monsters are real. Sometimes we are the monsters.

The creature hisses, a long, curling tongue licks the fear in the air. Lula grabs a plantain mallet from the sink and hurls it. The maloscuro growls as the mallet hits it square in the face.

"Stop! You two, get your sister and get out of here," Mom says, taking the mace from me. She stands in front of us like a human shield. She whistles, long and slowly. The maloscuro twists its long neck toward my mother. Its gleaming, black eyes are rimmed with diseased-yellow rings. With every sharp whistle, the beast follows my mother's movement toward the back door.

"Mom," Lula cries. Fat tears run down her face.

At the sound of Lula's voice, the creature snaps out of the trance. It snarls at Lula, raking long, black claws across her face. We all scream as Lula falls to the ground. She presses her hand to her bloody face and shuts her eyes against the pain. The maloscuro raises its claws for a second strike, and I know I have to do something. My heart feels like it's in my throat, beating a scream from my mouth. I jump in front my sister, my crazy, rude, wonderful, beautiful sister.

The air in the kitchen thickens like fog. Fear takes ahold of me. I fear this is my fault. I fear this power will only bring terrible things. I fear this is only the beginning.

I take everything I'm afraid of and shove it aside. It's like my body isn't even mine, a bright burning light surrounds me, flows through me and hits the maloscuro. I fall on my knees, shaking as I hold the barrier between the creature and us.

The kitchen rumbles with thunder. The charge pulls from my stomach. It both tickles and hurts, an invisible chord that links me to the magic and the maloscuro. I feel its essence and my skin crawls. It's malign, unwanted, *death.*

I cry out as my control on the shield weakens. The creature needs only a little bit of weakness to get in. A burning pain slashes across my chest and then instantly goes cold. The maloscuro freezes in place. Its wicked, wide mouth is open, like a bear trap ready to snap around my head. The rotting smell makes me gag.

"You froze it!" my mom marvels.

"I can't hold it!" Sweat drips down my face. Blood drips from the bleeding cuts on my chest.

"Get back," my mother says. She raises the mace over her head and screams to the Deos. She swings down hard. The spikes crunch against the maloscuro's skull. A wet splatter hits my face. She hits it again and again. When she brings down the mace for a final blow, our whole house trembles.

8

Shell of sea and cinder flame,

show us the enemy to blame.

Dirt of earth and wing of skies,

stop his heart and blind his eyes.

—PROTECTION CANTO,
BOOK OF CANTOS

When I wake up, I'm on the living room floor. Rose is laid out beside me, a pillow tucked under her head. Lula's on the couch next to me.

"You both passed out," Lula says. Her knees are drawn up to her chest. Her eyes are red and puffy. I don't think I've seen Lula cry this hard since Tristan Hart, the swim team captain, broke up with her last year.

"You're healed."

"Ma did it." Lula covers the side of her face with her hair. "There's a scar."

I put my hand on her arm, but she pulls away. I wonder if she blames me.

"Where's Ma?" I try to sit up, but everything hurts. When I look down, I see my shirt is ripped open. Four red scars mark my chest.

"I'm sorry," she says. "Your cut was deeper than mine. We couldn't heal it completely. It'll scar too."

I don't care about a scar. I care that my family is alive.

"Lula…" As my eyes adjust, I can see the bruises across her chest, the dark circles around her eyes.

"Don't. We had to heal you. We're blood, Alex." She hesitates but then holds her hand for me to take.

I squeeze her hand. "Thank you."

"Ma's Circle is here. They're cleansing the house and getting rid of—of that *thing*."

I stare at the ceiling, settling into the buzz on my skin. There's a huge spot where the paint is chipping away. Dad used to say he was going to fix it, but then he left, and every day, it gets bigger and bigger.

"I used to think Mama Juanita made them up," I say. "Just to scare us into eating her tripe soup."

Lula's laugh is wet and snotty, but it feels good to hear. "And then she'd promise a unicorn, but I'm still waiting on that one."

We lie still, listening to the tumble of shells across the kitchen floor. They absorb all the bad energy, and then they're sent out to sea for cleansing. I think of the maloscuro's head cracking open, the insides splattering all over the kitchen. I wonder if there are enough shells in the world to cleanse this house.

"Why is my face so stiff?" I ask her.

"Do you know what you did?" Lula asks. "You conjured an element. A storm. Mom says the energy fills your body and numbs you. I heard Lady say that we need to be careful. Some encantrixes use the recoil as a drug. They conjure just to get high or feel numb. But I know you're not like those brujas. I know you're not."

"I only feel the numb part," I say. "And thanks for your vote of confidence."

When the cleansing seems to stop and the whispers of their conversations carry my name, I decide that pain or no pain, I need to stand up.

"Alex." Lula whispers my name like a warning. "Get back here. That's a Circle meeting."

I ignore her and tiptoe to the door but don't announce myself. I stand at the edge and listen.

"You have to move up the ceremony, Carmen," a man tells my mother. "Before this happens again."

People mumble in agreement.

"We don't know *how* this happened," my mother snaps.

"I found a ring of black thorns tucked beneath the front and back entrances." I recognize Lady's smoky voice. "That weakened the barrier. When I went to touch them, they turned to ash."

"The maloscuros are not supposed to be able to enter this realm," the man says, "let alone the home of a bruja as protected as this. We've never been attacked like this before."

"*You* were not attacked, Gustavo," says my mom. "My daughters and I were."

"What happens to you," he says, "also happens to the Circle. Now's not the time to be stubborn."

My mom dismisses him with a curse. I think of her brandishing the mace. She looked ferocious, terrifying. It's a side I've never seen. I wonder what else I don't know about her.

"We need answers," she says. "Someone had to send that beast. They are not supposed to *leave* Los Lagos."

"Not without a portal," Lady says. "If other realms can sense Alejandra's potential, then I imagine this is only the beginning. An encantrix that strong has the power to change the world. Whether for better or worse is in the hands of the witch. It is the highest blessing of the Deos and needs to be treated as such. I agree with Gustavo. Alejandra's Deathday must be sooner. Tomorrow."

"What about after tomorrow?" a woman's high-pitched voice asks. "My daughter says Alejandra never attends your classes, Lady. Perhaps it's time you ushered her in the right direction, Carmen. After what happened to Rosaria—"

"You don't have to remind me what happened to my sister."

"Peace, Carmen." Valeria now. She's a seer, like Rose. She brings us ham croquettes and pan de dulce once a month. "We came here to help."

"Alejandra isn't the problem. This attack didn't start with her. It started long before, with Rosaria. We never found the cause of her death. Then Patricio's disappearance… There's something *more* to this. Rose was possessed. Someone spoke through her. It said, 'I found you.' It's coming for my family and I won't let that happen. Not again."

They fall silent. My mom never talks about my dad. After he left, a year went by before she stopped reassuring us that he'd return. The second year, she packed his things away. The third, she took his photos down. The Circle's silence tells me one thing: she hasn't stopped trying to find him.

"What happened to your family is beyond a tragedy," Valeria says. "But we can't make assumptions when we know so little. I'm afraid—"

"Afraid of what?" my mother says impatiently.

"I can't see Alejandra's future."

My mom gasps.

"I'm sure," Lady says, "it's all of the dark the maloscuro's brought in. Let's leave Carmen to tend to her girls. We will get to the root of this together. First, Alejandra must receive her blessing."

When they leave, muttering prayers for our safety, I stop hiding and step into the kitchen. My mom sighs heavily and sinks in her chair. Only taper candles are lit, elongating every shadow around us. She stares at the faded, flower-print tablecloth in front of her, then drinks tea that must be cold by now.

"You heard them," she tells me.

My body gets a hot flash from being caught. "I guess being supersneaky isn't one of my great encantrix powers."

I take the seat in front of her. She places a warm hand over mine and squeezes. I'm afraid to look her in the eyes. I'm afraid because everything I want is the opposite of what the Circle wants. I'm afraid that if I tell her, she'll love me less. She'll look at me with the same fear as my dad.

She pats my hand. "They're a bunch of old farts, but they mean well. I'm going to make some calls. The ceremony will be family only. Less people coming in and out. Less chances of something getting in again."

"We don't have to do this."

"Of course we do! Your powers are going to get stronger. The sooner you receive your blessing from the Old Ones, the easier it'll be to control your abilities. Don't you see what you did today? You saved your sisters. You saved me."

"Lula still got hurt!"

"A scar is a lot better than being dead. She'll learn that."

"Mom, please," I beg. "Please listen to me. I don't want to spend every day of my life looking over my shoulder. I don't want this."

She takes my face, kisses my forehead. She puts the dishes in the sink and braces herself against the counter, staring at the boarded-up windows.

"One day you'll learn."

She said the same thing to me nine years ago. I don't want to learn. I want to be free.

I wish all of my life could be as easy as calling on my dead ancestors for protection from the monsters under my bed. While I'm wishing, I wish my dad had never left. I wish no one would hurt my family ever again. I wish I were the kind of girl they all think I should be.

They've decided that tomorrow will be my Deathday. My ancestors will rise, and I will make my sacrifice. But I've decided something too. The Deos gave me this power. And I'm going to give it back.

9

The Book of Cantos is all a bruja needs.

Well, the book, and her wit.

—Jacinta Ferrera Mortiz

Aunt Rosaria liked to say, "Tell me your troubles. If there's a cure, it'll be in the Book."

The Book is our family Book of Cantos. My ancestor Jacinta Ferrera Mortiz was the first of my father's family to come to America. Her parents died on the ship to Ellis Island from Puerto Rico by way of Ecuador. She was five years old, and she didn't speak a word of English. They put her in an orphanage. All she had was a small briefcase full of home-sewn dresses that couldn't stand against the New York December winds, a doll, and our Book of Cantos.

I flip through the pages of spells, curses, the names of the Deos, the history of our magic, my family tree. It's all in here. Even depictions of cantos gone wrong. Many brujas and brujos find their deaths by trying to overstep the limits of their magic. If I'm supposed to be this all-powerful bruja, then I should be able to handle it. Mom says that you have to believe in that which you ask of the gods, and I believe in mine.

When I find the canto I'm looking for, my magic rattles inside me like a beast in a cage. I tiptoe through to our other supply closet, full of votive candles and shells and everything a bruja needs. I grab a single black feather from a female raven— the messenger of the Lady de la Muerte. She's a hooded woman with a cane, and the worst omen you get during a card reading.

The sky starts to brighten. Red stains the fat clouds that hide the sun. I'm running out of time. I feel like my future is slipping from my fingers. I want to do everything I can to hold on. My eyes burn as I read the text once again. I may not want anything to do with being a bruja, but I've always been a good student.

The depiction of the Banishing Canto is virtually recoil free. Side effects look like severe drowsiness and temporary paralysis. I'm prepared for the recoil to hurt. A moment of pain is better than a lifetime of being hunted.

Somewhere downstairs, I hear my mother's footsteps. Every morning at five, she puts on a strong pot of coffee and makes buttered toast.

I leave the Book of Cantos on my bed and start to get ready for today's festivities. I lock myself in the bathroom. I run the shower as hot as possible. I scrub my skin until it's red, and I wonder where cantos go. I wonder if there is an endless vortex or a big space dump where this stuff ends up. Every wish, every prayer has to go somewhere, right? I mean, do the gods even listen?

I lose track of how long I've been in the shower until Lula bangs on the door.

"Just because it's your party doesn't mean you can take your sweet time! I have to do your hair."

When I don't answer, all I hear is a grunt and what I presume is a hair flip because she can't storm out without a good hair flip.

I lather my body in rose oil and stand in front of the mirror to air dry.

"You can do this," I tell my reflection.

I put on a brave face and go to Lula's room, where my dress and flowers are laid out.

"Let me work my magic," Lula says, like we're regular girls getting ready for a regular birthday party instead of sister brujas ready to wake the dead.

Mama Juanita used to say that when you drop a spoon, get ready for company, probably from a vindictive woman. A fork—a handsome man. A knife—lock the doors and windows. Since I've literally wrecked our kitchen twice in a week, I don't even want to think of what's in store for me today.

Every single surface is filled with fat, white candles and pulsing flames. Dozens of brujas and brujos fill the house in their Deathday best. Lady's turquoise head wrap is tall, accented with dozens of tiny crystals. Great-Aunt Esperanza shimmers in the colors of a peacock with a fascinator of the same bird's feathers. Our distant cousins, the brujas from Lula's circle, are done up in chiffon skirts and silk blouses covered in glitter. You'd think it was their birthday and not mine. When I think of family, I think of Mom, Lula, and

Rose. When my mom thinks of family, she means everyone related to us by a single drop of blood or marriage.

I smooth down my simple, white dress covered in hand-stitched little flowers along the neckline. Traditional. Plain. Functional. It's going to get stained anyway.

"Rose, get back here!" I hiss.

But she leaves my side and dives straight for the tray of guava and brie empanadas.

Uncle Gladios makes a beeline for me. He holds my face with his grizzly hands. Traces of sweet sugarcane rum and cigar smoke cling to his clothes.

"You are a woman now," he says. "I *knew* there had to be great power in you."

I put on a smile when all I want to do is roll my eyes. It's always nice when your older male relatives tell you how great it is to be a woman *now*, like I was an androgynous experiment before. I duck out of his grip before he caves my head in.

The hugging and face pinching goes on for a while. Aunts and uncles and cousins touch my hair and dress and necklace. Suddenly I feel like there are too many people in my house. It's too loud, too much, too bright.

Old Samuel drags his conga drums across the living room. He wears a white tunic with tiny mirrors sewn across the chest. The mirrors are to ward off bad spirits because they can't stand to see their own reflections. Lady's deep voice shouts orders about where the ceremony will take place. Crazy Uncle Julio brought a lonely pink balloon, and it's already started to sag in the corner.

Lula comes over and holds my hand. She stands straight and

defiant as eyes linger on the scars on her cheek. Her hair is braided around her head like a crown, and instead of traditional flowers, she opted for a veiled fascinator covered in gems. She pulls on the veil to make sure it falls over her scars, and for the first time, I see a chink in my sister's armor.

"I'm sorry," I tell her.

"Not now." She holds my hand tighter, and we do a lap around the living room.

Lula elbows me hard and nods at the group of newcomers. She whistles just loud enough for me to hear.

"That's a drink of water and a half."

"Gross, we're probably related," I remind her.

Rose shakes her head on her way to the punch bowl. "No, we're not."

But when Nova turns around, dressed in a blue button-down that frames his broad chest and shoulders, the magic in my belly tugs, and a warm pain passes over me. His earrings wink in the light. I don't know if I want to keep staring at his smile or find a quiet corner where I can throw up. Who am I kidding? There are no quiet corners in this house. Not tonight. He looks down the hall, where I'm standing, but his gaze goes right past me.

Emma, a cousin thrice removed, stands next to Lula, hooking their arms together. Emma has small teeth and a pointy nose that gives her a look like she's always smelling something sour. "Oh my Deos, he's so fine."

"Totally fly," Mayi joins in, pursing her lips like she's getting ready to blow him a kiss.

"I heard he did three years in juvie," Emma says.

"I heard his parents were into some really bad juju," Mayi says. Her dark skin is like polished stone. Her long, dark hair comes down to her tiny waist. "That's why he lives with his grandma."

"You guys are holding out on me," Lula tells them.

Mayi turns to Lula. She hesitates, then says, "Want me to glamour your scars?"

Lula looks startled for a moment. She unhooks herself from Emma's arm, reaches for her veil, and adjusts it.

"No," Lula says. "But you might want to go to the bathroom. Your real nose is starting to show."

Nova looks over to where we're all staring at him. The girls all turn around quickly, except me. He smiles and licks his lips. A no-good kind of lick that says, *I'm going to get you.*

"Oh hey, Alex," Emma says, as if only just noticing me. "Happy early birthday."

"Are you ready to accept our Circle invitation?" Mayi asks.

"I think I'd rather clip Crazy Uncle Julio's toenails," I say as the front door opens again. "More people. I'd better go say hi."

Lula runs after me and pulls me into the corner near the stairs. She stares at the center of my forehead. "Are you going to be like this the whole time?"

"*What?*" I drop my voice to a whisper.

"Can you at least try to have fun?"

"We've never gotten along. Magic isn't going to change that."

Lula shakes her head. "You're just mad you can't go to that stupid party with Rishi."

"And you're mad at me because of the maloscuro."

"I didn't say that."

"You didn't have to. You won't even look me in the eye. You wanted us all to have our powers. Now look. We do. Maybe you want to spend the rest of your life hiding from monsters and watching the people you love die, but I don't."

She meets my eyes to prove a point, but only for a second. Her stormy-gray eyes flick to the side. "You're hopeless."

She leaves me for her Circle, and I stand alone against the wall. Old Samuel starts off with a song that has everyone dancing. The only good thing about this party is that I can hear my mother laughing. That alone is worth it.

I send Rishi a text.

Me: Change of plans. Family thing is ending early. Meet you at ten? Can I still be your date?
Rishi: Maybe.
Me: Rishi…I'm sorry.
Rishi: Just kidding. I can't stay mad at you for long. See you.

I find myself smiling for the first time today. Something like hope fills my chest.

When I turn around to find the bathroom, Nova's standing there holding two cups of fizzy, red punch.

"You're here." *Dear Alex, please stop being so awkward.*

"Brooklyn's best delivery boy, at your service." He smirks. His skin is so smooth. I wonder how often he moisturizes.

I take the drink he offers and smell it. Lady's special blend of fizzy sangria. Her secret is rose petals. She says nothing coats the senses quite like roses do. I should have worn roses in my hair.

Over in the living room, the girls from Lula's circle are dancing to the drums and Spanish guitar of Old Samuel and his band. Their hands twist in the air, like they're calling a forth a spirit. But this is only dancing. Except for Mayi, the show-off.

She spins in place, her skirt swishing around her dainty feet. Soft candlelight adds a glow to her brown skin. I want to hate it, but instead, I love the way it flows, the way her glamour magic makes us see things that aren't there, like the rain of flower petals that fall to the floor. My guests *ooh* and *aah* at her. They reach for the petals and their hands go through them. Just a trick of the light.

"You know, an encantrix has the ability to channel any kind of power," Nova says so close to my ear that it tickles. He smells like rain hugging the new green of spring. "You can do that too."

"I can't." Despite the roses in the drink, something inside of me is restless. The raven feather wedged in my bra pokes me. I remember the hideous face of the maloscuro. I shut my eyes, pushing down the surge of magic that burns the palms of my hands.

I run to the kitchen and close the door behind me. There's a draft coming from the boarded-up windows. I pace around the kitchen table. My dress feels too tight. The skin over my rib cage itches. When the door opens and Nova walks in, I jump. A spark of magic slips from my hold and the light bulb above us pops.

"Are you still planning on doing the thing we talked about?" he asks, looking over his shoulder.

"Are you going to talk me out of it?" While my eyes adjust to the dark, I fumble toward the cabinets for a spare light bulb.

"That's not my place. I already told you that you might not like the recoil."

"Then why are you here?"

I walk past him, trying to ignore the way my senses flare when I'm around him. I stand on the chair under the broken light. I try to unscrew the glass cover, but the knob is too tight.

"Free food, good music, cute girls. Gatherings are few and far between nowadays. Everyone acts like Deathdays are only big parties. But they're more than that. They're about getting the blessing and connecting with the Old Ones."

"You're wrong. Deathdays are about sacrifice and blood and binding yourself to a power that destroys."

He reaches for my hand. I pull away. "It's supposed to get better."

"How old are you?" I ask. The blown-out light bulb is stuck in there.

"Seventeen. Why?"

"Because I don't need someone my own age telling me that life gets better."

He's quiet for a little while. Out in the living room, the music gets louder, all drums and horns and wailing voices.

"I think I've lived enough for about two lifetimes." He sounds so worn when he says that. But he recovers his charm quickly. "I hope in the next one I come back as a billionaire playboy."

"The way the Deos work, you might come back as the billionaire playboy's toothbrush." I grunt, trying to twist the bulb, but it won't budge.

"Don't be stubborn," he tells me. "Let me help."

"I've got it."

He drags a second chair beside me and hops on it.

"What are you doing?"

My eyes have adjusted enough that the light from the living room lets me see the outline of his face. His cheekbones are perfect. His eyes are on the green side of the spectrum now. I can see myself in them.

And then the light comes on.

Nova pinches the air with his black-inked fingers. A soft, white light flows from his fingertips and fills the room. I can feel its warmth along my skin, brushing against my own magic.

"Oh," I say.

"Oh," he says playfully.

I want to ask him how he did that. How do you control something that is living inside of you, like a parasite, a virus? Like this growing thing that has attached itself to me without asking my permission.

"Come back to the party, Alex."

"Why can't everyone just leave me in peace?"

It's a hypothetical question, but in truth, I want an answer. A real, true answer.

"You're a brat, you know that?"

"Excuse me?"

His blue-green eyes are brilliant in the shadows. He doesn't even blink. "I always hated kids like you growing up."

"Kids like me?"

"You have everything. A mom that busts her ass for you. All the gifts of the Deos at your disposal. Look at all the people here for you."

"They're here for my mother."

"They're here for *you*. You have a legacy. They're family. You think your life is so tough—you don't know what tough is. If you knew what I've been through, you'd never sleep again."

I hop off the chair. My magic sparks between my fingers. "You're right. I don't know you. So do us both a favor and leave. You don't want to stick around for what comes next, trust me."

I hear him jump. Hear his footsteps walk around me and toward the door leading to the backyard. He shoves his hands in his pockets, turning around to look at me. "I guess you're not a fan of tough love."

"Not a fan of any love if it's coming from you."

Part of me wants to take it back. Out of everyone here, he's the only one who noticed me leave. I want to tell him to come back, but he's already gone. When Nova shuts the door, I look up at the light he left. It dims slowly, like a concentrated sunset meant just for me.

"There you are!" my mom says, running into the kitchen. She holds my face with her hands. She kisses my forehead. I take a deep breath, but I can't stop myself from shaking. "It's time."

10

When the bruja meets her dead,

she will welcome them.

She will open her heart

and know her true potential.

—THE DEATHDAY,
BOOK OF CANTOS

It starts in the dark.

My closest living relatives—my mother, Lula, Rose, Aunt Jeanette, and, from my dad's side, cousin Teresa and Maria—sit in a circle with me at the center. My feet fall asleep in seconds. Sweat clings to my lashes, blurring my vision with every blink. Somewhere in the dark is Old Samuel, tapping the drum skins, matching the rhythm of Lady's song.

Lady lights the stone bowl between us. She thanks the Deos for blessing me with such power. She's singing about the moon and sun and the balance of the earth. Then, the names of my ancestors are listed one by one and called forth to meet me.

The lights go out, but a different brightness fills the rooms. Soft, red, and warm. My heart booms—a terrible, bloody thing inside of me. My first instinct is to run. Lula widens her eyes at me, a quiet order to stop fidgeting. So I concentrate on the rattle of shells, on the *tsssss* of tongues against teeth. On the wisps of smoke rising to the ceiling. On the parakeet batting its wings in my hands.

"Carmen," Lady says my mother's name. "The death mask."

My mother dips her fingers in a bowl of white clay. She covers my face with it, blows on it to help it dry quickly. Her breath is sweet like rose punch. Then comes the coal. She traces the black of bone around my eyes, down my nose, my lips, my cheeks. We wear the face of the dead so the waking spirits feel at home.

Lady takes my hand and slices it down the center. I gasp and pull away. She grabs it back, and I force myself to stay still. For my counter-canto to work, I need my blood too. I look away and squeeze my fist. Warm wetness trickles into the fire. The fire burns acid green, which is strange. I see the confusion on Lady's face. She and my mother look at each other. Is it my canto? Every Deathday I've been to, the fire burns white once the blood is spilt. I fear I'm caught when there's a firecracker pop, and the green flame becomes true white. Relief washes over my mother's face.

Then, they arrive.

The temperature drops, announcing the presence of the spirits. The brujos and brujas of my family are hidden in the shadows beyond the circle. I can hear them singing along to Lady's song, louder and louder, voices rattling like thunder.

Mama Juanita once said there are many kinds of dead. Once you die, you can choose the way in which your spirit returns. Most opt for their younger selves. Others as they were when they died, no matter how gory. Others go straight onto their next lives. Some get stuck in a terrible in-between.

Even in death there is possibility, I think. If my father is dead, will he step forward?

The spirits show themselves. They dance and walk around me, cocking eyebrows at the small bird in my hands. I see my grandmothers and grandfathers, aunts and uncles, and others that have been dead for hundreds of years. One woman is as dark as night. A white wrap covers her head, and a cigar is clenched between her strong, white teeth. My heart squeezes painfully. Mama Juanita.

In my life, they're old, fading photographs, but now they're here and they're waiting for me, judging me, expecting me to be fulfill this legacy.

I grab the parakeet tighter. It bites and struggles to get free. It's stronger than I thought.

"Alejandra Mortiz," Lady says. Her face is more severe than usual, all rough lines and angles. "What do you offer the spirits of your dead in exchange for their blessing?"

"Blood of the guide," I whisper.

"We accept," they respond in a chorus.

I take the knife from Lady. The handle is ivory. The steel glistens with anointed oils. Press it to the yellow feathers of the parakeet's chest. I'm searching for two faces. Aunt Rosaria. She should be here. She's been haunting me all these years, so where is she when it matters the most?

"Alejandra," Lady says. "The dead don't like to be kept waiting."

But don't they have nothing but time?

I search for his face, but I don't see him, and I don't know if I'm relieved or not that my father's ghost isn't here.

"The guide," Lady says harshly.

I hold the parakeet up to my lips, kiss the soft feathers as it chirps a cry I want to return but can't. If I don't complete the canto now, then my life will be full of death and demons forever.

"It's okay, Alejandra," Mom says, seeing me stall. Her eyes are still bruised from yesterday's attack. I hope she can understand one day that I'm doing this so we can all be safe. "You can do it."

"Go on," Lula says.

There's chattering from the audience and the dead. I squeeze the knife tighter. I can feel the parakeet's heart racing under my thumb. I will never get a chance to do it again.

With trembling hands, I plunge the knife into the bird. It stops trying to fly. There's a smattering of applause. My mother lets go of a long sigh, as if all of our worries are now over.

But my canto isn't complete. I gave my blood and the sacrifice. Now, I retrieve the raven feather from its hiding place. My hands shake, and sweat drips down my face. Someone gasps, but I can't see who. I throw the feather into the flames. The dead stumble back in a great gust as the red light is replaced by shadow. White smoke billows all around us. I hear my name shouted from all over the room. The house trembles, as if a thousand fists and feet are beating at the walls.

"Alejandra!" my mother screams. "What are you doing?"

The smoke surrounds me and only me. Wind funnels into the house, bringing rain and lightning. But I sit still. I grab the bowl of coal. The feather chars and curls, then turns to ash.

"Lady de la Muerte," I shout. I grab fistfuls of ash and salt and draw a circle around myself, breaking my connection with the others. "Accept my offering. Protect me from my living. Protect me from my dead."

Windows shatter, doors fly open, the floorboards warp beneath me.

I cry out as my heart feels like it's twisting out of my chest.

Something is wrong. This wasn't part of the recoil.

"What have you done?" my mother asks me.

I don't have time to reply. Screams twist like cyclones in the room. A force hits me in the gut, and I fly backward. I push myself up as the floor beneath me rips apart. My feet dangle over the edge, and I see spinning black and stars, like the seam of space and time is coming undone.

"It's you." That voice again. The one that possessed Rose. It's coming from the portal. "I've found you."

Black tree roots shoot out and wrap around my neck, lifting me into the air and toward the vortex, where a creature is waiting. I see infinite, dark eyes hiding beneath a helmet made of bone. Lady de la Muerte? It can't be.

Then I hit the ground. My mother stands in front of me with a machete in her hand. Lady raises her hand and, with a blast of her power, sends me flying across the living room. My head spins. My throat burns where the roots crushed my throat. I try to push myself up, but my shoulder feels dislocated. My family blocks my path to the vortex. Dozens of roots slither out, like the heads of a hydra reaching for me. Instead, the roots snap around my family, living and dead.

"Mom!" I shout.

My mother screams as the black roots wrap around her waist and drag her into the vortex.

"Alex!" I hear Lula cry out for me.

There's a final boom, followed by total darkness and the end of the storm. My ears ring in the dead silence. I stumble in the dark, my hands bloody and stinging as I crawl through shattered glass.

I'm afraid to see, but I force my burning eyes open.

They're gone. Everyone is just *gone*.

In their place are dozens and dozens of scorched feathers. Every window is shattered. Every candle is extinguished. My mom always said, "When the Deos answer your call, they snuff out the lights."

11

Deos, take my offering.

Return my pain al olvido.

Return, return, return.

—CANTO DEL REGRESO,
BOOK OF CANTOS

hat did you do?" Nova's voice startles me.

I stare at his dirt-caked boots making their way toward me. He's still in that blue shirt.

I made them go away... I can't say it out loud. I touch the outline of feathers burned into the wooden floor, then the singed parakeet feathers that flutter around me.

I grab my face with my bloody hands. Tree branches tap at broken windowpanes, like long, thin fingers calling for my attention. My insides ache. My magic is slipping. Air swirls and thickens around me until everything is drenched in rain, washing the blood away, revealing stinging cuts all over my bare arms and legs.

I remember that I'm not alone. Nova is here. Nova will know what to do. I need them back.

Nova kneels down beside me and takes my hand in his. I hold

on to him and pull him toward me. Fear splinters the green sea in his eyes. He wants to flee. He looks at the open door. He breaks my hold, but I'm on my feet in a heartbeat. I pin him against the wall. His heart races beneath my palms.

"Alex, stop it. Let go."

My name sounds foreign coming from him. Alex. Alejandra. Who am I if I've lost them forever?

"You have to help me!" Desperation makes my voice shrill. "You have to help me get them back."

Nova stares at me in a way that makes me feel like a thing that crawled from the sewers. I'm a decrepit, crooked, beastly thing clawing at his feet. I am the thing that should be feared. I am the thing I hate most. *The gods ask too much*, my father said. But it wasn't the gods that did this. It was me.

"Alex, relax!"

"A demon just took my whole family, and you tell me to *relax*?" I shove him, his head snapping against the wall. He's taller than me and all muscle, but I can feel my strength growing. "You said it would work. This is your fault!"

"My fault?" he scoffs. He grabs my wrists, and I take a sinister pleasure in his shock that he can't make me budge.

"You have to know about this stuff. I know you do." My belly swells with magic. It chokes my heart, my lungs, burns tears to my eyes.

"Alex, you're hurting me." Nova's eyes are wide. Lines crinkle his features. His lips, dry, part. A strangled cry. My name. His heartbeat at the center of my palms. His pulse in my veins, slow and steady and bright.

I want to scream. My power rages, hateful and wonderful all at once. My family is gone, but the power is still there. They're gone and it didn't even work.

Nova falls on his knees. His hands pulse with a weak conjured light. He's trying to fight me. His light burns against my bare skin. I hiss, releasing him. Instantly, the wrinkles on his face smooth out, the color returns to his skin. The mini-storm I conjured dies.

My body buzzes with awakening. "I'm—"

"Don't say you're sorry!" He staggers away, then finally lies down in a pile of feathers.

I close my eyes. I've gone beyond feeling like I'm in a dream or a nightmare. I'm in a limbo of my own making.

"I could have killed you." I dig my hands into the dirty fabric of my dress. My mom was right. She should have sewn in pockets.

When he's regained his breath, when the silence becomes so unbearable that he has to say something, he mutters, "It's done."

Even without touching him, I can sense the way his muscles ache. There are bruises on his chest. I can't know that, but somehow I do. I watch as he moves toward the front door, so slow, as if treading water.

"Wait!" I push myself up on shaking legs. "Where are you going?"

He flinches as my fingertips brush his shirt. He turns the full fury of his eyes on me. "Home, like I should have in the first place."

"You can't just *leave*."

"I warned you, you might not like the consequences. I know you want to find someone to blame other than yourself, but you did this, Alex. What did you think was going to happen? The entire *universe* would change just because you don't like how your lot turned out? Well, guess what, princess? The rest of us don't get to choose. Why did you think you'd be any different?"

He keeps going. For a moment, I'm too stunned to move. Everyone I would turn to is gone and I just accidentally tried to kill the only person left.

"I don't have anyone else." What I want is for Nova to stay. I want that door shut. It's a spark in my mind, and in a split second, the command leaves my body. The door slams shut. Nova whips around, his hands glowing protectively.

"You can't keep me locked here." He looks scared. Big, bad street boy with tattoos covering his skin, and he's scared of *me*.

Part of me hates it. A whisper, deep in the back of my head, relishes in it. I can hurt him. I can make him feel my pain. It's so easy. That's the point of being an encantrix, isn't it? Nova said it himself: I can do anything. I can get my family back.

"Nova, please."

He rubs his close-cropped hair and exhales. "Tell me *exactly* what you did."

I open the door to my family altar. The black-and-white photos of my ancestors have changed. Their eyes are completely white. I grab the Book of Cantos and shut the door. Nova rights a coffee table that flipped over. It wobbles when I set the Book on it. I show him the canto. I describe what happened.

Mom, I'm so sorry, I think. Grief and guilt hit me like a wave, but I can't—I won't—cry in front of Nova.

"It was meant to *block* the blessing, like you said. Then

I combined it with a phrase from the Canto del Regreso and changed it a bit... I was offering my power to Lady de la Muerte."

Nova shakes his head. "How many cantos have you done in your whole life?"

"This is my first," I whisper.

"Thought so."

"Can you not? Just tell me they're alive. Where did they go? They can't just have vanished into thin air."

"Technically, they did," he says roughly. He flips through the pages of the Book of Cantos until he lands on a map that spans two pages. "But they also went somewhere. This is Los Lagos."

"How do you know that's where they are?"

"Look at the burn marks on the floor."

"Feathers." Feathers, feathers, everywhere. They flutter in defeated little tufts. They're burned into the floor and walls.

"Look where you were sitting in the circle."

I try to look beyond my parakeet's severed head and am thankful that there aren't any human body parts. I bend down and touch the burned marks of a craggy tree, just like the one painted on the back room door of Lady's shop. It's the symbol for Los Lagos, an in-between world I know nothing about except for bedtime stories of lost souls and fantastical lands.

"My grandma says that's where souls go to wait their passing, but there are also creatures that live there, banished from the Earth by the Deos."

"*Tell me* they're alive," I whisper.

Nova hesitates to speak. He sighs. "I'm not going to lie. There's a *chance* that they're alive."

"Chance?" My legs feel like jelly. I have to sit again.

"Well, if only their souls had gone, we'd be surrounded by corpses."

"A chance is all I need." I look to Nova, who traces the pages of the map. "Are you sure?"

"Our people don't have many other dimensions. There's the Kingdom of the Deos, which is our version of the Greek's Olympus, but I always figured that's a fairy tale."

"Oh *that's* a fairy tale," I say.

"The other alternative is that they're just gone, princess."

Los Lagos. Spirits and monsters and other realms. If there's a chance of saving my family, no matter how small, I have to take it.

"How do we get there?"

He cocks an eyebrow. "We?"

"You have to help me," I say, putting my hands on my hips and puffing out my chest. Very intimidating.

"Let's say I help you." He leans in closer to me, and now it's my turn to move back. "What do I get in return?"

"What do you *get*?"

"Yeah, what do I get? In case you hadn't noticed, everything in life, this one, the next, and the unseen—they all have a price."

I spit at the ground where he sits, and he chuckles. "You're disgusting."

"I like you, Alex," he tells me. He stands, and I follow. "You're difficult to like, you know that? But I do. You have a spark. Los Lagos isn't somewhere you just *go* unless it's life or death, and a brujo's got to eat. Don't take too long to think about it. The longer they're gone, the harder it'll be to get them back. That's just common sense."

My power crackles on my skin. I level my eyes to his. "I could *make* you."

Make him, whispers a little voice in my head.

"We both know you can't control your magic enough to make me do much." But when he can't hold my stare, I know that he's afraid. Maybe not of me, but of my power.

I hold my hands out at him. Nova steps back and readies his own. I want to break. I want to burn up with the anger I feel toward myself. I want to hurt him. Except…nothing happens.

Nova chuckles to prove his point.

"I hate you," I say.

"Join the club," he says.

What does a boy like Nova want? His arms are covered in tattoos. His blue shirt is new, but his jeans and shoes are worn to shreds. Other than his earrings, all the jewelry he wears is his blue prex. "How much?" I ask.

"How much do you have?" His voice is flat. I'd expected him to be more eager.

I think of the money in my savings account. I know very well that my mom won't be able to afford college for three girls, no matter how much she prays to La Fortuna. I guess…no one will be going anywhere if I don't get them back.

"I have five thousand saved up."

"You don't know who Los Lagos belongs to. It's not a walk in the park. And if I'm going to be risking this pretty face…"

I curse at him. "What are you talking about? The land can't belong to anyone. It belongs to the Deos."

Any trace of smile vanishes from his face. "Sure, the gods

created Los Lagos. But my gran tells this story of a creature who took over. It lives right at the heart of the land, where the Tree of Souls is. You saw it in the portal. The creature that you said tried to take you."

My heart is like a hummingbird in my chest. "What is it?"

"They call her the Devourer."

"I'm guessing she's not a unicorn princess."

He puffs out a laugh and looks to the sky, like he's asking for patience. Then he sets his intense eyes on me and I don't dare look away. It feels like the most important staring contest of my life.

"You were willing to risk your power to have freedom," he tells me. "Instead, you banished your family to another dimension. *You* owe them your life, but I don't owe them mine."

I can't stand to look at him, so I turn around. "My mom could give you more. She has some jewelry. Look around you. That's everything. That's all we've got."

He doesn't try to haggle, just stands behind me. Why am I so surprised? A guy like Nova is no good. Didn't Mayi say he'd been locked up? How could I even think he'd just help me? He doesn't owe me anything. He's right. I owe my family my life. I owe them everything I am.

"You've got yourself a deal," he says after a long silence. "I'll get you into Los Lagos. I'll take you to your family. But after that, you're on your own."

"No. You don't get a dime unless we make it back safely." I turn around to face him.

I hold out my hand. Nova takes it. The light he conjures hits me in the gut, but I push back with my own. It's the release I've been looking for. I can feel his arm shake as I hold it, but he won't let go either.

"Deal."

12

Drunk with their magics, brujas thought themselves as high as the Deos.

So the Deos slowly took away their powers,

leaving the brujas barely above humans.

Except the encantrix. The encantrix is always Chosen.

—THE CREATION OF WITCHES,
ANTONIETTA MORTIZ DE LA PAZ

While Nova runs off to gather an ingredient to create the portal, I shower and pour peroxide on my cuts. I could try to heal them, but I choose not to. I don't deserve it. I change into a black shirt and black jeans. I turn my backpack upside down and shake the contents onto the floor.

In the pantry, I grab a couple of bread loaves, apples, a jar of peanut butter, a dozen protein bars, and six water bottles. I start to think about how empty the house feels. That it hasn't been an hour and I miss Lula's teasing. I miss finding Rose in different corners of the house, reading her books. I miss the smell of my mother's midnight teas. Their absence is a punch in the gut, and it's hard to breathe.

There's a noise coming from the front of the house. Nova's

back. He runs in and shuts the door behind him. His shirt is speck-led with raindrops.

"What is that?" I motion to the shoe box rattling in his hands.

"Uhhh—"

The familiar squeak of a New York City rat answers for me.

"That's disgusting."

"Yeah, well you didn't have an extra parakeet." He sets the box on the table. The rat scratches and bites from the inside. Nova sets one of my mother's good luck roosters on top of it to keep the box closed.

"I'm not paying for a comedian."

He unbuttons his stained blue shirt, revealing a white undershirt that clings to his muscles. He winks. Blue eyes now. "I'll throw that in for free."

He grabs a mortar and pestle, then riffles through the pantry for a handful of ingredients. He works fast and confidently, grabbing a pinch of dirt from our cactus, a feather from the dead parakeet, ash from the charcoal bowl, and a vial of seawater. He grinds it to a paste and dots the cardinal scars of his face. Then he does the same to me.

"It's disconcerting to me that you know more about what's in my kitchen than I do."

"Don't use your big words on me, Ladybird."

"Should we bring a dictionary on our journey?"

"Do you *want* me to help?"

"Do you *want* your money?"

He wipes his hands on a dish towel. I wonder how badly his tattoo hurt.

"What else should I know before we go?" I ask.

"Be prepared for anything. Los Lagos is another realm. My gran used to tell us bedtime stories about a river of souls and a bloodred lagoon."

"That actually put you to sleep?" I ask, zipping up my backpack.

"Nah. But it got me to behave." His smile is all mischief. "For a little while."

I make a face at him. "I used to think Los Lagos was just a waiting realm for spirits between lifetimes."

He smirks knowingly. "Not all dead are created equal. Honestly, I find your disbelief a little unnerving."

"Do people actually believe in heaven? Olympus? There's belief and then there's wishful thinking. I'm allowed to be skeptical of things I haven't seen for myself."

"So young," he says. "So jaded."

I brush him off with a roll of my eyes. "Where will my family be in all this land?"

"The Tree of Souls," he continues, tapping the map the Book of Cantos is open to. "It collects power throughout the month. Then on the eclipse, well, that's when it gets ugly. Everything it's consumed gets turned into raw energy. The tree used to feed the land, but then the Devourer took over. She feeds off the tree now. The creature you described matches the Book of Cantos's description. I think it's safe to say your family is at the Tree of Souls."

"Why would the Deos create something like this?"

"Why do gods do anything?" Nova asks. "You can have your existential crisis when we return."

"Get to the tree," I say. I grab the Book of Cantos and rip the map out of it. "Simple enough."

"You wish. Everything in Los Lagos is designed to keep us from getting to the tree. Hope you're ready to use your bruja boxing gloves."

I feel for the whispering pulse of my magic. I'll make myself ready even if I don't feel so just yet. "I am. Are you?"

"Listen, Ladybird. If I can survive these mean streets, I can survive just about anywhere. I'll keep my promise. I'll get you to the tree."

"And you get your payment when we return safely."

He shoulders the backpack and picks up my dagger from the table. It still has blood caked on the blade. He wipes it off on his jeans, then bends down. With one hand, he takes hold of my ankle, and with the other, he slides the dagger into the loop of the outside of my boot.

"Just in case," he says.

When he stands, he's barely two inches from me. Every time I look at him, I find new scars. There's another one close to his upper lip.

I fold the map and slide it into my back pocket. I go to the storage closet and tuck the Book of Cantos under a loose floorboard. I take one last look at my home. My legs feel weak. I start to picture Lula and Rose and my mother.

"I'll get you back. I promise," I whisper.

"Come. We have to make the portal." Nova places a hand over the shoe box. The rat squeaks and scratches, like it knows this is his end.

"What are you going to do with your money?" I don't know why I'm asking.

He starts to speak, but something makes him stop. He runs out the door, where the sound of sirens fills the streets. He curses. We've thought about the supernatural threat but not the human one. Lights start flicking on in the neighborhood. I can still make out the impatient blare of traffic and the urgent whirl of emergency sirens. One of my neighbors must've called the cops after all the noise we made. Right now, I don't care about exposing our secret. I care about getting to Los Lagos.

"Come on!" Nova shouts.

I look back at my home. A metallic glint catches my eye. The pantry door is open, and my father's old mace lies on the ground. I run back in and grab it.

I follow Nova through the cemetery of old plastic toys and rusted bicycles that is my backyard. The wind is a cold slap against my face. It strips the scarlet and orange leaves from the tree and carries them through the rain.

"All right, Ladybird. Let's do this thing! Place your hands on the tree."

I do as he says. The bark ripples. It's warm and soft, like flesh. I can hear it whisper, like it's trying to tell me the secrets of the universe, its energy calling to my power.

Nova takes the squirming rat from the box, then pulls out a switchblade from his back pocket. It unfolds with a metallic snap. The end is curved upward. The sharp edges look like it's meant to rip though flesh. In a swift movement, Nova slits the rat's throat. He bleeds it all around the tree while chanting words I can't understand, and I realize Nova speaks the Old Tongue. He presses a thumb to his forehead. Then turns to me to do the same.

My first instinct is STOP DO NOT TOUCH ME RAT BLOOD STOP. But I realize I've set myself on a path I can't come back from. I'm surprised by the softness of his touch. I let Nova drag his bloody thumb on my cheek.

"Why is it always blood?"

"Blood is life, Alex."

For beings that don't bleed, the gods sure ask for a lot of it, I think.

He seems to find the terrified look on my face amusing.

"We'll be fine," he says.

"Nova…" The blue and red lights of police cars are nearer.

"Repeat after me," he says.

The bark bends, changes at our touch. There's the slip and screech of tires and sirens on the street in front of my house. I start to turn, to look back, but Nova stops me. He takes the dagger sheathed in my boot and slices my palm open. The sting makes me cry out. I squeeze it into a fist. Nova holds my bleeding hand to the tree's bark.

"By the Deos of eternity. By the blood of my blood. By the light of La Mama and the shadow of El Papa, I offer the blood of the wretched. Open a door to Los Lagos."

There's the slam of car doors. The rattle of our chain-link fence.

Nova shoves the dagger in my hand. "Stab the tree!"

I see my mother's face when I close my eyes. I bring the dagger over my head. *This is for every time I wasn't strong enough to believe.* Now belief is all I have left.

My blade slices into the bark. A brilliant light splits the tree open. I can feel its center connecting to me. My body isn't my own, like something greater is wrapping its arms around me and pulling me into the black hole.

I grab on to the sides. He expects me to jump into *that*?

Nova doesn't give me a chance. His hands press on my shoulders. He shoves me into the portal.

I scream into the void, down, down, down, into a pitch-black sky. I scream even as I feel Nova's hands holding mine. Can I still call it the sky if we're falling down? Whatever it may be—sky, space, a black hole—the wind is warm, and after a few moments, I relax into the fall. We're a tangle of limbs flailing in the wind. It's a relief to hear him screaming too. I catch glimpses of Nova as we pass by what can only be stars. He's staring right at me, smiling triumphantly. We've done it. We've created a portal and thrown ourselves blindly into it.

The sense of calm goes away when a light erupts below us.

His hands start to let go.

"Don't!" I shout, but the wind carries my words away.

We spin and turn over until I can't tell which direction we came from or if we're ever going to stop. All I know is our black hole seems to shrink, the walls closing in until we're in a tunnel made of space and starlight.

"Let go!" Nova says.

I hold on by the tips of my fingers. "Are you crazy?"

"Trust me!"

How can I trust him when he pulls his hands from mine and lets me go?

PART II

THE
FALL

La Mama and El Papa shaped Los Lagos to their liking.
A place for all souls and a home for the banished.

— ON LOS LAGOS,
BOOK OF CANTOS

Falling was the easy part.

Trying to open my eyes is not. Like there's a weight on top of them. When I try to sit, my body sends pinpricks of pain through my sides. My magic pulses weakly. I can hear it whisper to the surrounding trees.

I don't remember hitting the ground, though I'm cushioned by curly, dark-green grass that tickles my cheek. The copper taste of blood fills my mouth from where I must've bitten my tongue. I lean back on my elbows and take in the scenery.

The scarlet trees are so tall their lush, black leaves form a protective barrier that blocks out the sky. There's an energy here that feels as old as time itself. Whispers come from the wind weaving between branches, the trickle of water down tree trunks, and the chirping of insects foreign to me. Giant, heart-shaped plants shoot up from the ground, like natural shelter for the lazy snails dragging their shells on the rain forest ground.

It's familiar but not. The colors are all wrong. Like I was wearing a dull filter my whole life and now there are only the brilliant hues, raw and dark all at once.

"Nova?"

I stand through the pain. I give thanks to El Terroz by taking a bit of dirt and pressing it to the center of my forehead.

"Nova?" I say a little louder.

I clutch my crescent moon necklace for some sort of comfort, but it doesn't help. I don't know what I was expecting from Los Lagos, but a rain forest wasn't part of it. A whooshing noise catches my attention, like when the windows are open and my mom is driving down the highway. I move slowly toward a great big hole in the ground where a tree has split in two. Thick roots shoot out of the ground, as if the tree tried to pick up and walk away. I touch a root and feel the familiar warmth of the tree in my backyard. The black hole sucks in dirt and leaves and tiny worms, like an insatiable mouth. Its pull makes me lean toward the swirling void. Slowly, it starts to shrink. If Lula were here, I'd tell her it reminds me of my screensaver, and then she'd snicker and Rose would laugh.

Hands fall on my shoulders. I kick back. He grunts.

"We just fell through that," Nova says, pulling me back a dozen steps. "You do not want to go back out that way."

"Why not?" I ask, a wave of vertigo crashing over me. There's a black spot in my line of sight from staring at the portal. I shake it off and focus on Nova. "We can't just go home that way?"

"The portal is a one-way deal. It'll close on its own. You'd be falling with nowhere to go, Ladybird."

I punch his arm. "*Stop* calling me a bird."

He rubs his bicep, though I doubt it hurt. "I can't help it. You remind me of a flightless bird."

"Flightless birds are penguins and ostriches. And a ladybird is a *bug*, genius. That's not endearing."

"Fine. You're a falcon. You just haven't learned to fly yet."

For the first time, I notice the bruise on his cheek from the fall. It looks painful, yet it doesn't stop him from smiling. Does he think *everything* is funny?

"Come on," he says when I fail to respond.

Behind him is a small camp. There's a clear patch on the ground and a fallen tree trunk blanketed by black moss, where he's spread out our map, the mace, and a couple of water bottles. I'm suddenly incredibly thirsty and drink mine in almost one gulp. Nova chuckles, then refills it from a curled leaf.

"The map marks the safe drinking water," he tells me.

"That's good to know. How long have I been out?"

"Time is a human fabrication," he says, like he's reciting from a textbook, "and doesn't exist in Los Lagos."

I roll my eyes. "How many fabricated minutes on the ticking thing around my wrist was I out for, then?"

"Fifteen," he mumbles. "Thought you could use some rest before we get going. And check your ticking thing. It's not ticking no more."

I tap my waterproof watch, and sure enough, the numbers are frozen.

Nova walks over to sit on the tree trunk. He shifts all his weight to his right side when he moves.

"You're limping."

"I came down on my left side. I'm fine. It'll fade."

"What's that humming sound?"

"It's the magic of this place. Don't you feel it?"

I feel something, like a pulse so rapid all you hear is a vibrating sound.

"Los Lagos is a place of power. You have power, whether you want it or not. The land calls out to us. It's saying hello."

I stare at the brilliant-blue bug that looks like something out of a prehistoric exhibit. It scurries across the dirt, right past my feet. Then it opens up its hard shell, revealing wings. It flies around my head.

"Hello," I say, while Nova laughs at me.

"I wouldn't touch anything," he says.

"Is it poisonous?" I jerk away from the buzzing little bug. Then it loses interest in me and flies away into the trees.

"I don't know," he says, "but it's just common sense to not touch things unless you know what they are."

"You could always volunteer as a test subject," I muse.

"So could you."

The heat starts to rise. I can feel the air turning to steam. I sit beside him on the tree trunk, facing the map. It's the most precious thing we have right now. I touch the thick parchment, whisper a rezo for my family.

Nova nudges me with his shoulder, sending a spark of pain from the landing.

"We're here." He taps his finger on a dark sketch of land labeled Selva of Ashes. "It's a land unto its own, separating it from the rest of Los Lagos by a river. We have to get across the river, through the Caves of Night, take this middle path from the fork in the road that leads through Meadow del Sol, over this small mountain range called Las Peñas, and boom. We're at the labyrinth. Cake."

I want to hyperventilate and slap him at the same time. There's a black blotch above the Tree of Souls, at the center of the labyrinth, like someone set a pen there and let the ink run. "A small mountain range? Are you crazy? We don't have the supplies for that!"

"With your powers and my brilliant survival skills, it is cake, Ladyb—"

"Why can't we take the path on the left and cut across? There's an arrow pointing to it."

He holds the map up to my face and points. There's a sliver of a trail between a place called Bone Valle and the Poison Garden.

"What part of Poison Garden makes you think we should go there? And Bone Valle." *Vah-yey*. He puts an emphasis on that last word. "That's straight up what it sounds like. A valley of bones. Not to mention it borders Campo de Almas. Now, I may not spend a lot of time around them, but I've been told wandering souls can get pretty nasty."

I get what he's saying, but whoever drew this map made a direct line through the worst-sounding places of Los Lagos.

"It's the most direct route," I say, wavering on my instinct. I wipe the sweat from my brow. I drink more water. The insects that were surrounding us start to fly up to the canopies.

"Look," he says. "You're going to have to trust me."

"Yeah? Because you trust me so much."

"I don't," he says. "You tried to suck the life out of me. If anyone should have trust issues, it's me."

"I'm not the one who spent three years at a juvenile detention center."

"I'm not the one who sent her family to hell."

I stand and walk away. The tree canopy shudders and a thick, warm rain falls. I raise my face to the heavens. I know that Nova is right. I have to put all of my trust in him, not just because I've paid him, but also because he's all I've got. It doesn't mean I have to like it. I don't know why I'm so hard on him. If Lula were here, she would say this is why Rishi is my only friend. When I was with Rishi, I never felt like there was something wrong with me. Maybe it's because Rishi hasn't seen this side of me, the girl with the power. The girl with the selfish heart.

I wonder how my sisters are right now. I wonder if they're in pain. I wonder if this creature, this Devourer, is hurting them. I wonder if they'll ever forgive me. I wonder so hard that my own tears mix in with the warm rain, and it feels really good not to have to brush them away.

When the rain stops, soft, gray light filters through the canopies. Strange, fat, black-and-green birds weave between branches, higher and higher until I lose sight of them. Bright-yellow snakes slither around thick, red tree barks and race up, up, up.

Behind me, Nova's shoved all our things in the backpack. He shoulders the weight and comes up behind me. The smell of a just-put-out fire clings to him.

"Like it or not, Ladybird," he tells me, "we have to trust each other just enough. Not completely, but enough to know that I need you alive to get my money and you need me alive to get your family back."

"Good point," I say darkly. I have to keep reminding myself that Nova isn't helping me out of the pureness of his magical heart. When he looks at me, he sees a dollar sign.

And when I look at him, what do I see?

A boy with a handy switchblade, a borrowed mace, and more tattoos than you'd expect on someone so young. It makes him look older than seventeen, older than his dimples and casual humor suggest. I wonder what made his skin so tough, what made the cuts on his face. Our paths crossed the moment Lula's boyfriend almost ran him over, and now they're aligned, two freight trains side by side. When do we collide?

My face flushes as he pulls up the hem of his shirt to dry off his face, but between the heat and the rain, it's a lost cause, and he takes it off completely. His muscles are bulky and taut, like he works hard to stay so big. But his muscles aren't the most fascinating part. On his solar plexus is a tattoo of a sacred heart surrounded by thorny rosebuds and a brilliant starburst. Around it are more tendrils of black ink, same as his hands.

"Let's get one thing straight." He leans forward and a part of my brain tells me to pay attention to the way his abdominal muscles flex when moves toward me. "I don't know what I'm doing. I've never been here, and I made that clear. It's fifty percent suicide. But if we don't do this, you're already dead. And if I don't try to get that money, I'm dead too. Let's get out of this rain forest and through the Caves of Night. Then we can bite each other's heads off trying to pick a fork in the road."

"Fine," I say, snatching my water bottle from him.

"And another thing," he says. "No one needs to know the details of why we're here. Whatever or whoever we come across, just lie."

That should be easy enough.

Above us, a flock of the fat birds perching on a branch snap awake. Their eyes glow amber, their howls so human that it makes my skin go cold. They spread their wings and vanish deeper into the rain forest.

There's that smell of cinder again.

"Do you smell that?" I ask him.

Nova grabs my arm. He looks up to the canopy. There's smoke coming from a plant where a beam of light shines down. A pop of flame makes me jump. It burns fast and hard until there is nothing but a patch of ash where the plant used to be.

"Selva of Ashes," I whisper. For ashes, you need fire.

Another pop at our feet. We jump back. Nova stands directly under a beam of light. I can feel the anxiety bubble in my chest, and I scream. I push him with a blast of my magic. He hits the trunk of a tree. The place where he just stood goes up in roaring flames.

Nova jumps around the fire and grabs my hand. He doesn't have to say it. My legs are already moving.

We run.

14

Rain of fire, birth of ash.

Born again, the gods will clash.

—SONG OF EL FUEGO,
BRINGER OF FLAME

The Selva of Ashes goes up in flames around us.

No wonder birds and insects were traveling upward. But Nova and I can't climb. I'm not even sure if we're going the right way, but I don't stop running. We race across the beams of light, their heat pulsing against the ground. Even though I know it's coming, I can't stop from jumping every time a blaze of fire pops. It's like we're surrounded by land mines.

I thank La Mama that I decided to join the track team last year. I jump over fallen trunks like hurdles. I pump my arms at my sides. I'm surprised Nova is keeping pace beside me, and I can't help but think that he's had some practice at running from things too. He shoots me a challenging smile. He nods to the light ahead, where a line of trees in silhouette marks the end of the rain forest.

I run across a beam of light just as it explodes. It burns my shoulder, but I keep going. Fire is catching up behind us, and it licks at our feet. I feel the burn in my legs, my lungs, but the end is so close, I throw myself out of the line of trees.

Nova falls beside me.

We're out of the Selva, and the light-gray sky feels infinite.

"Oh my gods," I say, sprawled out on the ground.

"And here I didn't think I'd get in my daily cardio," he says between heavy breaths.

I cough and get up. My adrenaline is buzzing and so is the magic around us. The entire floor of the Selva has caught flame. We watch as the underbrush burns quickly to ash. Then it stops. Then, the sky breaks and the rain comes and washes away the black ashes, revealing dark-green buds.

"Why is this land separate from the rest of Los Lagos?" I ask Nova.

"Not sure." He's still trying to catch his breath. "Let me add that to my list of Los Lagos mysteries."

"Okay, genius." I put a hand on my hip. "How do we get across the river?"

Now that the Selva of Ashes is behind us, we can only look forward. At the end of the rocky bank is a silver river that gleams in the gray light. The river rushes in an undulating current. On the other side is a black line of caves. The Caves of Night look more like an impenetrable wall. The bank, the river, and the caves—they all go east to west as far as my eyes can see. It makes the land feel so expansive, like it'll never end no matter how far we walk.

Nova closes his eyes and leans his head back, his face toward the open sky. It really is beautiful, like a black-and-white photo. I inhale the cool, salty air, and allow myself to sink into the reality of this plane.

It startles me when I look at both ends of the horizon. The moon and the sun are out at the same time. On one end, the sun is a white circle hidden behind the overcast sky. On the other side of the horizon is a sideways, slender crescent moon, the points facing up. Something swells inside me, a faded memory of bedtime stories about them reaching across the sky to join together—La Mama and El Papa. I touch the moon necklace between my collarbones.

"Is that our moon?"

Nova stands beside me. His boots crunch the gravel. "Yeah."

"But that's not our sun?"

He shakes his head. "The passage of 'time' is marked by the movement of the moon and sun across the sky. They travel from one end of the horizon to the other, bypassing each other. That's a cycle, what we'd call a day. Every cycle, the moon and sun get closer and closer to each other."

"Like the story of La Mama and El Papa traveling across the galaxy to find each other." I used to love that story as a kid. The two major Deos were once separated by their enemies, and so they had to reach across the heavens, creating night and day.

"Exactly," he says. "When they eclipse, that's when the Tree of Souls takes all of its energy and metabolizes it. Then, the Devourer feeds on the power for herself."

"How do you know that?"

"You'd know too if you went to Lady's classes." He takes out the map and flips it over. "Also, it says so right here."

There are a few notes scrawled in nearly illegible handwriting.

I wonder who it belongs to. My father? Aunt Ro? Maybe Mama Juanita. I remember her sitting at the kitchen table when she thought everyone was asleep. She had a cigarillo in one hand and her fountain pen in the other. Usually, a bruja writes their initials after an entry in the Book of Cantos. The map of Los Lagos, and the notes scrawled on the back, are unfinished, anonymous.

"Wait," I say. "If the Devourer is siphoning out the energy, wouldn't that kill the land?"

Nova stares at the shore across the silver river, clutching his prex. He rubs the blue stones one at a time. My mother does that when she's uncertain and when she's praying.

"I don't know, Ladybird. What I do know is the moon and sun are still far apart. We have time. We'll have to see how fast the cycles pass to mark our pace."

"You can say *day*, you know."

He shakes his head and walks west.

I start to follow, but I see something moving in the water. I walk to the edge of the riverbank. My boots kick gravel into a current so fast it doesn't even ripple. I try to find a sense of calm in the rushing water's silver waves. I reach my hands to touch the salty water, but Nova yanks me back. I fall on my butt.

"What the hell?"

His face pales as my foot dangles over the river, silver waves licking at the tip of my boots. He grabs me again and drags me back a few feet.

"Don't touch things just because they're shiny."

"I wasn't." I push myself off the ground and dust the moist earth from my pants.

He makes a deep guttural noise that makes me think of my neighbor's pit bull.

"Do me a favor. Let's have the rain forest that sets itself on fire be our warning for the rest of our time here. Don't touch anything. You don't know what kind of water this is. You're not back home, Alex. We're in another *dimension*. If I can't make that clear for you, then you're dead, and I'm dead with you."

I cringe at the smell of burning rubber. I look down to find a hole at the top of my boot where the silver water splashed me. Right. Don't touch anything.

"Welcome to Los Lagos, Ladybird," Nova grumbles as he leads the way. "Come on."

We walk at a safe middle distance between the edge of the rain forest and the edge of the silver river. The clouds thicken in dark-gray mounds above us. Every shadow, movement, and splash makes me want to jump out of my skin. What else is going to get set on fire? Is everything here made to kill? I take off my shirt because of the thick humidity and stuff it in our backpack. In minutes, I sweat right through my tank top.

"Did you see that?" I point to the water. "There's someone in there. I saw it before."

"You saw what that water did to your boot. I don't think it can sustain life."

I know what I saw but I drop it. A light rain starts to fall, which makes our walk more slippery.

Nova searches the horizon with a frustrated scowl. "The ferry-man is supposed to be somewhere here."

If the water burned a hole in my boot, how does it not burn a boat?

As the rain gets progressively harder, the rain forest to our left shudders as lightning strikes.

"There!" Nova points ahead.

I grab hold of him and together we run, trying not to slip as the earth softens under our boots. We take turns almost falling, but when the golden glint of something bobbing in the water becomes clearer, I'm the one pulling him.

Disappointment comes swiftly. "That isn't a ferry. It's an over-size rowboat."

"It's a small Viking ship," he says. But even he has to admit it wasn't what we were expecting. "This can't be right."

Nova takes a step onto the golden pier that goes out a few yards over the river. The gold boat has a curling bow and stern, and high sides that might prevent the passengers from getting splashed with the corrosive water. There are four oars resting across a bench, and it looks like it seats up to six passengers.

"Hello?" I shout. I realize I probably shouldn't announce myself like I'm at the bodega.

Then a man appears from thin air.

"I'm right here, girl," he says in a raspy voice. "No need to shout at the wind."

I take several steps back until I collide with Nova's chest. His hands fly protectively to my shoulders.

The man isn't exactly a man. He's got the face of an old man, yes. His moss-colored skin looks rough to the touch. His eyes are like swirls of gold, and when he smiles, two perfect rows of gold teeth flash back at us. His torso is hidden beneath a long, black cloak that's caked in mud at the hem. He hobbles when he steps toward us.

"Fear won't get you very far in these lands." He extends a furry finger that ends in a sharp, black nail. He breathes deep, as if he smells a perfume he likes. "Though…perhaps your magic could."

Nova steps in front of me, to block me from the creature's golden gaze. Nova's posture changes. He digs one hand in his pocket and relaxes his shoulders like he's not afraid. He tilts his chin up.

"You the ferryman?"

The creature tilts his head from side to side, amused. He moves like molasses and speaks just as slowly. "I am Oros, the duende of the River Luxaria. I provide crossing to the other shore."

"Shut up." Nova's sudden enthusiasm makes me panic. Where did my street-savvy brujo just go? Instead, he looks like he's about to jump on the creature's lap and list everything he wants for Christmas. "My grandma told me you guys were all extinct."

The duende makes a sour face. He keeps that long, craggy finger pointed in my direction.

"Most of my kind was sent here by El Terroz, Lord of the Earth and its Treasures. He is our father and protector. I am charged with passage across the Luxaria, or as common witches call it—Lover's Lament."

"Lover's Lament?" I look at the hole in my shoe. "Why do they call it that?"

Oros hobbles to my side. I follow his gaze to the silver water. "Watch."

"For what?" Nova says, impatient.

I nudge him in the ribs.

"Impatience will get you killed almost as quickly as fear, boy."

I wrap my hand around Nova's wrist. His fingers ball into a fist. His magic pushes against mine. It's a weird feeling to recognize it.

"Girl," the duende says to me. "You saw it before."

I step onto the pier. I get on one knee to look closer. Nova says my name in warning, but I'm not in any danger. Not from this distance at least. I was right. I did see a face in the water before. When I inhale the salty breeze, I'm overcome with a wave of yearning. I have the overwhelming sensation that I might break down and cry, so I take several steps back and blink against the sting in my eyes. I realize the salt in the air isn't sea spray. They're tears.

"It's a river of souls," I say.

"Takes some travelers ages to figure that out," the duende says. "Your heart must be calling out for long-lost ones. These souls take the shape of water, tangled forever as one. With each splash and wave, they try to break free."

One soul leaps from the mass, and a silver hand slaps the pier right at my feet. She pulls herself up with one arm. Her beautiful and ghastly face is covered by a wet tangle of matted hair. She tilts an open mouth to the sky and howls. She breaks a hand off of the undulating mass of souls around her. Her elbows are sharp like spikes, and she digs them into the pier to pull herself farther up, long, pale fingers reaching for me.

I kick, and the rubber of my sole melts when it touches her head.

My power is on alert, sensing my despair. It swells in my chest, but something stops the magic from coming forward.

Not yet, a voice whispers.

Oros's heavy feet run up behind me. With a swing of his golden staff, he knocks the soul back into the mass making its way downstream.

"Why are they like this?" I ask. "I thought souls pass on eventually."

"You'd think that, girl," Oros says. He pulls on a golden rope to bring the vessel closer to the pier. "These end up here because they're unable to let go of their human lives. When they try to harm the living, Lady de la Muerte herself sends them here."

"Are you trying to tell me that this entire giant river is made up of souls that can't let go of their…loves?"

"Why is that so hard to believe?" The duende puts a foot on the boat to keep it steady. "You're seeing it with your own eyes."

"She's a hard one to impress," Nova says.

Oros's smirk is a terrible, dark thing that makes me want to turn back and jump into the infinite portal that leads to nothing. "What brings you young travelers to the Selva of Ashes?"

Nova and I exchange looks. My whole mouth feels dry. *Lie faster*, I tell myself.

"We're hunting for supplies in the Poison Garden," he says with a smirk.

"All this way? I do hope your dealer is making it worth your while."

"Listen, old man," Nova says, "as long as those things don't touch us and we can get across, I'm good."

Oros ponders, tapping a black nail on his chin. "Used to be people paid me to cross the Luxaria with a promise of their first-born or the tears of their first love. Even a little taste of magic. My services are costly, after all."

Taste of magic?

"Well, we don't have firstborn children," Nova says irritably, "or the tears of our first loves."

"Not yet you don't," Oros says, like a warning.

A silver wave rises high into the air. Arms and faces try to pull away from the imprisoned mass, but an invisible force pulls them back down.

"Isn't it obvious?" the duende says. He smiles, and the gold in his teeth is blinding. When his cloak parts, I get a good look at the reason for his limp. He's got a gold foot that stops at the middle of his calf.

His eyes fall to the pendant around my neck, the tiny gold crescent moon necklace I've worn my whole life. I grab it protectively.

"What's wrong, girl?" Oros snaps. His patience is running short. "The man who gave you that wasn't worthy of your love—what's left of it, at least."

My father gave this to me when I was five. I was obsessed with the night sky. I'd take my mother's silver eyeliner and draw stars on my cheeks and a crescent moon on my forehead. Then, on my birthday, my father gave me a tiny box. He told me that I could wear the moon forever.

My father left. I know the truth. I'm not like Lula or Rose or my mother. I don't believe that he'll return. And this duende knows, like I do, that every day, some of that love slips away a little at a time.

Suddenly, he's right in my face. His dark-gold eyes are expectant.

"Hold up, hold up," Nova says, pulling at his earlobe. El duende turns an irritated glare toward Nova. "My moms gave them to me for my thirteenth birthday."

He looks back and forth between us, weighing the diamonds on his palm. The duende smiles when they twinkle.

"It is nearly satisfactory," he says finally. "But she wears a truly remarkable piece, and it's been so long since I've had the opportunity to *help* lost travelers." Oros's eyes fall on my necklace again. He licks his lips with his dark tongue. I wonder what will happen when the rest of him turns to gold and how that happens in the first place.

"Plus," Nova says, taking off his prex, "my family's not powerful like hers, but you can feel how long our lineage is."

"Nova!"

"Stop," he whispers. "I got this."

Something about this pleases the creature. Because he's not a man—he's a hideous, greedy creature that belongs in this ashen, cold land. It's a hateful thing, and this is a hateful place.

"We have a deal." He snatches the prex from Nova's hand. "Now get onboard."

Nova helps me get on, straddling the pier and the edge of our boat. It moves under my weight and then again when Nova sits in front of me.

Then, Oros unhooks us from the pier and gives us a push with his staff.

"What are you doing?" I shout.

"I do not cross, girl." He shakes his head. "I cannot cross."

"You little sh—"

"You said you'd take us!"

He shakes his head in that slow way. The oars start slipping from their metal rings. I grab on to them before they fall into the silver river.

"I said I *provide* crossing. And I have." He waddles farther up the pier and waves. "Give the boat a push back if you get to the other side."

15

Where is my love?

Swimming in the River Luxaria.

Has he forgotten me so?

—FOLK SONG,
BOOK OF CANTOS

I 've never liked duendes." I curse and grab the oars.
"Trickster, lying—"

"Forget him," Nova says.

"I'd like to tear that old beast to bits." Empty threats are comforting when you're sailing across a river of vengeful souls.

The closest to rowing I've ever gotten was the rowboats in Central Park. Here, the current is quick, trying to drag us downstream and away from our destination. It takes a few tries, but we sync up our rowing.

"You don't think this is romantic?" he asks dryly.

I make a face at the back of his head. Our blanket of gray sky turns dark. Out here, the cool wind provides a reprieve from the dense heat created by the Selva.

A crooked, white hand reaches for the side of the boat and threatens to capsize us.

"Ignore it!" Nova tells me. "Row faster!"

How do you ignore fear that makes every muscle in your body freeze? It's so much easier to give in to fear. I've done it. After Aunt Rosaria, I refused to leave the house. After Miluna, after my father, I couldn't bring myself to speak. I didn't have anyone depending on me then. I force myself to push through the burning in my arms. And soon enough, we're too fast for the ghoulish hand to hold on to, and in a swift push of our oars, it lets go.

"Do you work out?" Nova looks over his shoulder at me.

"Are you kidding me right now?"

He chuckles. His eyes are so bright, like tiny stars gracing his brown skin. It's hard not to notice how pretty they are. But Nova said it himself. I can't just go running for something because I think it's pretty. After seeing my mom hurt so much, I told myself I'd never get fooled. My dad had pretty eyes too. The same stark gray as Lula's. Me, I got plain brown eyes to match the plain girl I've always wanted to be.

Nova turns back around and faces our destination. "Relax, I'm not hitting on you. I'm just impressed that you aren't tired yet."

I *am* tired, but I won't slow us down.

"If you must know, during the fall semester, I do indoor track, volleyball, and weight lifting."

"Weight lifting?"

"Don't seem so surprised. It's an easy class. The teacher is this old meathead. He looks like a fifty-year-old Ken doll."

"Gross, you think he's hot."

"I do *not*." I can feel myself slowing down. Nova's breath is

122

ragged. I know he's trying to distract me, to make me laugh so we keep going, and I appreciate that.

"It's not like I bench two hundred pounds or anything. But I like keeping my legs strong for when I run."

"What about in the spring?" He looks over his shoulder at me again. A crooked smile appears. "Outdoor track?"

"Yes. And pole-vaulting."

"Damn, girl. I never would've guessed."

"You can guess all day long. You don't know a thing about me."

He sucks his teeth. "I'm just saying. You're kind of uptight. I shouldn't be surprised that you like sports where you don't have any teammates. I would've thought you'd spend all your time in the library. But then I saw you in that dress."

"Don't try to flatter me, *princess*." My voice is hard, but I think my cheeks might be melting off, and I'm glad he isn't facing me.

"And it just so happens," he says, "I'm adding another five hundo to our deal."

"What?" I miss three rowing beats and now we're scrambling to get back in sync. My voice goes up an octave. "Why?"

"That's how much my earrings and prex cost."

"You know," I say, "I did you a favor. You dress like you're in an R&B music video."

"The ladies happen to love it."

During my party, Mayi and Emma, even Lula, were drooling over him.

"How about," I suggest, with a smile, "the next beast we come across, I let it eat you?"

He shrugs, sweat dripping between his shoulder blades.

That's when I notice the marks on his back. I've been so busy cursing Oros and the skies and staring at the shore we're rowing toward that I didn't see what's right in front of me. Long, violent scars crisscross from his neck to his lower back. I wonder when this happened. I wonder if he would even tell me the truth.

"You could go back to Oros and give him your little moon," he tells me. "But you wouldn't, would you? I'm going to let you in on a little secret, Ladybird. If you can't learn to sacrifice the small things, you'll never get the thing you're after."

I focus on the silver waves that undulate beneath us, the dark shore that starts to take the shape of caves. One step closer to getting to the labyrinth.

As we keep going, every face that I see in the wave fills my heart with more hurt. I regret the choices I made that brought us here. I regret putting my family in danger. I breathe the sorrow in the wind, and its breaks my concentration.

"Alejandra—" the souls call to me, cut off by the wind.

"Alex," Nova says. "What are you doing?"

I realize I've started to lean toward the water. The oar starts to slide through the ring holding it in place. I lunge for it, but filmy, silver hands reach up and grab it. I manage to grip the top of the handle, but they're so strong.

"Nova, I can't hold it."

"Let it go!"

The souls pull the oar out of my grasp. On the other side of the vessel, the souls yank the other oar from my grip. The momentum makes me fall backward. My head hits the ledge so hard I'm afraid to open my eyes out of fear of seeing stars. What was it Oros said? *If* you make it to the other side.

"Take my oars," Nova tells me.

I step around him to swap seats and start to row. He unzips the backpack and grabs the mace club by the handle. He swings upward and smashes the first hand that tries to climb over the side.

"To your left!" I shout as another soul pushes itself over the side. The spiked head of the club slams into its face, and it flies back into the river.

"Thanks." He turns to me with a flashing smile that doesn't last. His eyes widen when he sees something behind me. He jumps over my seat, rocking us precariously. I try not to look back, to focus on rowing, but his screams are distracting.

"It's like Whac-A-Mole for the dead," he says, panting more and more with every swing.

There's no way he can handle every one of them on both ends of the boat.

"Keep them away with your light!"

He looks at his palm. The worry crease on his forehead is deeper than ever. He shakes his head.

"My powers don't work like that," he says. "I can't hold it for long."

"You have to!"

He stands, holding his inked palms up to the sky. He conjures a light that halos his entire body. It pulses with energy, spreading all around us.

For a while, it works. The light kisses my skin and warms the cold breath coming from the silver river. Then he starts to weaken. He grinds his teeth, like he's holding on to a great weight. He falters.

And so do I.

My head throbs where I hit it. My thoughts are a messy stream of faces. My family. Oros. The dead of the river. I can't tell if the voices I hear are in my head or not. Except for his voice. Nova says my name. It's a desperate thing, and I know if I don't focus, we're lost. I row and row and row, despite the fire in my muscles and the pain in head.

"*Alejandra.*" The voice I heard before comes again, like someone searching for me in a crowd. I can almost see her. It isn't coming from the river of souls. It's something else—someone else. When I look up, hoping to see her familiar face, all I see is death.

The skeletal, silver face lunges at me. The boat has come to a slow, painful drag. The withered creatures are pulling apart from their eternal soup and clamoring for us. They cling to the oars as I struggle to row. They cling to the top of the stern and the golden dragon's head at the bow.

Nova screams my name. With his magic exhausted, he picks up the mace again and swings. I channel the magic inside me, but it's thinning and weak, and I can't get ahold of it. What's the point of being what I am if I can't use it when I need it to save my life?

The hungry soul bends over the side of the boat, its body a disfigured, warped mass of bone. I can feel the cold of its being, the angry force that keeps it moving. Those deathly hands reach for me, inching closer to my skin. This can't end before we've even started.

My voice is a hoarse scream and I grab the soul. I hold its skull.

It's like nothing I would have ever thought touching a soul would feel like. The skin on my palms bubbles and burns. When I close my eyes, I see my mother wrapping her arms around me after I burned my hands on the stove. I know that's impossible, but I feel her now, warm and comforting. And when I open my eyes, I know it's the memory I needed to channel my magic back from its hiding place.

Power erupts from my chest in a blast of fire. I can feel the heat of it on my face. The magic rushes through my veins and lights up my senses. With all my strength, I push the creature back into the river, and it writhes and cries out in the terrible wail of the damned.

Above us, the sky crackles; the lightning looks more like the sparks at the end of fried cables. Rain descends on us, hard and fast. Without oars, the river is an angry rush that starts to push us off our path.

"Alex—help me."

My red, raw hands tremble. Nova can't fight them all, and it took so much of my energy just to push *one* of them away.

"There has to be another way," I shout.

The winds get stronger now and carry the whisper of my name with them. I can't see her, but I can feel her spirit in the breeze that wraps around me. She's been calling me since we got on the river. Aunt Rosaria. I *know* it's her. I can't tell if she's haunting me or guiding me.

I pull on my magic. I reach out to the wind and grab it. The wind itself latches on to my power. The gust is so strong that our boat is lifted up into the air and away from the silver hands that grasp for us. So strong it nearly knocks me overboard, but Nova holds on to me like an anchor.

"Nova!"

He takes my hand, and I let my power flow, our magics melding together like metals under fire. Up in the air, we're safe. I wish I could look at us from a distance—a flying, golden boat sailing across the River Luxaria.

"This is amazing!" he shouts over the moaning wind.

I squeeze his hand as we climb higher and higher, and I think there is nothing as wonderful as feeling like you can fly.

"We're not slowing down." Panic takes over my sense of triumph. "We're about to pass the shore!"

I let go of Nova's hand. The wind cuts out around me, and I fight to rein it back in.

"Just a little longer, Alex," Nova tells me. "You can land this thing."

"It isn't a plane," I shout.

"We have to jump," he says.

I shake my head and cling to the sides of the boat. We spin in a funnel of air. Doubt clouds my mind. I had it under control, and now I've lost it. The black beach is fast approaching.

"Hold on!" he shouts. For the second time today, we're falling.

My muscles seize and spasm from the recoil of my magic, so I'm unable to shout, *I can't!*

But when he wraps his arms around me, I realize he isn't telling me to hold on to my magic or the ship.

He means, "Hold on to me."

Like a shadow, she crept across the land.

Like a weed, she took hold and grew.

— On the Devourer,
from the journal of
Rosaria Vargas

The first time I saw my dead aunt Rosaria, she was beautiful.

Brujas don't lay their dead alone in wooden boxes. We build them shrines and equip them for what comes next. When I was little, I thought it was a grand thing. I didn't realize the bodies were dead. I didn't realize we filled their mouths with flowers or put gold coins on their eyelids so they wouldn't reach the afterlife empty-handed. Little eyes don't see the consequences of adults.

"Why are you here?" I ask her now, here, in this wretched land. Here in Los Lagos.

Aunt Rosaria is a vision in her white dress. Her lips are red and plump, as when she was alive and dancing and full of wonder. Her soft-brown eyes sparkle against the stormy skies of a world I wasn't sure I believed in until now.

She shakes her head, a sad smile on her face. She's talking, but I can't hear her. Everything that comes out of her mouth is like radio static except for one word. "Stubborn."

I reach for her face, but I touch smoke. Aunt Rosaria dissolves into the air, and when my eyes can focus, I realize I'm seeing things that aren't there. Maybe insanity is part of the recoil.

I sit up and regret it. My body aches in ways I didn't think were possible. I feel broken. Three back-to-back days of training broken. Zero sleep after bloody dreams broken. Stiff neck after riding the Coney Island Cyclone broken.

I grab a clump of damp sand. Run it through my fingers. Black grains stick to my skin, and I remember that I hate the beach. No matter what, even at the end of summer, I find sand everywhere.

But this isn't a Brooklyn beach. It isn't summer. And it isn't familiar. Our golden vessel is sideways. A battered Nova tries to right it.

"Help me push this back into the river," Nova says.

"Why? That guy was a dick."

"Magical trade is all about the technicalities," he says, shaking his head. "I should've seen it. He provided crossing, and we got ourselves across. I don't want to have to keep watching my back because we stole mad gold from a duende. Do you?"

I don't tell Nova he's right because I'm sure he's keeping count.

My palms are still missing a layer of skin, but I help Nova right the boat on the river. It sails cleanly into the layer of mist that's settled over the water. At the shore where the sand is darkest, we watch as hands stretch up in soft waves where surf should be.

"Are you sure you're okay?" he asks.

"Doesn't matter. We have to keep going."

The thing I love about Nova is that he lets things drop. Rishi would poke and prod until I told her everything that was on my mind. Rose would stare in silence until I confessed, like the time Lula and I ate her stash of chocolate. Lula would simply demand I tell her what was wrong. Nova picks up our backpack and walks ahead of me, holding on to the mace with a firm hand.

We walk for a long time across the sandy shore, stopping only once to eat some bread and split an apple. The apple skin gets stuck in my teeth, and I try to wash it down with water. The heat is sweltering, and our lips are dry from thirst. I could drink everything in our backpack, but we still have such a long way to go. We consult the map, and it shows there's an opening to the Caves of Night.

A giant bird with a long, wrinkled neck and hooked beak perches on a nearby boulder. Its dull-brown wings sag. There are naked patches where the feathers have fallen off. It pecks at the boulder. It looks so skinny, but right now, our food is precious. I take the piece of bread in my hand and throw it to the bird.

It never touches the ground. The scavenger swoops in the air and gobbles the sliver up in a single bite.

"Those things give me the creeps," Nova says, walking ahead.

"We almost got our hides melted down by a river of souls, and a hungry bird gives you the creeps?"

"It's in the eyes," he says. "Something's not right about them. I bet if either of us dropped dead, these birds would be tearing at our flesh before we got cold."

"Then we'd better not die."

He looks back once, only to take the backpack from me. I told him we could take turns, but he wants to act all chivalrous. I want to point out that asking for another five hundred for the payment to Oros wasn't chivalrous, but I guess it's fair. We got each other across the river, and that's what matters. For all we snap at each other, I can count on him to not let me die. It's a symbiotic relationship, like a shark and a remora fish. Only I'm not sure which one of us is the shark or the remora just yet.

After we walk for what feels like hours without finding the caves that are marked on the map, I start to feel less thankful. It's silly to think of it as hours when our watches have stopped ticking. But we do see the sun and crescent moon travel across the sky, starting from opposite ends. When they reach the highest point of the sky, I decide it marks noon. I fiddle with my watch and discover something.

"Yes!"

"You see the opening?" Nova turns around expectantly.

I shake my head. "The timer on my watch still works!"

"How does that help us?"

"We can keep track of our movements." I pick up two round stones and hold them apart. "Okay, so the moon and sun start on opposite ends of the horizon, right? Like these two stones. Each time they reach noon, they get a fraction closer together. I'm setting a timer to see how long it takes for a full cycle."

"You're giving me a headache." He turns back around and keeps walking. "Don't make yourself nuts, okay?"

"*Excuse* me for wanting a little bit of order in my life."

He turns around, crossing his arms over his tattooed chest. He's all bright eyes and smirking lips. "Where has all this order gotten you so far?"

"Where has the lack of it gotten *you*?"

Looking at his naked chest makes me forget why we're even fighting. It's not for the same reasons Lula and I fight. We fight because we're sisters. Nova and I fight because both of us want to be right. What's the alternative? Oh, right—being friends. Rishi is my best friend, but even with her, I kept a part of myself hidden. I was Alex Mortiz, the girl that never cut class, that was always on time, that always did her homework.

Who can I be with Nova? He gets to see a side of me that's never been tested, that no one has ever seen, and I'm not so sure he's earned that. It makes me nervous and worried and unsure. What if I don't like that version of myself?

"You're pretty when you're stubborn," he says.

"You're just pretty dumb."

He feigns a shot to the heart but laughs all the same. I want to reach out and press my finger to his dimple. When I was a kid, I always wanted dimpled cheeks. I used to push the rubber ends of my pencils into my cheeks for hours, hoping they'd make lasting impressions.

"Your power is to conjure light?" I ask.

He takes a step back. "Where did that come from?"

"I'm sorry," I say, unabashedly staring at his chest but not for the obvious reasons. There's something different. "It's just the black ink on your tattoos look like they move."

He laughs and starts to close the space between us. He stretches his arms behind his head and looks off to the side. "If you want to check me out, you only have to say so."

133

I groan and walk around him. "Why do I talk to you? Let's just find the stupid cave opening before I throw you in the river."

"Empty threats will get you nowhere," he says, but he takes out the map again. He looks from the parchment to the wall of stone. He runs a hand across his close-cropped hair. I wonder what it feels like to touch. I bet it feels fuzzy.

"According to this map, we passed it. It was supposed to be directly across from the golden pier."

"Don't forget we got dragged downriver for a while. How can we have passed it when all of it looks the same? We are literally between a river of souls and a hard place."

A loose rock falls at my feet. Above us, the bird I fed before is back, and it's brought company. A dozen decrepit birds fly in circles above us. Feathers fall from their molting bodies, and my skin crawls when I think of the parakeet back home.

"That's why you don't feed the strays," Nova says.

I ignore him and focus on our rocky problem. In desperation, I start pushing my hands against the wall, hoping to find a secret passageway. When nothing gives, I slump down to the black sand.

"Maybe we could try to climb up and over?" I suggest.

Nova takes his T-shirt from his back pocket and uses it to mop the sweat from his face.

"It's too smooth and vertical," he says. "There isn't much to grab on to. Besides, we don't have any rope. I don't know about you, Ladybird, but there are only so many times I can fall from great heights without breaking my beautiful face."

"Helpful," I say.

More and more birds start to land around us, their wrinkled, sagging necks cocking their heads to the side.

"I don't think that's a good sign," Nova says, now focusing on the birds.

I focus on the shadow that passes over us. My heart leaps when I think it's the eclipse. I look at the gloomy, dark sky. The moon and sun are on opposite ends of the sky.

I tilt my head back farther still. Creatures climb down the wall, gracefully defying gravity. Black claws dig into stone and tails wag like whips. A low growl, followed by the yowl of a predatory feline. Lips pull back to reveal foot-long canines. Green eyes glow against the gray sky.

"What is *that*?" I ask him, taking careful steps backward until I collide with Nova. I swear I can hear his heart racing right through his chest. He holds his knife with a white-knuckled fist.

"I'm going out on a limb and say it's what you get if a saber-toothed tiger and a snake demon had a baby."

The giant feline advances on us. I gasp and hold out my hand to summon a soft pulse of energy. It's a weak, thin ripple of magic that vanishes as quickly as it appears. I'm still recovering from my last use of magic.

"Alex, get down!" Nova shouts.

I throw myself back on the ground. Nova's knife hits the saber-toothed thing straight through its forehead, burying in it down to the blue hilt. The beast writhes, falling straight down the wall and onto the black sand. Then, it pushes itself up. It shakes its head and flings the blade from the gash. The blade tumbles in the sand, warped into nothing but a piece of scrap.

I scramble back and pull my dagger from my ankle. I've never used a knife for anything other than butterflying a chicken cutlet and then during my Deathday. It feels foreign in my hand.

Nova raises his mace, and we stand shoulder to shoulder. We can't keep backing up because that'll take us into the river. But we can't walk forward because there is nothing but wall and the flock of molting birds all around us.

"I count three more cats," Nova says.

"Cats is an understatement."

Nova grins. "There could be more. I'll distract them with my light, and then you run."

"Don't be stupid. I'm not going anywhere without you."

Wings flap and birds caw and the sky churns. The rock wall begins to tremble.

Nova looks at me, and I reach for him. I can try to channel my magic into him. We *are* better together, stronger. But he does it without me. His light is a brilliant thing that erupts around us. It's like a flare, and it dies just as quickly.

Then, a new kind of pain rips through me. Sharp talons dig into my shoulders. I'm pulled into the air in a hard jerk. I can hear the rattling sound of stones tumbling against each other, and I realize, the wall is opening up.

I scream for Nova. Veins of light swirl around his forearms, leaving behind black burned marks. They're not tattoos but marks from his magic...

Nova falls face forward on the sand. The birds around us take flight, squawking and zooming around in a wide, protective circle. Maybe the pain is making me delirious or maybe I'm just not built for this land, but it looks like one of them shifts in midair. Her wings elongate to a massive wingspan, and hands with claws form at the tips. A long neck gives form to a human head with a black beak and black eyes. It isn't until she's looking at me that I realize I'm six feet in the air.

The bird woman flies to Nova and grabs him by his shoulders. She opens her beak and a terrible cry sends a ripple across the river. It's so powerful that the beasts tumble against each other. It takes them seconds to get back up. They get low to the ground, ready to pounce. The biggest one opens its mouths to reveal a long, red tongue.

More and more of the fowls shift into half-bird, half-women form. They fight and slash their talons at the saber-toothed demons.

Somewhere in the back of my head, I know these bird women are avianas. Lula used to tell me if I didn't give her my dessert, she'd feed me to them. As they drag us into the open mouth of a cave—the Caves of Night—I can't help but think that, unwittingly, my sister kept her promise.

17

When mortals defy the Deos,

heads roll from sunset to dawn.

—FROM THE JOURNAL OF
FERNANDIO NERUDA

The aviana's claws dig deep into my shoulders. My screams echo in the sparkling caves. The caves! Nova wasn't wrong. There *was* an opening. It was just hidden. The walls tremble as the entrance shuts, leaving us to fly in the dark. There is only the flap of wings, the rush of water, and the scent of burning cedar.

When I stop struggling against the creature and let myself be carried, it's just like what I imagine the free fall of a skydive to feel like. My eyes adjust to the hazy, yellow glow coming up ahead. The insides of the caves are dazzling, like someone chipped away pieces of rock to reveal the glittering bits of gold and crystals that pulse with light.

The ground gets closer and closer, and we aren't slowing down. The aviana releases me, and I fall to the ground with a hard thud.

"Alex!" Nova shouts.

I open my eyes despite the pain in my skull to see his hands reaching for me. The bird woman carrying him swoops down past me. I hold my hand out, but everything aches. I manage to graze his fingers, and then he's gone, into another dark hall.

"Where are you taking him?" My voice is as weak as the pulse of my magic.

I can't sit up, so I fall right back on the ground. A loose stone digs into my side. From down here, I can see the layout of the cave. The ceiling goes up so high there's no telling where it ends. The avianas flock to large cavities in the stone walls, and I realize those are their nests.

A few feet away from me is an enormous statue. I recognize the likeness from Rose's tarot deck—El Cielo, god of the sky. He's always depicted with great wings and a crown of feathers around his smooth, bald head. Here, he stands with arms stretched out toward the sky and his wings stretched down to his taloned feet.

The large bird that carried me lands at my feet, blocking my view of the statue. Her large talons change into feet with feathers growing at the ankles. I catch a glimpse of strong, muscular legs before the pain in my head forces me to shut my eyes again.

"We do not allow men in the caves," she says.

I finally succeed on my third attempt at sitting up. Four other avianas flank the one who carried me. In their half-human, half-bird forms, they look even more battered and beaten than before the attack. One of them looks feverish and weak but tries to remain upright.

"What were those creatures?" I ask, rubbing my shoulder.

The bird woman studies me with her unnerving gaze. "Saberskins. They hunt along the wall. Not that there is much to hunt anymore. What is your business here, bruja?"

Her face is more human now, though her striking features retain the likeness of a bird of prey. She's terrible and wonderful to look at, with soft, bronze wings that grow from the bottom of her arms and reach down to the ground. I wonder if they ever get tired from such a weight. Instead of hands, she's got long, red talons. When she sets her hands at her sides and paces on the natural dais around me, I notice her hourglass figure, naked except where feathers form natural sort of clothes. Her movements remind me of a hawk watching its prey with luminous, dark eyes. Unlike the others, she's strong, and I can tell without a doubt that she's their leader.

"My friend and I," I say, "we're trying to get across the caves."

"Is that all you seek?" She's almost completely human now, with the exception of her bronze wings.

I remember the story Nova told Oros. *Lie*, I can hear Nova saying. Then why are my words failing me?

"We wish to get across the Caves of Night."

"Why?" She leans closer to my face. This close, I can see myself in the dark pools of her eyes.

"To—to get to the Poison Garden," I say. "We do not wish to harm you."

"Harm us?" The aviana's wings expand. "We are avianas, Daughters of El Cielo and Guardians of His Treasures. You cannot harm us. Nor are you the first mortal to come into these lands to attempt to reap its wealth and die on its paths."

When I look at the other avianas, I don't see guardians. I see hunger and weakness. If it weren't for their leader, we wouldn't have survived the saberskin attack.

"Please," I say. "My name is Al—Alejandra Mortiz."

"I know who you are," she says. "And I know your tale is a lie. I can smell it on you the way I smell your fear and hear the rattle of the dead that trails at your feet. Now, tell me, Alejandra Mortiz. *Why are you here?*"

Footsteps echo through the cave, but the aviana still waits for my answer. The guards behind us flaps their wings as a girl pushes past them and onto the dais.

I feel cold from head to feet. It *can't* be her.

"Madra," she says, putting a hand on the aviana's shoulder.

Madra, the leader of the avianas, turns around and opens her arms to let her wings open to their full span.

"I told you to stay in your nest," Madra hisses.

It can't be her. It's a spell. A mirage. She twists hers hands, freshly painted in henna, and smiles nervously. I want to run to her, but find I can't move. She gets past Madra's wings and throws her arms around me. The air escapes my lungs, and as my thoughts spin, I find it hard to breathe.

Rishi.

And she's got *wings*.

18

It's really you!" I hold Rishi so tight, she grunts and asks for air. I have so many questions I don't even know how to start. I step back and hold her face gently. Her nose isn't swollen anymore, and the bruise around her eye is covered by makeup. "I can't believe it."

"Rishi," Madra says, more like a scolding mother. "You were to wait until I questioned the intruders."

Rishi lets go of me and turns to the aviana. Rishi's in a long, lace black dress, tattered all along the bottom, and her purple boots. Then there's the small matter of her wings. I reach out and touch them. They're long and black and soft. And totally fake. I can see where the elastic loops are for the arms, but her long, black hair covers that.

"I *told* you, Madra. She's not an intruder. She's the one I was telling you about. The girl I was looking for." Rishi talks to the bird as if they're longtime friends.

Then again, Rishi does have a way of taking strangers and making them feel like they've known each other for years. She did the same thing to me on the first day of freshman year when she found me crying in the girls' bathroom. I'd gotten myself lost and then found the nearest hiding place. She walked me to class and then showed up afterward to help me find the next one. Now she's here, and even though I know it isn't safe for her, a part of me thanks the Deos she is.

"What about the man?" Madra asks.

Rishi shrugs. "I don't know. Maybe if we back off a little, Alex can fill us in on the rest."

"Us?" I ask. "Rishi, how did you get here?"

She hooks her arm around my shoulder. "Same way you did."

The ruffle of feathers interrupts her, followed by the heavy thud of an aviana falling forward. She tries to push herself up but her body shivers.

Madra runs to the guard and examines her face. "Jesla? What is it?"

All over the cave, the bird women flap their wings and hoot and caw for their fallen sister.

Rishi holds on to my hand, and I squeeze. A sense of familiarity and comfort washes over me.

"Madra," two more avianas whimper before falling to the ground.

Madra lifts her face to the dark endlessness of the caves. Her mouth shifts into the golden beak of a hawk. Her cry is loud and full of pain.

Now's my chance to take Rishi and get out of here. But then, what about Nova? How will we find him? How will we get out?

Madra sweeps the first aviana that fell, the one she called Jesla, into her arms. She gives instructions to take the others into the caves below.

Then she turns to Rishi and me. "You two! Stay here."

With a great flap of wings, the avianas disappear farther into the caves.

"Tell me everything," Rishi says.

She leads me to a stream flowing inside the caves. The water glows blue, reflecting the phosphorescent green moss clinging to the side of giant boulders. She fills up a waterskin.

I'm so thirsty. I lower myself at the water's edge and drink as if there isn't enough of it on this earth to quench my thirst. It's the purest water I've ever tasted, and when I've had my fill, I sit back on the cool stone. Rishi sits across from me. Her nose ring sparkles like the gems in the cave wall behind her. I want to touch her face to make sure she's really here. But I hesitate. My magic flutters in my stomach again. I reach for the loose strand of hair falling over her face and tuck it back. Rishi is *here*.

"It's so good to see you."

She purses her lips and scowls. "Nice try. I'm still mad at you for standing me up."

"The Ghoul Ball," I say. "I'm so sorry."

"Don't be sorry," she says. "Just don't do things to be sorry *for*. Now that you don't have a choice, tell me. What the hell is going on?"

So I tell her about my family. About the magic of the brujas and brujos that exist in the world. About my Deathday and how I tried to send my powers back to where they came from. I tell her about Nova and how he's helping me. When I'm all caught up, she just stares.

"Wow," she whispers.

"Wow?"

"This is so cool."

"I don't think *cool* is the word I'd use."

"Alex, you're crazy. Why would you give up your powers? Imagine all the things you could do!"

"You don't get it." I pull my hand from hers. "Magic destroys. It's only brought my family pain and death and loneliness. I thought I could break the cycle. Instead, I made things worse. I *know* what I did was wrong. I didn't think about the consequences. That's why I'm here to fix it. But I can't do that without Nova."

We're quiet for a long time, listening to the hooting whispers of sleeping birds in nests high above and the *ribbit* of frog-like creatures that catch bugs from the stream.

"Your turn," I tell Rishi. "How did you get here?"

"By the time I realized you weren't coming, I called your house. No one answered, so I decided to just go yell at you myself. So then I pulled up to your house and there's police circling the block and an ambulance. The doors and windows looked broken. They put that yellow tape up all over the place. I went in through your neighbor's yard and climbed over the fence. The tree in your yard was doing this really weird thing, like it was breathing from the giant hole in its trunk. I could hear you screaming when I got real close. You and that guy. Also, *where* did he come from and how come you haven't mentioned him before?"

"Wait, wait." My head is swimming. "You just jumped in after me?"

"Of course I did," she says. "I thought you were in trouble. Really, Alex, how could you not tell me about this? I *knew* your family was into some weird stuff, but in my head, it was like voodoo or Santeria or like Scientology or something. This is real magic. *You* are really magic."

She says it with such furor that I don't want to contradict her.

"When I jumped into the tree, I thought it would lead me to you."

"Nova said portals are unpredictable. A one-way trip."

"I don't know anything about that. I just remember I started falling through the sky, over this silver river. I lost a lot of feathers on the way down. One wing is a little loose." She shimmies one shoulder to show me. Then, in a low voice, she quickly adds, "Madra caught me before I fell in the river. They made me an honorary aviana because of my wings. I told her I needed to find you, but she said it isn't safe out there."

"She's right," I say, sounding more like Nova than I'd like. "We have to get you home. I'll find a way to get Nova and get out. Then we'll figure out a way to make a portal for you."

"I'm not going anywhere," she says. "I came because I thought you were in trouble. You made a snake come out of a boy's *throat* for me. I'm not going to leave you in some Neverland dimension with a guy you don't even know. Look into my eyes and tell me you don't want me here."

I make an exasperated sound. "I *do* want you here."

"Then what's the problem?"

"The problem is that if you get hurt, I wouldn't be able to stand it."

"So you care about what happens to me but not about what happens to that guy you're with?"

"His name's Nova," I say. "I hired him as my guide."

"Well, that's fine because I'm here for free."

She smiles smugly, and I can tell I've lost this argument. Rishi might be almost as stubborn as Lula.

"So it's settled," she says. "Did you bring any food? There isn't much to eat around here."

"It's in our backpack. But Nova was carrying it last."

"I think I saw where it fell." She takes off in a sprint, her black wings bouncing against her shoulders.

I take this second alone to compose myself. I press my hands on a boulder of shimmering stone. This land has a heartbeat. It's faint, but I can feel it. It helps calm my fried nerves a little. What am I going to do to get us out of here? What if the avianas never let us leave?

Get a grip, I tell myself. *You are taking Rishi and Nova and you're going to keep going.* I reach into my back pocket for the map, but when I can't find it, I realize Nova must have it.

"Over here!" Rishi shouts from the other side of the cave. She holds the backpack in the air.

I return to the dais, where molten feathers litter the ground.

147

There's blood where the injured avianas fell. When I was hurt by the maloscuro, Lula and my mother healed me. Maybe these creatures have their own healers. The scars on my chest burn at the memory of that hideous, grinning face, those bloody claws.

We find a spot that's relatively clean to sit and eat. I munch on a protein bar while Rishi tears into the bag of beef jerky. Avianas fly down from their nests in their bird forms and stand around us like seagulls at the beach. I remember the hunger in their eyes. Some of them have lost all their feathers. I can see their rib cages poke through skin, and my hunger goes away.

I take the two loaves of bread, the beef jerky, and the apples. I leave them out on the dais.

"Go on," I tell them.

They swoop down on the food in a mad frenzy. It's gone in seconds.

Rishi smiles at me. I forgot how much I missed her smile, like there's an infinite well of happiness inside of her. I forgot how good I feel just being in her company.

"Why are they like this?" I ask Rishi.

"The way Madra tells it," she says, "it's too dangerous for them to go out. There's some bad juju on the land. It wants the avianas to join her side. The avianas won't, so the creature is starving them out. They call it—"

An involuntary shiver passes over me. "The Devourer."

"Yes," Madra says, flying around us until she lands on the dais. "That is the creature who's ravaged these lands for her own power. That is the creature you seek, isn't it?"

"It is." There's something about Madra that makes me want

to stand perfectly still. Nova was right. There's something about their eyes.

"Are the others okay?" Rishi asks.

Madra turns to the statue of El Cielo and bows her head. My mom does that with the statue of La Mama when she's asking for strength to deal with three daughters. Madra shuts her eyes and mouths a silent rezo.

When she finally turns to me, her shoulders sag with defeat. "I beg you. Nothing is worth journeying to the Devourer. Her cruelness has conquered many souls across Los Lagos. Those who refuse her remain hidden, scavenging to live. You will only find death."

"I have to," I say. "She has my family."

Madra is quiet for a bit. She takes to pacing again, then comes to a stop in front of me. "What do you know of these lands, bruja?"

I shake my head. "Only the notes in my family's Book of Cantos. My friend has our map. Can you let him go? We mean you no harm."

"He will be released when I give the word. Men are not allowed in the Caves of Night."

"What about this guy?" Rishi says, pointing to El Cielo. "He looks like he has all the man parts."

"*Rishi*," I say through gritted teeth.

Madra actually smiles. "The Deos are more than male or female. They are both and neither at the same time. They are the creators and destroyers of the worlds. Tell me, Alejandra Mortiz, what does your witch book say of my kind?"

Now that the food is gone, the birds have returned to their

nests, but their eyes are still cast down at us. So much for a speedy getaway.

"There's a story about the daughters of El Cielo," I say, like I'm reciting from a history textbook. "He was Deo of all the Skies. The avianas were made to protect the riches of the world from being stolen. But they failed and were banished from the mortal realm."

"Failed," Madra repeats. "I did. I let a man whisper in my ear. I let him into the caves. I let him have the treasures of El Cielo. For that, my curse is to never change. Never age, never die. But not my sisters. They can grow old and sick and *hungry*. I do the best I can, but the land around us is dying. I can only hunt so much without the saberskins coming for us."

"What about the others you were talking about?" Rishi asks. She turns to me and elaborates. "There are these tribes that live underground and refuse to give their lands to the Devourer."

"There are few tribes of creatures left who still fight," Madra says. "The rest of the land is filled with ghosts and others who gave up long ago. If you continue on your path, you may lose more than your life."

"I'm the reason my family was taken," I say. "I have to make things right. No matter what happens to me."

"Why don't you come with us, Madra?" Rishi suggests. "Alex is going to free her family, and you can free your lands."

Madra shakes her head. "My duty is to my people. Their survival is all I live for."

"But, Madra!"

I take Rishi's hand to pull her away from the aviana. "Rishi, drop it. Let's just take Nova and go."

A sharp whistle pierces the air. Madra turns away from the statue of El Cielo and to the right, where a group of avianas hold Nova by the wrists. A dirty cloth has been shoved in his mouth.

"What are you doing?" I start to run to him, but Madra's wings expand and push me onto the ground.

The avianas bring Nova forward. His eyes widen when he sees me. Then he frowns when he sees Rishi. He shakes his head and screams through his gag. The avianas speak in sharp cries back and forth.

"Madra, please," I say.

Madra puffs up her chest. Her face is inches from mine. "Do not plead with me for a boy who does not know the meaning of honor. If you would plead, plead for yourself, Alex Mortiz."

"What happened?" I start to step forward, but Madra's wing knocks me back again.

"I have allowed you into our home," she says, her body shaking with anger. "I have saved you from death. I have made an exception to keep this man in our caves."

The avianas empty Nova's pockets. Dozens of glittering crystals and gold fall at his feet.

Madra's black eyes are endless. She grabs my shoulders with her clawed hands. "But I *cannot* abide thieves!"

19

Sana, sana, the body endures.

Cura, cura, the soul of the pure.

—HEALING CANTO,
BOOK OF CANTOS

The avianas grab the three of us in their talons and throw us into the one of the highest nests. Dried leaves and branches are woven into a makeshift mattress, and a fire burns in a stone bowl.

"What did you do?" I punch Nova's chest.

He grabs my wrists to pull me off him. "How was I supposed to know the gems weren't up for grabs?"

I yank my hands free from his hold. I point my index finger, like the barrel of a gun, at his face. "You just ruined everything! How are we supposed to get out of these caves? They could have helped us."

He turns away from me and sits on the makeshift mattress. "How? A bunch of starving birds are going to storm the labyrinth with us?"

"You're the one who told me not to *touch* shiny things. But you think with your pockets, don't you?"

"I didn't think they'd see me take a few gems in a *cave full of them*!"

"Shut up, Nova. You're not even sorry." I kick a stone away from us. It flies off the side of the nest. We listen to it fall, hitting the sides of the caves like a penny in an empty jar. I count ten seconds before it lands.

"Let me talk to Madra," Rishi says. "I think she'll listen to me."

"Who the hell is this?" Nova thumbs at Rishi.

"Relax, protein shake," Rishi says. She crosses her arms over her chest and looks at Nova like he's a fly that drowned in her soup.

"Stop," I hiss. I stand between them like a shield—though I'm not sure who I'm more afraid for, Rishi or Nova. "Nova, this is Rishi. She's my—she's my best friend. She jumped into the portal after us and wound up with the avianas. Rishi this is Nova. He's a witch, like me. He's my guide."

"I am a *brujo*," Nova corrects me. "And this isn't going to fly. It's one thing that I have to look out for you. I'm not about to babysit some *sinmaga*."

"What did you call me?" Rishi closes the space between them.

My head throbs at the temples. I turn my back to them while they bicker. How does my mother put up with Lula and me when we get like this?

"How sweet," Lula says, clear as a bell. "They're fighting over you."

"Did you hear that?" I whip around to find her face, but she isn't there. I know I heard her. It was like she was standing right beside me.

Nova and Rishi ignore me. They're like a pack of wild dogs barking at each other.

"I've known Alex for two years," Rishi shouts at Nova. "She can trust *me*."

"Clearly you didn't know her very well if you didn't know about her powers."

They fall into some indecipherable shouting when an even louder sound stops us all. There's a scream coming from deep within the caves, where they took the injured avianas.

"Hurry," Lula says again, her voice fading. "You know what you have to do."

"Lula?" Her name is an echo in the sparkling caves. I'm officially going crazy.

Behind me, Nova and Rishi are in each other's faces. Rishi's face is tilted up to him. She's a rabid wolf. He's a lion with an alpha complex. And they're both idiots.

"*Silentio*." I whisper the curse. *Silence*. My heart races from using that bit of magic. My lips are numb. I didn't know I could do that.

They move their mouths, but nothing comes out. Rishi touches her throat and tries to scream, but only a whooshing gasp comes out. Nova punches the wall.

"Madra!" I shout. I call out her name until she flies up to our nest.

"What?" she asks impatiently.

"How are your girls?"

She flaps her bronze wings. Despite her stoic face, I can tell she's worried. If it were my mom, she wouldn't be able to sleep.

"What did you do to your companions?"

"I'm not sure," I say honestly. "I just couldn't think with their fighting. That's not why I called you. I want to strike a bargain."

"I don't have time for bargains," she says, turning to fly away.

"What if I can heal them?"

Madra takes me to the injured avianas. Three of the bird women are laid out on rock slabs. They shiver from head to talons, clutching flimsy blankets. One has blue lips. Her head is turned to the side, and her eyes are shut. Sweat and tears roll down her face.

"You have the healing gift?" Madra asks. She stands in the center of the room.

"I'm an encantrix," I tell her.

She raises a single feathered eyebrow. Her dark eyes appraise me, like she's seeing me in a new light.

"Finally, some truth to you."

"I did tell you the truth. I'm here to rescue my family from the Devourer. I'm an encantrix. I will heal them, but you have to do something for me."

Magical trade is all about technicalities, I recall Nova's words.

"I assume you want your freedom?"

"I am not your prisoner, and neither is Rishi. We did nothing wrong. Nova was the thief, and you took back the gems. I'll trade Jesla's life for Nova's."

Madra doesn't blink. "Why would you trade for such a man?"

"That is my business."

"Very well. And the other two?"

"You will tell us the safest path to the labyrinth." I'm starting to sweat under her steady gaze.

"That I cannot promise. These lands change as power changes. Lands that were safe could be under the Devourer's control. There is much we cannot see from within the caves."

"Then you'll look at our map and update it. Even you must know the terrain from your hunts."

"Hadrigal's life for the map," Madra says. "What will you ask for the third?"

"Nothing," I say. "I will heal her because it's the right thing to do."

Madra bows her head to me and walks out. "If you should need me, just call."

I've seen my mother and Lula heal a thousand times. I take Jesla's hand in mine. Her wings are a deep blue, like the sky before night falls. She's mostly in her bird form, though her eyes are still very human. A sickly green film clings to their lashes, and her breath is ragged wheezing when I press my hand to her chest. Her pulse is weak.

"What did you get yourself into?" I ask myself. I wish Lula were here. She'd know what to do in a second. She never hesitates when I'm hurt.

My mom likes to say that belief has to be unyielding. Part of what makes magic so powerful is that the bruja believes in her canto. She believes in what she's trying to do.

"You're really deep in it now," Lula says.

I jolt back as my sister appears beside me. I reach for her, but she's not like Aunt Rosaria's haunting spirit or the damned of the Luxaria. She's a flicker, like a screen projection.

"You're really here."

"Don't *touch* my apparition," she snaps, sassing me with a roll of her eyes. The rude gesture fills me with so much feeling that I want nothing more than to hug her.

"Are you…" I can't bring myself to finish the sentence.

"Alive? Yes, no thanks to you." She looks behind her like she's afraid to get caught. It's just the three avianas and us. "At least you figured out a way to come after us. You don't hate your family that much after all."

"I don't hate you." The shame I've felt since I performed the canto returns. How can I face them all again?

"You don't love us." Lula points her finger at my chest. The anger that marks my beautiful sister's face breaks my heart over and over. "How could you after what you did?"

"I'm trying to get you back. I'm so sorry."

Lula turns her attention to the right, looks at someone I cannot see. She sucks her teeth. "Fine, I'll leave her alone."

"Who are you talking to?"

"Ma, that's who. Typical, you send your whole family, living and dead, to a next-level realm, and she still forgives you."

"She does?"

"I won't," she says. "I'm never going to. Especially if you don't hurry up and fix this mess."

"If you haven't noticed, I'm a little busy trying to figure out how to heal."

"I'm the one who put the idea in that thick head of yours." Her face brightens with a mischievous smile—typical Lula, so clever. "You're a difficult one to reach. Rose's been trying her best to help us connect with you, but it's like you don't want to be found. You're impossible."

"I get it. I'm scum."

"Lower than scum."

"Lula, please. I told Madra I could do this, but I don't know how."

Lula sighs, resigning herself to being my spiritual guide. Even she places her hand on my face. Her hand is warm and goes right through me.

"When you use your power, what's the first thing that comes to mind?"

I think about the first time my powers manifested. I was afraid when Miluna attacked me. I was angry when I conjured the snake. Then there's fear. Fear that made me fight back against the maloscuros, that made me fly across the River Luxaria.

"Fear," I tell her. "Anger."

"That's usually the key to physical powers." She walks around the room, holding her hands over Jesla's shivering body. "Healing is different."

I wipe the sweat from my forehead with the back of my hand. "I'm having a bit of a hard time finding my Zen, if that's where you're going."

"Healing isn't just about being calm." She's made a full lap around the room and returns to me, hovering her palm over my chest. It makes the pain from my scars subside. "What did you feel every time I've mended your bones or cuts?"

"Warmth."

"That's love, Alex. That's the love I have for you. Replace the anger and fear and just think about the person you're trying to heal. You're an *encantrix*. You can channel all the gifts from the Deos. They're right at your fingertips. You have to stop being afraid of yourself."

"What if I can't do that? What if I just keep being afraid?"

"I'm scared too. You don't know what it's like here. We're trapped, and there's nowhere to go. It takes so much energy to project myself to you, but you need to know we're counting on you. We know you're going to do everything you can to come get us. You don't know how strong you are."

I press my hand on Jesla's chest. Her pulse is a whisper. I can fill myself with love, right? People do it all the time. Mom and Lula do, so why is it so hard for me? When I close my eyes, I see the maloscuros. I see the bloody parakeet in my hands. I see everyone I love lying in a heap, just dead bodies.

"Sh," Lula whispers in my ear. "Don't do that. Remember the times Dad took us to Coney?"

I shake my head. "I don't want to think about Dad."

"Well you have to, okay? Because we loved him once, and he loved us too. Remember, Alex. He'd take us every Sunday night to the boardwalk. We'd fill up on corn dogs and popcorn until we were too full to walk and we'd just lay there on the beach watching the sun set."

"I remember." Sometimes it's hard to find the good memories.

"It's love, Alex. Love is you jumping through a portal despite your own safety. Love is Mom singing in the car and Rose making tea when we're sick and even us fighting because we're blood, and no matter what you do, I'll *never* forget that you are my sister."

I let the magic uncoil from the pit of my stomach and flow through me. It's different than the other times. Brighter and stronger. It leaves me in a flood, connecting to Jesla. Her eyes snap open, and she gasps for air. Her back arcs, like there's something inside her fighting against my magic. I move my hand over the claw marks from the saberskins. They've been cleaned, but they're still bleeding. I focus on the brilliant light that links me to the aviana, my magic embracing her, calling her back from the darkness. When I feel her heartbeat kick up to a normal rate, I let go.

"Easy," Lula says. "The recoil is going to kick in soon. Move on to the next. You can do it."

My mind spins. I try to grab Lula's hand, but I forget she's only a projection of herself.

"Don't go there," she tells me. "Not yet."

There are white spots in my vision as I stumble to Hadrigal. Her black wings hang over the sides of the stone slab. Her eyes roll to the back of her head. I can feel her fading quickly, so I press my hands over her heart and send a shock right into its center. I can hear Lula cheering me on, telling me it's working. I can feel my healing energy flooding Hadrigal, returning the color to her cheeks, mending the cuts over her chest until she has the same pearly scars I do.

I fall on my knees, my head spinning like a carousel.

"Come on, Alex," Lula says. "One more. You're a natural, don't you see? Way better than I ever could be."

I choke on a laugh. "Am I dying or something? You're being really nice."

"I can't hold on, Ale. Hurry."

"Lula?" It's hard to breath. She looks over her shoulder, her apparition getting weaker.

"Oh no... It's coming back."

"Is it the Devourer? I'm going to kill it."

Lula erupts in an earsplitting scream.

"Lula!" I reach for her but I grab air.

She's gone.

I crawl on my knees to the next table. I lower my ear to the aviana's open beak. The breath is as faint as mine, but I have to find a way. I repeat Lula's words. *That's the love I have for you.*

Love is Lula. Love is my mom. Love is Rose. Love is in this power that I never asked for but courses through my veins like the blood of my ancestors.

When I hear the sharp intake of the aviana, I let go. All three of them are awake.

I fall on my face. I'm not ready for the recoil, but I brace myself. I shut my eyes and think of my family.

"I wish you could see me now."

20

All roads lead to the labyrinth.

—FROM THE JOURNAL OF
ROSARIA VARGAS

hen I wake, I feel like I've slept for a hundred years. Rishi sleeps in the fetal position atop a pile of leaves, and Nova sits beside me. We're back in the nest.

"It's funny," I tell Nova, "having to remind myself that this isn't a dream."

He nods but doesn't look at me. He leans his head back against the cool wall, watching the avianas in their bird form, flying around the statue of El Cielo.

"You could have died," he says.

"You told me an encantrix can do anything."

He looks off to the side, avoiding my eyes. "Experienced ones. Not ones who barely know how to control their power."

"I had to do something to save your skin. A simple thank-you would be nice." I sit up and stretch the stiffness out of my body. I'm covered in tender bruises, but it was worth it to know that my family is safe. For now. "Madra's going to help us with the map. Let's get our things and keep going."

I stand to walk past him, but he takes my hand in his. He stands, towering over me. He brushes my tangled hair back and cups my face. His eyes are greener in this firelight.

"I'm sorry," he whispers.

I shake my head. "Why'd you do it, Nova?"

He starts to smile. I bet he can't help it. I bet his smile gets him out of and into all sorts of trouble.

"You and me?" he says. "We come from different worlds. I have nothing to my name."

"What about your grandma?"

He shrugs dismissively. "I'm just another mouth to feed."

"That can't be true."

His hands slide down from my cheeks to my neck. I wonder if he can feel my heart racing.

"Not everyone's got a family they'd die for," he says. "If I thought it'd get you in trouble, I would've thought twice about stealing. Okay?"

"I can't get all righteous on you," I say, "though I'd just like to point out that you're the one who told me not to touch anything."

Eye roll. "We cool?"

Rishi clears her throat. She's leaning on the wall opposite us. How long has she been standing there without me noticing?

"Let's get this donkey show on the road," she says.

"I think you mean dog and pony show," Nova says.

Rishi looks him up and down. I guess they've stopped yelling at each other, but that doesn't mean they've called a truce. "Since you're here, I'm pretty sure I mean donkey."

. ❦ .

We say good-bye to the avianas, leaving them two-thirds of our food supplies. Madra walks us to a tunnel that leads out of the caves. It smells dank and is lit by torches.

"I do not think it is wise to journey to the labyrinth," Madra tells me. "But I honor your loyalty to your family, Alejandra Mortiz. I will take a look at your map."

I unfold the map for her to see. Her hawk eyes follow the ink rendering of Los Lagos.

"The opening to this cave is on the map," I say, "but if you hadn't come to our rescue, we'd never have found it."

"Many witches and humans alike have come to these lands. Some seek to steal its treasures. Others seek to make deadly pacts with the Devourer—the desperate searching for their dead. We used to offer passage to those who landed on this side of Los Lagos, but we closed the caves off long ago."

"What changed?"

"The Devourer's strength grows every eclipse. My kin and I attempted to band with the other tribes this side of the labyrinth. Our loss was nearly total. The Forests of Lights were burned to the ground. Now they are wastelands. The desert land of Bone Valle was created from an old witch village during the first rebellion."

"First?" I ask. "There's been more than one?"

Madra nods somberly. "You ask why we do not join you. We have lost everything to the Devourer. All we can do is try to stay alive. Even now, the dead earth of Bone Valle encroaches on our territory as the Devourer feeds off the Tree of Souls."

"That's horrible," Rishi says.

"What if the Devourer could no longer feed off the tree?" I ask.

"That is a question that has cost thousands of lives." Madra looks to Rishi with motherly love, then to me with her usual stoic face. "I do not have to remind you she is at the most risk."

"I get it," Rishi says. "I'm human, blah, blah."

"Your disregard for the dangers of this land tells me you do not, as you say, *get it*. But your path is your own to take."

"Hold up," Nova says, making a *T* with his hands. "If we take the fork on the right, that means we end up at the Forest of Lights. You said that was burned to a crisp."

"Yes. The Devourer won't chase after you in a wasteland."

Nova looks unsure.

"You asked for my advice, and I am giving it to you. Follow this tunnel to the other side of the caves. The path leads to the fork in the road. Keep to the right path through the Wastelands del Este and to the mountain pass. Be wary. Your presence here is known. Servants of the Devourer roam the land and report any strangers they see."

"The maloscuros," I say.

"Among other beasts," Madra says. "The saberskins, the giants guarding the labyrinth, and sea monsters swim in Mar del Fin. Travel swiftly and look twice at anyone or anything. Los Lagos is a fluid land, and so are its inhabitants."

I feel like I'm walking myself off a plank. A chorus of off-key caws mark our final good-bye.

"Remember." Madra's deep voice follows me and echoes against stone. "At the fork in the road, keep to the right path. The Devourer does not free the power she takes. Be careful you are not caught by her shadows."

I find myself turning to Nova, who starts to lead us into the tunnel. And I think to myself, *It's a good thing I've got a boy made of light.*

21

In the woods, I found the love de mis amores.

He was there at the end de mis dolores.

—FOLK SONG,
BOOK OF CANTOS

We walk down the tunnel in silence. Rishi kicks stones out of the way. They roll like dice down our path. Nova cracks his knuckles over and over. I think the lines on his arms are stretching farther up. Why won't he talk about it? I think about the recoil of my magic. I examine my hands. All I've had to show so far are bruises that have begun to fade. Passing out isn't exactly my idea of fun, but I wonder if it's better than permanent marks.

I listen to the steady hum of life beneath the tunnel. The stones, the minerals, even the stream that runs through the caves. I can feel all of it calling to me like a long-lost friend. Madra said the Devourer is sucking up all the life from these lands. If there is nothing left, would she try to find a new place to destroy?

"You all right, Ladybird?" Nova asks, not looking back at me.

"Just wishing I'd brought a bottle of painkillers."

"Why can you heal others but not yourself?" Rishi asks.

"We're not supposed to use our powers for our own benefit," I say.

"That sucks."

"It's not so bad," I lie. I should say, *It isn't as bad as Nova's*, but I don't. I wonder why my recoil is different from his. My mom says there aren't truly evil or good brujas. That our powers are the same blessings and it's up to us to choose how to use them. Perhaps the marks come when a brujo uses his powers for bad. They cover Nova's hands, forearms. They ring around his heart… Maybe I'm trying to see a good in Nova that doesn't exist.

Rishi picks up her pace to walk at my side. She's a funny sight in her black dress and broken black wings, but that's what I love about her. She's completely and unabashedly herself, no matter who's around.

"You're practically a bird," I say, playfully tugging at her hair.

"That's what I want to be in my next life," she says. "Being people is too hard sometimes. I just want to shower in birdbaths and fly like the wind."

Nova looks over his shoulder briefly. His bright eyes trace my face. Then he shakes his head. Whatever he might have said is dispelled into the dark of the tunnel. He keeps walking with his hands in his pockets.

"Where did tall, dark, and ugly come from?" Rishi whispers.

Ugly is the last word I'd use to describe Nova. He walks with his head down, and I try to picture him walking down the street. If I saw him walking opposite me, before I knew him, I'd probably cross to the other side. Now that I know him, I *want* him walking with me.

"Rishi, be nice."

"I guess if you're into muscles and tattoos or whatever," Rishi says.

"He's a family friend."

"If that's what you call a hired lackey." She makes a face. "It's like I'm seeing a whole new side of you. I'm not *complaining*. It's just that you've been this kind of blurred version of yourself and now what I see is more crystal clear."

"Are you freaked?"

"Do I look freaked?" She looks at me, trying to pull me into a staring contest.

I shove her playfully. "Not enough."

Her wings brush against my arm. Nova looks at us again.

"I'm glad you're here though," I tell her. "You have to know that this isn't a fairy tale."

She slings her arm around my shoulders. "You're magic, Alex. You're like my human shield."

Nova reaches the end of the tunnel first. Tiny creatures flutter through miles and miles of sharp-green grass as tall as Nova's shoulders. The ring of sun and the crescent moon travel across the swirling, purple sky. I'm thankful the gloomy, gray rain is gone. I'm thankful the moon and sun aren't close enough to eclipse. I'm thankful we still have time.

We cut through the wild grass. It practically swallows Rishi and me whole. Nova could pass for a disembodied head walking across the top of the emerald-green sea. Giant flowers grow in brilliant shades of red, yellow, and orange. We use our knives and the mace to part our way and keep the flower's thorny vines from scratching our skin. Still, when we reach the road at the clearing, my arms are covered in dozens of thin scratches.

The road here is dusty and sunken in, like thousands of feet have walked across it. Who were they? I wonder. What were they searching for?

Nova reaches for something around his neck—his prex, but it's gone. Instead, he kisses the back of his thumb. "Thank El Papa for our passage."

Rishi gives me a sideways glance and shrugs. I've got no one to ask blessings to because I know in my heart I don't deserve it. Instead, I lower my head and ask El Guardia, Protector of All Living Things, to watch over my family.

We get to the fork in twenty minutes. I press on the sides of my watch. When it beeps, Nova's eye twitches, but he doesn't say anything. Instead, he stares at the paths in front of us.

"I'm not sure about this," he says.

"Madra said to take the right path," I say.

"Why are you so eager to trust the birds over me?"

Rishi coughs into her hand and says something that sounds like, "*Thief.*"

"Let's look at this objectively," I say. "The left path leads to the trail *I* wanted to take between Bone Valle and the Poison Garden."

"I don't know how I feel about bones or poison," Rishi says.

"See?" Nova asks.

I scoff. "*Now* you agree with each other."

The left fork looks bulldozed, cleared of trees and rubble.

"Now let's look at my path," Nova says, pointing to the one in the middle. The way is green and vibrant, lined by lush trees. White butterflies flutter by the dozens. When the wind blows, petals and leaves fall to the ground. Fuzzy animals that remind me of overgrown hamsters race from tree trunk to tree trunk. "It's goddamn angelic is what it is."

"I don't know about you guys," Rishi says, "but that third one, the 'right' one we're supposed to take, doesn't look so hot."

She's not wrong. The third path is out of my worst nightmares. The trees are dry and black, like used coal. Thin and tangled like barbed wire, and just as prickly. A hunched, furless cat scatters up a tree with something dead in its jaws.

"I'm not just doing this to contradict you," Nova says. "We don't know Madra. For all we know, she could be leading us into a trap. The Meadow *and* the Wastelands lead to the mountain pass. Let's take the way that looks less likely to kill us."

"But—"

"You paid for a guide, Ladybird. So let me guide."

Doubt makes my thoughts spin. I reset my stopwatch to keep track of our next leg. "It seems too easy."

"We deserve a bit of easy, don't you think?" Nova smiles, and it lights up his whole face.

Rishi raises her hand. "I like it easy."

Madra did tell me to *look twice*. The more I look at the path on the right, the more it frightens me. A tiny imp creature lazily drags a bloody bag over his shoulders. It glares at us with black eyes, bares a row of tiny sharp teeth, and hisses, "*Intruders.*"

The middle path sings with light and life. One step closer to my family.

Finally, I hold my hands out and say, "After you."

22

Look twice, my child,

for shadows change

and so do faces.

—REZO DE LAS BRUJAS

S o far, so breezy," Nova says, whistling as we walk.

Their good mood is a wordless shift that happens when he flanks me on the right and Rishi on my left. It's like there was never a different path or option. This was the only one.

As we walk, my magic tickles my skin. Something about these woods is magnetic. I want to reach out and let my power free, but I hold back.

"I wonder if the rest of Los Lagos looked like this once," Rishi says. She picks up a white flower that fell from a tree and tucks it behind her ear. "Before the energy-sucking monster started destroying everything."

"When I was little," Nova says, "my gran used to say that Los Lagos began as a waiting place for spirits. La Mama and

El Papa created it for the afterlife. But then the land took on a life of its own. It became solid. Grass and forests began to grow. Mountains formed, prairies shifted, and lakes and rivers cut across them all. The Tree of Souls was always the heart of it. Then the Deos sent animals and half-beings that didn't belong in the human realm anymore."

"Like the dodo bird?" Rishi asks hopefully. Out of every extinct animal, she wants to see a real-life dodo.

Nova chuckles. "Something like that. People came after that. Brujas and brujos were banished here. Some even came on their own, seeking to build a new life."

"When did the Devourer show up?" I ask. Tiny animals on the trees shudder when I say the shadow creature's name.

"I don't know," Nova says. "Maybe she was banished here or maybe she was here from the start."

"I wish Madra were less cryptic," I say. "I think the answer to defeating the Devourer is in the tree. Maybe we'll come across another one of the tribes Madra mentioned. Maybe we can get real answers."

"Maybe." Rishi is half listening, half petting tiny, green fairies that jump on branches and walk alongside us. They come in all the colors of the forest, with gossamer bodies and slick, bald heads crowned with thorns. They seem to make it a game of seeing who can get the biggest bite out of us.

One opens its tiny pink mouth and goes for my face. I pinch her leathery skin and hold her up to my lips. I blow at the fairy, like she's an eyelash at the tip of my finger. As she floats away, I wonder if I should've made a wish. Nova, on the other hand, flicks at one that lands on his shoulder. It hits a tree but recovers quickly, spitting in our wake.

"It's hard to think of Madra being afraid of anyone," Rishi says. "When she caught me in the middle of the sky, I thought I'd died and gone to heaven. Not that Hindus believe in *that* heaven, but you know what I mean."

"Monsters are the origin for a lot of human myths," Nova tells her. "Like angels."

"Madra isn't a monster!" Rishi says. "Madra is doing the same thing as Alex. She's trying to keep her people alive. *The Devourer* is a monster."

I remember the night of my Deathday. The portal opened up, and she was on the other side, waiting, her face hidden by the horned skull of a hideous beast. *I've found you*, she told me.

"I wonder what the Devourer looks like beneath that bone helmet," I say. "The Book doesn't have a sketch."

"The avianas described her as a 'terror in the night,'" Rishi says. "I'm not sure I want to find out what that looks like."

"In a place of magic like this," Nova says, "power doesn't always have a single shape. It just *is*. Maybe the Devourer is a beautiful woman one moment and a winged demon the next."

"I suppose it shouldn't matter *what* she is," I say, "as long as I can defeat her."

Rishi makes a pondering sound. "What if she has a million eyes or poisonous fangs or, I don't know, a flaming sword. What if she's human?"

Nova looks at Rishi curiously. "Is something easier to destroy if it doesn't look human? Like, you'd kill a spider because it scares you, but you wouldn't kill a person if it destroyed some-one you loved?"

"That's different!" Rishi shouts. The flower in her hair is drooping.

"Not all monsters *look* monstrous." There's so much sadness in his voice that I want to ask how he knows that. "Sometimes they're perfectly normal humans. Sometimes they're so beautiful, you would never suspect."

He holds up a branch so Rishi and I can pass without it hitting our heads.

"We have to be prepared for any form it takes shape."

"I'm prepared," I say, sounding bolder than I feel. "The Devourer consumes power. What if there's no tree to take power from?"

"Destroy the Tree of Souls?" Nova stops walking for a minute. "You'd destroy an entire realm to save your family?"

"That's not what I said." I keep walking without looking at him. Suddenly, I'm annoyed at Nova. My eye keeps twitching, I'm sweating, and I'm hungry. "Whose side are you on?"

"I don't exactly like Sir Lights-a-Lot," Rishi says, "but he's got a point. Without the Devourer, the tree can give life back to Los Lagos. You could save more than your family. You could save the whole world! Or rather, this world."

They don't understand, a tiny voice says. I listen to the wind rustling through the perfectly green trees and perfectly blooming flowers. *Not one of them understands this power.*

I walk faster, leaving them behind.

"Alex, get back here," Nova shouts.

"Just give her space," Rishi tells him. Their voices are amplified in my head, like I'm hearing them over a stereo.

"We really shouldn't separate."

"You don't know anything about girls, do you?"

"I know enough."

Rishi scoffs. "She's overwhelmed by how enormous this task is and scared because everything is trying to kill us, and hello, you don't exactly have the best bedside manner. I know Alex better than you. Back off."

"You know her better? Clearly not well enough that she trusted you with her secret."

I can't take it anymore. I pick up my pace, sweat dripping down my chest and spine. I wish I could outrun their voices, my memories, my sins. When my legs burn and Nova and Rishi are shouting for me to wait for them, I stop. I grab my knees and catch my breath.

"There's my Olympic runner," Rishi says, patting me on the back. "I don't know about you guys, but all this talk about destruction has me hungry. I had a dream the other night that I was eating a tray of empanadas by myself."

"You'd have to get in line," Nova says.

My mouth waters at the thought of the food we had at my party—the trays of lasagna, hayacas, towers and towers of pastelitos and ham and cheese croquettes, fried sweet plantain with melted cheese, crackling pork belly over salty beans and yellow rice.

"We're here," Nova says.

Up ahead, the trail gives way to the Meadow del Sol. The trees form a perfect ring around the clearing. The sun and moon shine an ethereal light, so everything looks overexposed. There's a long, wooden table at the center of the meadow.

"You know what I find weird?" Rishi asks.

"You, the girl with fake wings and purple combat boots, think something is weird?" Nova asks.

Rishi turns her long nose up at him and continues her thought. "Madra kept talking about the other tribes, but we've been walking for hours."

I look at my watch. "Two and a half to be exact."

"But we haven't seen anyone. It's not like when you walk around Brooklyn and you see people coming and going."

"You're forgetting one thing," Nova says. "Some creatures prefer to see, not be seen."

"Oh great, I love getting creeped on by supernatural creatures," Rishi says.

"Maybe your voice scared them away," Nova tells her.

"If anything's scary around here it's your face." Rishi skips around Nova, ripping flowers from the ground and throwing them at him. He grumbles and slaps them away.

I shield the light from my eyes with my hand. Something shiny glints on the wooden table in the meadow. The sweet smell of freshly baked bread envelops me, and my belly growls so loudly, I'm sure a galaxy far, far away can hear. "What's that?"

As we get closer, I see the table is carved out of a fallen tree that's been cut in half. Toadstools and long grass rise up from the ground to create natural chairs. I can smell bread, but I don't see it.

Rishi squeals and claps her hands together. "It's a tea party."

"I don't see any tea," Nova says.

I turn my face up to the sun and moon and welcome the sweet

breeze. My nose tickles with my magic. There's a strong power all over this meadow.

Nova pokes the toadstool with his foot, and when he determines it'll hold his weight, he sits on it. "This reminds me of the stories of the Kingdom of Adas."

"What are adas?" Rishi asks. *Ah-dahs.*

"They're fairies," Nova says. "But they live in a different realm. They're pretty as hell, but I wouldn't want to meet one. They have giant banquets and party all night. I got invited to one in Central Park, but it's just not the same."

"How come *we* don't go to magical parties in Central Park?" Rishi asks me.

"Because if you eat fairy food, you're stuck there," I say. "Also, because *no.*"

"What, in Central Park?" Nova scoffs. "You only get stuck if you're *in* the Kingdom of Adas. Only an ada can take you there."

"Shut up," I grumble, but then so does my stomach. "I'm so hungry."

"Well, if you hadn't given all our supply to the avianas, we'd be feasting on beef jerky and stale bread right now, wouldn't we?"

Rishi mimics him as he speaks.

Then, their faces draw a blank. They jolt from their seats, slowly retreating from the table.

"Alex," Nova says, locking his eyes—blue and green and slightly terrified—with mine.

I see them too late, but maybe they were always there. What was it that Madra said? Look twice.

I blink rapidly, and it's like clearing a hazy film from my sight.

From the trees, the shadows, the tall grass, creatures emerge all around us.

My mother told me it's rude to stare, but they are wonderful and fearsome to look at. Real fairies from the Kingdom of Adas. Tall, slender green pixies with shimmering wings and black, almond-shaped eyes. Their fingers are long, like flower stems, ending in leaves where nails should be. Snow-white women with skin like leather and smooth, hairless heads wear crowns of thorns and pale roses. Dresses made of thousands and thousands of dry flower petals that rustle in the breeze like unearthly ghouls.

I want to keep looking at them when a voice startles me.

"What do we have here?" a smooth, silky voice, like the drizzle of honey, asks.

I turn around, but there is no one there.

"Don't be afraid," he says.

When I turn back around, everyone is sitting down, like I missed their movement in the blink of an eye.

Look twice, I remind myself.

At the head of the table, where the roots of the fallen tree create a high, twisted chair, is a man. His chest is bare. His skin is tan. There's a tattoo of the sun over his heart. His face is stunning in that symmetrical way, like his maker carved him from stone and wouldn't stop until it was perfect. But the truly startling part is the curved horns that sprout from his temples and sweep into twisting points around his head.

Gold, silver, and leather bracelets decorate his wrists, and dozens of bauble rings adorn his fingers like knuckle-dusters. My dad had a knuckle-duster from when he was younger. It's in the bottom drawer of my mom's dresser wrapped in a yellowing handkerchief.

"You like my rings?" the horned man asks.

"I'm not much of a jewelry person," I say, and instantly hate how nervous I sound.

"Just the one," he says, pointing at the moon around my neck.

"Are you hungry?" a girl asks. She's got wild curls and light-brown skin that is run through with green lines, like a birch tree. She wears the same set of bracelets as the horned man. She points to three empty seats. "Join us."

"Thank you," I say, "but we were just resting. We didn't mean to intrude."

"Then keep on walking," a girl mutters. Her skin is red as lava with splotches of black. Her eyes are dark and too far apart, giving her the look of a human salamander. When she huffs, smoke comes out of her nostrils.

"Rodriga," the horned man says. His voice is hard and cutting. Everyone at the table jumps. "Is that the way we treat our guests?"

Everyone at the table looks down at their laps.

"Hey, now," Nova says in his easy way. "No worries. We've still got a lot of terrain to cover. We're heading to Las Peñas to mine for minerals. We'd best get a move on."

"Do you know what happens to travelers who come here in search of treasure?" Rodriga asks.

On the other side of the table, one of the pixies is letting Rishi touch her iridescent wings.

"Enough," the horned man says. "I am Agosto, Faun King of the Meadow del Sol, and these are my kin. We live here safely away from the wicked birds near the river and far away from the Bone Valle."

I don't like that he called the avianas wicked, but I stay quiet.

"I insist you join us," Agosto says. "Regain your strength. You look parched and ready to fall over."

Nova and I look at each other. I don't want to insult this horned man. Behind the pleasantry, there's steel in his voice. His knuckles are thick with calluses that come from repeatedly beating on things. Like my dad's from his boxing days.

Nova holds my hand. He applies the tiniest pressure, but I know he's urging me to sit. Make nice. Avoid ruffling any more feathers, so to speak. Then we can plan our escape.

"Okay," I say. "But only for a bit."

Agosto waves a hand across the air and a decadent banquet appears. "Eat."

Se fue, mi'jita, past the unseable door.

If I listen to the wind, I can still hear her laughter.

—CLARIBELLE AND THE KINGDOM OF ADAS:
TALES TALL AND TRUE,
GLORIANA PALACIOS

Dozens and dozens of plates appear across the table. The meadow people raise their arms and cheer. A lonely cloud momentarily passes over the sun, leaving us in shadow. My vision flickers for a moment; then the cloud passes by, and we're basked in white fairy light again.

Nova and Rishi take the empty seats between two winged adas. The only seat left open is the one to the right of Agosto. He motions to the empty toadstool with his ornately decorated hand.

"I'm sure your journey has been exhausting," he tells me. "The path to the mountain is not an easy one."

I nod. Words. Where are my words? Looking at Agosto is unlike anything I've ever experienced. He is perfect in his beauty and strangeness. He's a wild, horned forest king and an angel all at once.

"I hope you find rest here," he says.

The Meadowkin don't need to be told twice to eat. They dig in to heaping piles of plump, purple fruits and down sweet mead. White, fluffy cakes drizzled with honey and sprinkled with fat, sparkling sugar crystals. Roasted meat sizzles, surrounded by tender root vegetables the color of blood and bone.

"Are you serious?" Rishi shouts from the other end of the table. A stack of fluffy roti appears in front of her. She rips it up and dips it into a cast iron pot of dal. "It tastes just like my mom makes it."

Agosto leans back in his twisted throne, an ornate wooden goblet in his hand. His full lips curl up, showing he's pleased. "We have everything you could ever dream of having."

"That right?" Nova leans over the table. I'm afraid he's going to say something offensive or rude. Instead he says, "Then I dream of a fat ass steak."

"I'm so glad you said 'steak,'" Rishi says with her mouth full.

And sure enough, a sizzling hunk of prime rib appears in front of him complete with disco fries.

A frail man with the head of a mouse leans over Nova's plate. In his thin voice, he says, "Ooh! Looks good. Is that what you eat where you're from?"

"Nah, I usually eat whatever's on the dollar menu."

The mouse man grins and stuffs his mouth with cake. His wrists are too small for some of his bracelets, and when one of them slips, I notice black-and-red wounds ring his wrists.

"Something the matter?" Agosto asks me.

I shake my head, trying to mask my worry when Rishi gets up

from her seat and comes over to my side. She curtsies to Agosto, then sits with me. We barely fit on the same stool but that doesn't stop her from trying.

"I want you to try this," she tells me, holding a slice of fruit shaped like a perfect star. "These are my favorite in all the worlds."

I take the sticky star in my hand. It's perfectly green with a single seed wedged in the center. When I take a bite, juice rolls down my chin, and then we're in a fit of giggles at our messiness. I wipe my lips with the back of my hand.

This place is a dream, a voice whispers. *This place isn't real.*

But I want it to be real. I want to feel this happy always. I want to be in the light.

"I'm glad I'm here with you," Rishi tells me.

This place brings out the warm brown in her skin, her shining eyes. Rishi has impossibly long, black lashes and perfect eyebrows I've not so secretly coveted.

"I wanted to tell you something else," she says, "but it's the strangest thing…the thought fell out of my head."

Rishi's always distracted. She's like a magpie, searching for shiny, pretty things. She gives me a quick peck on the cheek and goes back down the table, making new friends.

When Rishi leaves, Agosto returns his attention to me. He leans his face toward me with total interest.

"Go on," he tells me. "I know there's something you want to ask me."

There are tons of things I want to ask him. Like, where does this food come from? Why do they all wear the same bracelets? Why does Rodriga the salamander girl seem to hate me? Even as she tilts her bowl of soup to her lips, her eyes never leave my face. What does Agosto know of the Devourer?

He waves his hand and a second wooden goblet appears. The liquid is dark and smells bittersweet, like berries gone too ripe. My tongue is so parched, and my belly makes hungry noises. The journey is catching up with me, pressing down on my shoulders with a terrible ache. Why can't I be like Rishi and Nova, happily eating and telling stories about where we come from? They make the streets of Brooklyn sound magical and wondrous. Why does it take being far away from home to finally miss it?

I drink from the wooden goblet. I've tried wine once, on a dare from Lula. It was Lady's Alta Bruja wine and they were blessing a newly married couple. Just like that time, this wine causes me to scrunch up my face at the tartness. I look down the table to see if Rishi or Nova want some, but they seem to already have their own goblets, complete with rose petals floating atop the liquid.

Agosto finds my reaction to the wine amusing and laughs. I decide I rather like his laugh and the way tufts of pollen float around him. One gets stuck on his long lashes. I reach for it and free it. He watches me. Blinks. His smile is a riddle. His face is a dream. I can't seem to take my hand away from his face. My fingers trace one of his horns.

I jerk my hand back.

"It's okay," he tells me. "You're curious."

I fear I've turned as red as my wine. "Why aren't you in the Kingdom of Adas?"

He thinks on the question. Even his serious face is beautiful. He looks into his goblet like he's searching for the right answer. I

186

realize maybe that wasn't the right thing to ask. In a world wholly new to me, that seems to hold so many secrets, what *is* the right thing to ask?

"We are exiles," he whispers.

"Oh." I bite my lip, searching for something to say. Then, because my brain seems to be on delay, I settle for, "I'm sorry."

"Don't be." He takes a small drink. The red liquid stains his lips. "It was long ago. We refused to bow to a vicious king, and so we left. These lands have changed over time, and our meadow grows smaller. But it is the only home we have. We've been here so long that I don't consider myself as coming from the Kingdom of Adas but from here. Don't you think it important to have a land to call your own?"

"I think so. My mother's family were run out of their lands in Spain and fled to Mexico. My dad's ancestors were African slaves in Ecuador. They went to Panama and then Puerto Rico. Somehow, my blood comes from all over the world and settled in Brooklyn. Brooklyn is my home."

"Brook-*lin*," Agosto says. "I rather like that word."

I laugh wholeheartedly, right from my belly. It's such a good feeling that I can't remember why I don't let myself do it more often.

"It's so beautiful here." I tilt my face to the light. I start to feel like I've forgotten something, but I'm not sure what. I realize my goblet is empty and I'm a little disappointed. But when I blink, it's full again.

"You say you're traveling to the mountains?" Agosto asks. "I should warn you. There are nasty giants in those parts. Oh, and do avoid the Laguna Roja, unless you can breathe underwater. Los Lagos might be home to me, but all places have their dangers."

"Is the labyrinth dangerous?" I ask.

A sad smile tugs at his lips. He leans into his seat, a throne suited for the Meadow King. "No good can come from that place."

"Have you been there?" My heart shoots up to my throat.

"Long ago." Agosto takes his goblet and drinks deep. His lips are stained purple. "I was searching for someone. But the labyrinth has a way of taking you in and never letting go. It is a dark place, a damned place. I find it's better to stay here, in the meadow, where I can always find the light."

"What if you didn't have a choice?" I press on. "What if you had to go back?"

The faun king laughs heartily. I love the sound of it. "Eat, now. You must be famished."

I *am* hungry. Who knows when we'll have food again on the rest of our journey? But there's something wrong about the roasted chicken in front of me—the skin is perfectly crispy. The potatoes are soft and smothered in rosemary and sea salt. It's just the way I like it. But when I lean forward, I don't smell the rich spices.

I smell dirt.

The magic within me stirs. I press my hand over my racing heart. I've used more magic since we arrived than I have my whole life. I can feel my power getting restless, as if it had a taste of freedom and it won't be caged again.

"Your power is calling to the meadow," Agosto says.

How does he know that? "Do you have magic?"

He turns his head from side to side. "Once. It was taken from me."

"By who?"

"My brother, the Bastard King of Adas. The last great thing I could do for my people was find them a new home." He pats my hand gently with his. "There's so much I wish I could do for them still—so much I'm willing to do."

I take Agosto's hand and squeeze. I can't imagine that an immortal being such as him needs the comfort of a girl like me, but I know his pain. The feeling stirs inside of me until I start to feel like I'll come undone.

"Excuse me," I say, standing from the table.

"Wait." Agosto takes my hand in his. Despite his calluses and scars, his touch is surprisingly soft. For a moment, I pretend he's someone else. I look down the table, and the thought startles me so that I pull away.

"I'm just getting a little warm in the sun," I assure him.

He kisses the back of my hand. "Don't go too far. It isn't safe out there."

The sound of a snake hissing follows me as I walk away. When I turn around, Rodriga is leaning over Agosto's arm, vying for his attention. She waves her arms in the air, but all he does is look into his wine goblet.

I start to walk down the table to Nova, but he's on his second steak, and I've already forgotten what I wanted to ask him. Where are my thoughts going? It's like Rishi said. They fell out of her head.

I walk to the edge of the meadow to find some shade. My stomach contracts painfully. I sit down and hit my head against the bark of the tree. Can it be that I've resisted my magic for so long that I simply just can't recognize the difference between a stomachache and my own power?

"Lula," I say. "I really need you to come back."

It isn't Lula who appears. It's my mother. Right in the middle of the field. Her hair is still haloed by bright-red flowers that match her lips. Her white dress is stained with dirt.

I jump up to my feet. I need to run to her. I need her to forgive me. Need her to tell me I'm going the right way. I need my mom.

Just like Lula's apparition, my mom flickers. Unlike Lula, she doesn't stay. I run to her open arms but a shadow appears behind her. I can hear her shout my name once before she vanishes. My shaking hands close around air, and I can feel the magic pounding up from the pit of my belly. *That's my magic.*

And it wants out. I listen to the heartbeat of the ground. It whispers a welcome. My magic builds in me like a song, and I let it play along my skin.

Listen, the little voice tells me.

What am I listening for? There is only a meadow full of laughter and cheer.

Look, the little voice says.

What am I looking for? There are my friends and the adas. There was a woman there. She was wearing roses. I felt like I knew her. I felt like…

"Encantrix." Agosto calls for me, walking on powerful hooves. He takes my hand and helps me stand. As the sun and moon set, the meadow is bathed in firelight. "Are you well?"

"I'm better than well," I say.

"I wanted to give you one last gift before you carry on with your journey."

He hands me a wine goblet and offers me his arm. This time the wine isn't bitter, and the roses coat my senses. *Nothing coats the senses quite like roses*, someone said.

"Journey?" My thoughts drift away like clouds. "I wouldn't dream of going anywhere."

24

The bleeding heart

cannot survive the night.

—Bleeding Heart, Herbs, and Flowers,
Book of Cantos

The dark brings out its nocturnal critters—owls with glowing, red eyes. Marsupials scratching their way up trees. Fireflies by the hundreds. The sky is painted the deepest blue, moonless, sunless, and covered in shooting stars.

Every time I blink, I see something new. Agosto leads me back to the center of the meadow, where a white fire erupts. There's a great cheer, followed by music. A band of adas play instruments made of hollow branches and shimmering cobwebs. Agosto spins me in place, our fingers sparking with magic. Wine sloshes over the rim of my cup, and I bring my hand to my lips to lick every falling drop.

This *is what a party is supposed to feel like*, I think.

The Meadowkin and my friends gather around. Agosto bows in front of me and pulls me into a dance. I never dance. I never liked it before. A hazy memory sifts through my crowded thoughts:

Lula and Rose dancing circles around me, too little and too happy to care about looking foolish. They would love this place. They would love to see me happy.

"There's somewhere I have to be," I say.

"I will get you there," Agosto tells me. His large hands close around my waist and lift me into the air. "But first, there is someone who wishes to dance with you."

Agosto bows again, winking at someone behind me. He holds his palms out and a flute appears. It twists at the ends like vines of ivy and has dozens of little holes. He brings it to his wine-stained lips and blows. I can't imagine how something so delicate can make such a powerful sound, but it does.

"You owe me a dance," Rishi says, tapping my shoulder.

My insides tickle, like the moment you plunge down a roller coaster. I walk around her in a circle. She rests one of her hands on her hip, her weight shifted to the side, all attitude. The gem of her nose ring winks at me from every angle. My little magpie.

"Would you accept a fairy fiesta to make up for the Ghoul Ball?" I hold out my hand. I've never felt this bold in my whole life. It's like the magic is pulling the strings and I'm just allowing it.

Rishi shrugs a shoulder playfully. Her black wing looses a handful of feathers. Something in my mind clicks, and I reach out with my power. Rishi gasps as the wings bind together, longer and fuller.

"Oh, Alex!" She spreads her arms wide and jumps on me.

I ignore the twinge in my spine where the recoil grips me like a vice. The throng of dancing Meadowkin spin and glide around us. It's a chaotic waltz, everyone moving together but separately around the flames.

Rishi twists her hands in the air. The long, dark waves of her hair sway over her shoulders. Her skirt billows when she spins, and when I look at her, I consider that magic can be a beautiful thing.

Overgrown dandelions perk up from the ground, like they wait for the cover of darkness before showing themselves. I reach for one. Hold it up to my lips and blow. The glowing white seeds disperse in tiny bursts of light.

"I could stay here forever," I say. "My power feels different here. It feels *right*. I've never had that before."

The music slows like a caress. Rishi takes my face in her hands. Her long, black lashes create spidery shadows down her cheeks. Her midnight eyes flick down to my lips, and when she sighs, I know she was eating peaches. My heartbeat multiplies, like there's a tiny heart at the end of all my fingers and toes, between my clavicles, inside my ears, and at the tip of my nose.

"Hey!" Nova's cheery, booming voice cuts across the meadow. He zigzags between the fairy people. He slings his arm around our necks.

Rishi's face scrunches up, irritated.

"Ladybird, where have you been?" He grabs me around my waist and lifts me into the air.

When he tries to go for Rishi, she spins around and says, "I'm going to get us more wine."

"What's gotten into you?" I ask him.

Nova's *playful*. He pinches my cheek and seems to be dancing to a rhythm in his own head. In the firelight, his eyes look like they're glowing.

"Isn't this great?" he asks. "It's like Christmas dinner. Not at my house, but probably at your house. My Christmas dinner is a grilled cheese and tomato sandwich. Some years, I put bacon on it. Maybe, if I wish it, the magic tree table will give it to me. I'll make one for you. It'll change your life. We can share with Rishi, but I don't think she likes me very much."

"Pardon." An ada with a blue face and silver hair bumps into Nova. She clutches her stomach and makes a run for the line of trees, a rank smell trailing behind her.

Look, a little voice whispers in my ear.

I shut my eyes and try to focus. My mind feels like cotton. Cotton candy. Pretty cotton candy, pink and fluffy and melty on my tongue.

"Earth to Alex," Nova says, squeezing my nose.

I slap his hand away. "What?"

"Look at me," he says. Maybe Nova was the voice I heard just now. Maybe I'm imagining things. "Look at what the meadow is doing to me."

Nova holds his arms out. The black burn marks I mistook for tattoos are changing. His glossy eyes are full of hope. "They're getting smaller. Can you believe that? This means I might have a chance."

"What do you mean 'a chance'?"

His smile falls, and he jerks back, like he can't believe he just said that. "I—I can't remember."

Look harder! the voice yells.

I whip around to search for the source when a cold splash hits my face. Red berry wine trickles down my neck. I wipe it out of my eyes and spit the droplets that make their way into my mouth.

The music dies, replaced by whispers. Hundreds of eyes turn to stare at me.

"What the hell was that?" Nova turns to Rodriga. The salamander girl throws her goblet on the ground.

I hold up my hand to Nova. This isn't his fight. It's mine.

"Come on, encantrix," Rodriga says. "Let's see that power fly."

"What's your problem?" A dark coil of energy wraps itself around me. I could unleash it. I could make her hurt.

"Your weakness. Your lies. Your fear. I could smell it on you before you entered the meadow. You get to sing and dance and fall in love, while the rest of us have to be *this* for eternity."

My anger snaps like a whip around her throat. I can feel her struggle for breath. Her pulse slowing in my veins.

I gasp and let her go. This isn't me.

But it is, the voice in my head whispers.

Rodriga coughs, managing a weak laugh. "Maybe there is hope yet."

I grit my teeth and keep my fists balled at my sides. "Why can't magical people ever say what they really mean?"

"My Meadow King," Rodriga hisses. Agosto is walking across the meadow. "I'm bound to him and the meadow. You don't belong here, wretched girl. Get out before it's too late."

"But—"

"Rodriga!" Agosto shouts. His face is all shadows. His powerful, hoofed legs stomp across the meadow. His voice is a thunderclap. "I *warned* you."

His fists hit her in the chest. She flies back and slams into a tree. The air around her splinters for the blink of an eye. She grabs her side and then slowly picks herself back up.

"Did you see that?" I whisper to Nova. Nova shakes his head. He holds his hand out, like he's telling me to keep whatever I've seen to myself.

Agosto's dark eyes trace the perimeter of the meadow, then fall back to me. "I am sorry if she has displeased you. Please, eat."

Eat? How can I eat after this? At his command, dozens of adas run to the banquet table.

A fat bird with thorns coming out of his side lands on Agosto's shoulder. It squawks in his ear, but Agosto shows no sign that it bothers him.

"Excuse me," Agosto says. He conjures his flute and begins to play. The notes sound rougher, deeper than before.

Despite the openness of the meadow, it starts to feel small, like the trees are encroaching. A shadow howls in the wind, sending shivers along my skin. *You don't belong here, wretched girl. Get out before it's too late.*

Too late for what? My senses are groggy, like I'm waking from a long, long sleep. I know something isn't right, but part of me still wants to believe in the spell of the meadow. Spell.

It's all a spell.

Wretched girl. That's what I am. That's why I'm here in the first place. A jolt runs through me like lightning. My mind clears, and all at once, I can see their faces—my family. My mother. My mother was *here* and I turned my back on her again.

Wretched girl.

Too late.

"We have to go," I shout at Nova.

"Wait." Nova presses his hand to his stomach and shakes his head. "I'm going to be sick."

He doubles over and throws up at my feet. I rub his back until he stops. I try to help him stand, but his knees give out and we fall on the grass.

"I can't," he cries.

"I'm going to get Rishi. Wait here."

I search for her in the clusters of adas but can't find her. The stench of rotting fruit is overwhelming. When I look down at the banquet table, all I see is moldy bread and fruits cracked open like skulls. Feverish fingers scoop the sloppy meat down their gullets. Fat tears run down their faces as they binge on the rotten feast. All the while, the music plays on. The adas stomp their hooves, claws, and feet to the rhythm of the flute and the strum of golden strings.

"Rishi!" I scream for her.

Rodriga's words start to make sense. I fell for the spell of the meadow. *We have to be* this *for eternity.*

Then I see her.

Panic rushes through me as Rishi extends her arm to a fairy girl. The acrid smell of rot and bodily waste makes my head spin. *Look twice.*

The bracelet in the ada's hand changes, and I see it for what it really is.

I break into a run, but I know I won't make it in time. I hold my arms out and blast a shot of raw power at the ada. She flies back into an invisible barrier between two oak trees. The air fractures like a crack in a windowpane. Her bracelets are replaced by rusty manacles.

Blink. The glamour returns and they're bracelets again.

Blink. I can see the adas for what they truly are—gaunt, thin, wrinkled. I wave my hand over the banquet table and find the glamour. I tear it down so the table reveals itself to all. The creatures wail and scream and cry. Nova squeezes his temples with his palms. Rishi gets on the ground and heaves.

"No!" The adas turn away from the banquet. "We cannot see! We cannot see!"

The table is nothing but rotting wood, the plates of rank food covered in slick, fat maggots.

The flute in Agosto's hands disappears.

"You keep them here," I tell him. "Why?"

The faun ambles toward me. His muscles ripple in the break-of-day light. The Meadowkin behind him cower.

"Is that what you see?" Agosto asks me. He is no longer the wild king of the forest I first saw. It's as if all the wonder and hope has drained from his voice.

"You said you brought your people here for a better life, but you're torturing them!"

Agosto tries to grab for me, to stop me, but I smack away his touch. My magic collides with him. He's glamoured too. I can feel the magic around his aura. He shakes his head, but I've already gone too far. I break away his facade, revealing the shackles around his own wrists. The chain drags from the roots of the tree at the center of the meadow. Agosto sinks to his knees, like the weight of his horns is too much.

"Encantrix," he says. "I'm trying to save us all."

"By trapping me here?"

"I had no choice. She instructed us to keep you here. The way you saw the meadow when you arrived—that is how we used to be. Before we defied her. Before we lost. She will come for you. She will take everything you love. Your power can change everything. Your power—"

Agosto snaps his head toward the hiss coming from the trees. The winds change, bringing a terrible cold with them. Shadows whisper in my ears.

"She is coming." Agosto jumps to his hooves and grabs me by the shoulders, pushing me to the border of the meadow. "Run to the Wastelands. Just run!"

"I can't leave without them!" I try to shove the faun out of my way but he's too solid. I scream for Nova and Rishi, but they're too sick to understand, eyes glazed and smiles plastered on their faces. They don't know we're in danger. They stumble in my direction, listening to the ghost of the adas' songs.

"Fix them," I tell Agosto.

He shakes his head. "The only way is to purge the poison."

"Poison?"

I grab Rishi's arm first and wrap it around my shoulder. I turn and Nova trips over his own feet. I can carry one, but not the other.

A collective gasp falls across the meadow. The adas retreat, the same way they appeared, into nothingness. *Blink.* They're gone.

"I told you," Rodriga hisses, her salamander skin changing to solid black as she gets on her knees, bowing to the shadow that cyclones at the center of the field.

I beg Nova to get up. I beg Rishi to run, but I'm losing them. Fear slithers into my body, pushing away at my magic. I can feel my power recoiling, hiding in the comfortable place I've always kept it.

"Agosto, help me!"

He can't. He's on his knees, hands splayed forward in submission as the great black cloud takes shape. Shadows curl like tentacles around a figure cloaked in a bloodred dress. The material hugs her like death, and a helmet of bone and metal hides her face.

She takes small steps, practically walking on air, and stops where Agosto is crouched. "You never learn, do you?"

Then she pulls out a spear and drives it through the center of his hand.

25

Hide me in your sombra,

mother of the dark.

—REZO DE LA OSCURIDAD,
LADY OF SHADOW AND DARK DEEDS

Agosto's screams fill the silence of the Meadow del Sol.

The Devourer walks past him, her movement like the rattle of a snake, each footstep reverberating in the deepest parts of my heart. She advances toward me like a turbulent storm.

"You're the one causing all the trouble," she says, stopping a couple of yards from me. Her posture is calm, the same stoicism I found in Madra but none of the patience. I can feel the magic that fractures around her. I can feel that it's stronger than me. "Speak, child."

This is why I'm here—to confront this creature and save my family. But standing before her, I've lost my nerve. My mouth is dry and my body is frozen. I can't even reach for my magic.

The Devourer floats up from the ground and flies a lap around me. The black tendrils of her hair lick at the air around me. She breathes deep, a wolf memorizing her prey.

"I have something that belongs to you," she whispers.

"They aren't *things*," I snap.

"So you do have a tongue," she laughs, standing closer to me still. The sky is lightening into a brighter blue. The moon and sun show themselves. "I'm going to enjoy ripping it out."

What am I supposed to do with Nova and Rishi helpless on the ground? I could run. I could leave them behind. Nova would do it if it came down to us versus him. At least, that's what I tell myself.

The Devourer looks at my friends and clucks her tongue as if we're a joke to her. "This is what you've brought to challenge me? You don't know the way of Los Lagos, Alejandra Mortiz. Power comes at a great cost, yes. But what is the price of banishing it? Did you stop to think that your power is connected to your blood—the living and the dead that are tied to you? I thought I was getting your power, but then, they tried to protect you. I can feel their essence in the Tree of Souls. What can you give me in exchange for your family?"

My life.

I don't say it aloud, but it's all I have. She knows it. She mocks me when she says, "Would you like to make a trade? You for them? Why would I when their power is so *delicious*? Why would I when I can have all of you?"

Nova pushes himself to his knees. He looks up at the Devourer like he's in a dream. He starts to crawl to her. I grab him by his shoulders and pull him back.

The Devourer laughs darkly, moving past him and over to where Agosto is whimpering from the spear through his hand. The Devourer pulls the spear free and Agosto's scream is so loud, every bird hidden in the circle of trees takes flight.

"Come on, encantrix," the Devourer says. "Show me what you've got."

I reach for the mace handle in my backpack. It's too cumbersome and heavy to be comfortable, but it's all I've got now that my powers have recoiled from me.

The demon witch tilts her head to the side and says, "Curious."

"Alex," Rishi groans on the ground. "I feel sick. I can't see."

"Get down!" I shout at her.

I step forward and swing the mace. The Devourer is quick as a shadow and moves back before I can complete my swing. She laughs and hits me in the gut with the butt of her spear. I fall to my knees, the wind knocked from my lungs until it burns.

"Pathetic," she spits. "You are the encantrix descendant of the Great Mama Juana Mortiz?"

Her movement is frantic. Her hands shake. There's something wrong with her. A tick to her face, like she's talking to someone I can't see.

I take this moment of distraction and swing the mace at her kneecaps. She falls forward, catches herself on her palms, growling. She throws her spear on the ground. As she stands, she pulls on her magic. She raises her hands to the sky, and the wind picks up and howls around us.

"I was promised the power of a savior," she says, "but all I got is a girl."

204

"I'm sorry," I whisper to my family. I backpedal, scramble on my elbows to get away from her. "I'm sorry."

But the blow never comes. Agosto stands behind the Devourer. He pulls on his chains, slings them around the witch's throat, and pulls tightly. The clouds above us start to shrink as she scratches his arms with her long, hooked nails.

The Devourer makes a terrible choking sound. The rest of the meadow is completely still, the other adas hidden except for Rodriga. She pulls her chains on top of Agosto's. Together, they keep the demon bruja restrained. I can see her eyes glow red with fury beneath the bone mask.

"Go!" he shouts. "I can't hold her for long."

"Agosto—"

I drag Rishi to the edge of the meadow before my arm muscles burn and I can't go any farther. Nova staggers toward us, and I fear I truly will have to leave them behind.

Fight, the voice in my head growls.

Lula's done all my fighting for me. Ever since we were little, she was the one to step forward and punch girls or boys who threatened me. Rose fights the visions in her head every day. My mother—my mother is the strongest woman I know, battling the sadness and grief that comes with raising children alone. All I've ever done is run from things that scare me.

A deep growl shudders through the trees. The Devourer has recovered, and then there is a terrible crunching sound. Agosto's and Rodriga's screams pierce me right down to my bones. I tell myself that they were trying to keep us there for the Devourer. But I saw the desperation in Agosto's eyes. The chains that make him a slave to the creature. They're trying to help me.

There might be hope yet, Rodriga said.

I pull Rishi and Nova behind a tree. I cover them with giant leaves and then run back into the meadow.

The Devourer flips Agosto and Rodriga over her shoulders. The adas are tangled in their own chains. I raise the mace to strike, but when I swing, it slips out of my grip. The Devourer's blast slams into my chest and I land on my shoulder.

"Your heart gives you away," the Devourer tells me. She turns around to face me. "It's like a warning bell the way it beats so loud. So scared. I'll gladly rip it out for you. Save you the trouble it'll give you down the line."

"Funny," I say, pushing myself up. "I was going to say the same thing about your mouth."

I pull on the anger and fear I've felt all my life. I pull on the hope that always feels like it's slipping away. My magic surges through me, fills me with a power stronger than ever before. I blast the Devourer in her stomach. She deflects it with a wave of her hand, but I catch the worry that sparks in her red eyes.

I find myself smiling because I put that worry there. I'm not running.

Unlike so many times before, I call on my power willingly. It's an instinct I can no longer ignore. I'm a wild thing, shooting sparks from my fingers. My throat burns from screaming as the Devourer slaps me with the force of her power. It stings cold all over, and I fall and freeze. I shudder as my magic warms me, my muscles seizing as they thaw.

My vision is filled with red. The Devourer stands over me. Black wisps trail at the ends of her long fingernails.

"You're strong," she whispers in my ear. "But I'm stronger."

I flip to the side, narrowly missing her foot to my face. I jump for the silver handle hiding in the blades of grass. I wrap my magic around the mace until it looks like a weapon made of lightning. I swing it at her head. The Devourer's face snaps to the side. Her hand goes to her mouth, where a thin line of scarlet blood runs down her chin.

She touches it, holds out her fingers to examine the red droplets. Is that fear I see in her eyes?

A sinister laugh makes me jump. Agosto crawls on his elbows toward us. One of his eyes is swollen shut. I can't tell where all the blood is coming from, and then I see the hole in his head where one of his horns has been ripped out.

"You are weakening," Agosto says. "How long since you've fed, Xara?" *Zah-rah.*

"I don't answer to a mortal's name."

"Gods don't bleed," I say.

The Devourer turns her rage on Agosto. He won't survive a second round. I can already feel my muscles cramping from the recoil, but I try to ignore the pain and stand between them. My power pulses at the center of my palms, ready to strike.

The Devourer hesitates, then tilts her face toward the light that comes from the sun and moon. What she sees seems to please her. She places her bloody finger to her lip and smiles a cruel smile.

"The difference between you and me, Alejandra, is that I've lived a long, long time."

"That's not the only difference," I say.

"It's my turn to shape the galaxies. And you're so focused on mourning your lot that you don't see how insignificant you are in the end. Don't worry. You will *beg* me to end your pain soon enough."

She conjures a great, black cloud. I run toward her, screaming at the top of my lungs as I blast my power at her. It booms like thunder and pierces a hole through her cloud.

She's gone.

I release the magic I've built up into the sky, and I relish knowing that I drew first blood.

26

She is the light in the hopeless places.

She is the sky when the night blazes.

—Rezo de La Estrella,
Lady of Hope and
All the World's Brightness

My mother used to pray to La Estrella, the daughter of La Mama and El Papa who birthed all the stars in all the galaxies. For a little while, after my dad's disappearance, my mom erected an altar for her. She bought a statue of a woman with skin like the night sky, eyes silver like stars, and a blue dress draped around her body. She bought fruits and candles and a starling bird in a cage. It took up an entire wall in the kitchen and none of us were allowed to touch it.

But then the candles burned, and the bird got sick, and the food rotted, and one morning, we woke up and the starling was dead. That was the day my mother lost hope and donated the statue of La Estrella to someone else that needed it.

Here, in the Meadow del Sol, as the adas emerge from their hiding places, as the Faun King kneels before me, I collapse. The brightening sky still sparkles with fading stars, and so I pray to La Estrella.

"Forgive me," Agosto tells me, crawling toward me. He takes my hand in his. His shackles drag behind him. He can't stand up, and for the first time, I notice the terrible angle of his broken leg.

I take a deep breath and get on my knees, fighting the recoil that wants to crash over me. I dig my left hand into the dirt and feel for the pulse of the land. I take energy from it, let it filter through me and into Agosto's wound. The gash closes and the blood dries. The swelling around his eye decreases, and before I can move to his ankle, he pulls me into a tight embrace. He's so big, so muscular that I'm surprised at how gentle his touch is.

"Forgive me," he repeats.

I shake my head. It's not that I'm not forgiving him. It's that I can't speak right now. My power is on autopilot, searching for his broken bones. I hiss when I hear the snap in his ankle. Then comes Rodriga. The adas have made a bed of flowers for her. There's a gash in her side, but it isn't fatal. Her hand has been torn off. I shut my eyes. *So much blood*, I think. *There's always so much blood.*

Blood is life, Nova said.

I let out a shaky breath and heal her. For a long time, the salamander girl stares at the stump where her hand should be.

"You came back," she says. "Even after everything."

"Yeah, even after you threw that wine at me. It's a good thing I'm already filthy."

Rodriga laughs, then winces in pain.

There's a noise off to the edge of the meadow.

"It's just us," Nova says, walking in with Rishi.

"Thanks for joining us," I say.

"I feel like I've been hit with a sledgehammer," Nova says. Then, when he sees Rodriga's wound, his face blanks.

"How does your foot taste?" Rishi asks him, heading straight to the center of the meadow where I'm surrounded by the adas.

When I turn around, there are more of them, all chained to the trees that create the meadow ring.

Nova walks silently behind Rishi. "What happened?"

"While you were sleeping off your drunk?" I stand, and suddenly all the adas stand too. I take a step closer toward Nova, and they follow.

"That's normal," Rishi says.

"Not fair, Alex," Nova says. "I didn't know what their food would do to us. We're in Los Lagos, not their fairy realm."

I don't know why I'm picking a fight with him, especially now.

"It doesn't matter," I say. I turn to Agosto. "What do you know about the Devourer? You called her by her human name."

"There is much to tell, encantrix. Perhaps we should wait until you are...better?"

I don't know what he's talking about until the recoil slams into me. My knees buckle, and I swear my head is splitting open. Rishi lunges for me, and I lean all of my weight on her.

"No." I shake my head. "Now."

"Very well." Agosto raises his hands and the ground trembles. Grass and flowers grow thick and twist into a tall chair. Agosto motions for me to sit.

"Do you know why the creature feeds?"

"Because it's hungry?" Nova says darkly.

Agosto looks him up and down. His lip curls, but he composes himself. "Because the need for power is endless. You feel it too. Your power is free in the meadow."

"Does the meadow do something to us? Does it make our power grow?" I wrap my hands around the roots of my chair. My magic connects with the essence in these living things, and it calms my nerves.

Agosto shakes his head. "No, but the meadow allows you to put away other worries long enough to let your magic come forward. Look at how you bested Xara."

"Who's Xara?" Rishi asks.

"The Devourer's real name," I say.

"Long ago, that was her human name," Agosto says. "She was just a bruja then, banished here by the Deos for a crime we'll never know. She simply appeared. Some, bewitched by her beauty, pledged allegiance to her. I admit, I was one of them. Others staked their claim on their own lands and shunned her. The Bone Valle used to be the Valle Azul, a sect of brujas and brujos that dedicated their lives to the ancient ways lived there and in the mountains. They saw the Devourer as an intruder. The more land she possessed, the more the tribes defied her. The witches were the ones who planned to kill her. One of their seers saw the threat. But they did not act in time. Overnight, the sky was red and the earth was scorched. The Valle Azul became a desert, their bodies left in heaps.

"She claimed the heart of the land as her fortress and raised the labyrinth around the Tree of Souls. You see, the tree feeds the land. Without the life of the tree, the land cannot be replenished."

"What happened to you guys?"

"I disobeyed her." There's a quiet shudder that passes through the adas. "We were one of the first to welcome her, but the more land she burned and sucked the life out of, the more I feared. We allied with the avianas and remaining tribes. We lost. The birds stay in their caves. The starlarks hide beneath the earth. As for us, she wouldn't let us get away. There are entire generations who will never know what it's like to roam Los Lagos freely. They'll never know what it's like to sleep under the shade of the Forest of Lights or run through the Valle Azul. Yes, Xara spared us. But our lives are a punishment every day and every night."

"Why didn't you let her take me?" I ask. "Your job was to hold me here until she arrived, wasn't it?"

Agosto looks down. He tilts back and forth, like he's adjusting to the absence of one horn.

"Because you remind me of someone," he says.

"Who?" I press.

"An Alta Bruja of old. Her name was Kristiñe. She wanted to return Los Lagos to the way it was before Xara started feeding off the Tree of Souls."

"Hold on," Rishi says. "Why don't your Deos stop her? If they created this land, can't they just undo what she's done?"

There's a snicker. "Do your gods grant easy wishes?" Rodriga asks.

"The last time I checked, they were busy." Rishi's cheeks are pink with embarrassment. "But something this evil has to catch someone's attention."

"It's gotten her attention," Rodriga says, pointing to me. "The

Devourer sends her demons to search for great power because she can't do it for herself. She found you. You wear the symbol of El Papa on your chain. The Deos chose you for this."

"This was just a gift from my father. Not the Deos." I shake my head. "I've never been the bravest or best bruja in my community. I'm just a girl."

"Don't say that," Rishi says. "Look at everything you've done."

"Encantrix," Agosto says, trying to get my attention to focus. "To free your family, you must release them from the tree. The tree is the key to Xara's defeat. You have the power and the freedom to challenge her the way none of us have before, and perhaps once you save your family, you will free Los Lagos as well."

I press my palm to my chest. Feel my heart racing. If my family were with me, they'd say that this is my destiny. A few days ago, I would've brushed off the thought that fate weaves the strings of life together. Today, I'm one step closer to making amends for my betrayal. The Devourer wants to hurt me, but I can return that favor. It's more than just the Tree of Souls. Her destruction reaches this meadow and the avianas. Where will she go when there's nothing left to destroy?

I hold out my hand, and Agosto takes it. I hold his dark stare with my own, and for the first time since we arrived, I feel like I'm on the right path.

I walk with him to the center of the meadow, where the banquet tree table is now empty. Since I broke the glamour, the source of the chains is in plain sight. There's a spike staked deep into the wood.

"I've tried, encantrix," Agosto says, tugging on the metal. "I try every day."

"But I haven't." I wave my hand over the wood. The traces of the Devourer's power writhe against my own.

I rub my hands together, and a ball of blue energy burns between my palms. I pull power from the soles of my feet, the pit of my stomach, and my fast-beating heart. I picture the Devourer's face, hidden under a mask of death, and I let my power go. The table splinters into a thousand bits, and blue flame rains down. A sharp pain stabs my heart, and for a moment, I can *feel* the Devourer's wrath.

Agosto struggles to breathe. He looks down at his hands in wonder. The manacles come undone, and the chains fall to the ground. The adas weep from joy. They embrace each other. They kiss my hands and feet. They run past the circle of trees and shout at the top of their lungs.

"Now," I tell Agosto, "show me the path to the labyrinth."

27

I believe the Deos fight as fiercely as they love.

—Philomeno Constancio Cruz,
Book of Cantos

Before we go, the adas surround me. They want to touch my hair and hands and feet. They cry and pinch themselves to make sure they aren't dreaming.

"Bless you," an older ada tells me. Her hair is silver as starlight and her dark skin is wrinkled like a raisin. "Bless you a thousand times, encantrix."

"You are the visage of La Tormenta, wife of El Cielo," another tells me.

I want to pull away, to tell them that I'm still far away from winning, that this is too much. But their hope is pure, and I've let myself go without it for too long.

Then it's time to go, and I wave my final good-bye. I fight the exhaustion in my bones. Mama Juanita used to tell us the story of La Vieja Tollussa, who put herself in a hundred-year sleep to outlive her enemies. But when she woke, her body had kept aging and ached too much to move. She used the last of her power to turn herself into a caterpillar because her journey was still not complete. As we leave the Meadow del Sol and take a path east, I carry that thought with me.

Agosto leads the way, followed by Rishi and Nova. I bring up the rear in case we have any surprise attacks. Though from what Agosto says, this place is deserted. We cut through dry weeds and patches of scorched woods. It's colder here than in the other places we've traveled. Thorny vines, like black barbwire, wrap around the base of trees. Agosto calls this place the Wastelands del Este, what once was the Forest of Lights. The ground here is dry ash littered with tiny, gray pebbles, every tree an unmarked grave.

"Why are we going east?" Nova asks. He's been moody and suspicious of everything the Meadowkin have said since I freed them. Granted, he has his reasons. I ate fruit and drank the wine, but it wasn't nearly as much as Nova and Rishi. It made me forget where I needed to be. It made Nova think that his marks were healing. He walks with a semipermanent frown to my left while Rishi is unusually quiet to my right.

Agosto looks over his shoulder at Nova. "Because Kristiñe hid the path to Las Peñas. I do not have the power to find it, but I believe the encantrix can. I will take you to the Alta Bruja's temple."

"You've been in that meadow a long time," Nova says. "Sure you remember which way to go?"

The faun doesn't answer. As we walk by, he lets his hands touch the burned tree trunks until the palms of his hands are as black as Nova's.

"Long ago," Agosto says, "the trees were majestic and white as the moon. When the fires came, they consumed everything. It was a living flame, out for blood."

"What are these symbols?" I ask, tracing a rune in the bark.

Agosto hobbles over to me. "It is the mark of the starlarks. They lived in the Forests of Lights before."

"It's hard to imagine anything living here," Rishi says.

"All lands change for the worse when the people do not fight back. Now there is nothing left."

"But if the Devourer drains the land dry," Rishi says, "what'll she do for power?"

"Move on to the next realm," Agosto says.

A dark thought grips my heart. *It is my turn to shape the galaxies.* "If she had enough power, could the Devourer leave Los Lagos?"

Agosto nods.

From here, the scenery starts to take shape. The trees give way to a steep downward slope covered in tall, yellow grass. The land undulates in rolling, purple hills that stretch into the flat lands of the horizon. Polished stones jut out of the ground, like the crooked teeth of the earth. Off in the distance, there's a ring of enormous pillars that remind me of Stonehenge. The Alta Bruja's temple. There's so much grass around the stone pillars that it looks as if the earth has begun to swallow it up.

The sky is a powdery blue with swirls of purple clouds. The breeze carries the scent of lavender and wildflowers. It's amazing that the same land that is home to the River Luxaria and the Wastelands can also be home to this. I wonder, if we return home after being gone for so long, will it look different to me?

But one look at the worry on Agosto's face takes my smile away. We get closer to the edge of the forest where we reach a dead end.

"What's wrong?" I ask.

"The land," he says. "It's different."

"Are you sure we didn't go the wrong way?"

Rishi bites her bottom lip. "You said it's been a while since you left the meadow. Maybe we did go the wrong way."

I grab the map from Nova's back pocket. It's been folded and unfolded so many times, the edges are starting to fray. I find where we are on the map. The edge of the Wastelands, west of Laguna Roja. North of us should be Las Peñas, and beyond that, the heart of the land—the labyrinth. But it isn't.

"It seems Kristiñe hid more than the path," Agosto says. "She hid the entire mountain."

28

The Deos don't act for us.
The Deos act through us.
—PATRICIO MORTIZ,
BOOK OF CANTOS

How do you move a mountain?" Nova asks.

"You know how they say if the mountain won't go to you," Rishi says, "then you go to the mountain? Maybe the mountain really did go this time."

I smile, and Nova gives her a long look.

The wind whips around us, like it's pushing us back to where we came from. My stomach is in a thousand tangled knots. I wet my dry lips, savoring the crisp air. The earth is dry in patches and bright green in others. Stone paths cut across the land, creating a patchwork quilt. As much as I want to laugh at Rishi's joke, I have to wonder: *Where is this mountain?*

"When I was little," I say, "my dad used to say, if he ever lost me, he'd just follow the starlight we leave behind."

Rishi turns to me with sad eyes. "You never talk about your dad."

"I don't know where that came from. He was talking about us running around the supermarket or the mall. Still. I just remembered."

Rishi takes my hand in hers but lets go when Nova wedges himself between us. "Well, Captain, it's not dark enough for starlight."

I purse my lips. "Says the boy *made* of light."

"I'm not *made* of light," he counters. "I conjure it."

I roll my eyes and step closer to the edge of the cliff. The way down is steep and rocky but not unmanageable. It's quiet here except for the rush of wind and Agosto's heartbeat in my ears. I can still feel his essence from healing him, a side effect of touching someone with my power. Like when I tried to hurt Nova back home. It makes me think of what the Devourer said to me, that she could hear me because of the fear in my heart. Why can't I feel a trace of her power?

"It's strange," I say.

"Which part?" Rishi asks.

I point to the horizon. "It's not hot here, but the air on the horizon ripples like there's a heat wave."

"Wouldn't that be the Bone Valle?" She squints and holds her hand like a sun visor over her eyes. "If I didn't want someone to come into my lair and I was this powerful bruja, I'd make sure no one would see it."

Look twice. Nothing in Los Lagos is what it seems. The land is fluid, yes, but even if the Devourer destroyed the mountains of Las Peñas the way she's destroyed so many other things, we'd still be able to see the labyrinth.

I raise my hands and feel for the glamour on the land. I remember Mayi from Lula's circle uses her powers to change her eye color and straighten her nose all the time. But sometimes, when I look at her from the corner of my eye, or between blinks, the glamour reveals itself. That's small magic. Magic used for vanity doesn't end well, my mom would say.

Even from miles away, I can feel the ripple of magic across the land. I relax my eyes, and for a fraction of second, the ghost of a mountain ridge appears. Then a force pushes against me, like a punch to the gut. I gasp for air and stumble back.

"What is it?" Agosto asks, rushing to my side.

"What do your bruja eyes see?" Rishi asks dramatically. Then she gives Nova the finger when he snickers at her. So much for their truce.

"It's there. It's hidden behind a glamour." I take Agosto's outstretched hand and pull myself up.

"What should we do?" Nova says. "We could walk straight for it. When we get closer, you can pull the glamour."

I shake my head, unsure. If I can feel its strength from here, I don't know if it'll get any better. "What if I can't?"

"I beg your pardon," Agosto says, "but pulling the glamour won't be enough. This is what the Devourer wants. Walk straight to the mountain and be unable to pass. Walk around it and end up in the Bone Valle. Disrupt her magic, and she'll come right at you, and I fear she'll take greater precautions now that she knows she underestimated you. You should make for the Hidden Path."

"Um," Rishi says, raising her hand as if we're in the middle of class. "Okay, but how do we make it the Un-Hidden Path?"

222

"Before our rebellion, Kristiñe created the path through the mountain to let other tribes pass. Their plan was to attack unseen. But their own people betrayed them, and as they crossed, the Devourer ambushed them from both sides. The Alta Bruja, leader of the tribe, used the last of her power to curse her traitors with immortal life. Gouged out their eyes and buried them beneath the earth. The Devourer found them and dug them up. She healed their bodies by linking their life force to the earth. She called them her 'blind giants,' guards of the labyrinth."

"How can they guard anything if they can't see?" Rishi asks.

"They don't need eyes to find you," Agosto says darkly. "Sight is the most easily fooled of all our senses."

I look at Nova, who stares at the horizon. I wonder what's going through his head right now. He looks more worried than I've ever seen him before.

I follow the twisting trails down below with my eyes. We could get lost no matter what. Los Lagos is as much a labyrinth as the Devourer's maze. As the sun and moon start to reach their peaks in the sky, nudging closer to eclipse, their light bounces off the henge below.

"Head for the temple. Alta Bruja Kristiñe erected the circle of stones and called it the Heart of the Deos."

"Why's it always the *heart* or the *eye* of something?" Rishi asks. "You notice that? There are so many body parts that don't get enough love, like earlobes and belly buttons."

"*Rishi.*"

She shrugs in her I'm-only-just-saying kind of way.

I find myself touching my necklace to feel the familiar weight of knowing I was connected to someone—the way I used to when I missed my dad. I'm starting to get that feeling back.

"I take it you're not coming with us," Nova says to Agosto.

The Faun King shakes his head. "I must return to my people. Take them to safety. I fear Xara will retaliate soon."

He takes my hand and presses it to his lips, then his forehead. "I hope to see you again, encantrix."

I don't wait to watch him go. I take off, running down the hill.

The temple is bigger than anything it seemed from up the hill. The stones are great pillars weathered by wind and rain. I press my hand against the groves and dips in the stone, the carvings of different moon phases and constellations. Sparks flare between my fingers.

Night falls as the moon and sun pass each other across the sky and set. Stars emerge behind thinning clouds.

"This is incredible," Rishi says, standing in the center of the temple with her hands stretched toward the sky. "My parents do all the ceremonies in the world, but I never thought I believed in anything. After this, I might have to reconsider."

"You're going to start believing in the Deos?"

Rishi grins. "Or I could just put all my faith in you."

I get closer to her. Her brown skin is bathed in the starlight. Her long, dark hair is windblown and wild around her shoulders. Something in the pit of my stomach falls, and when she smiles at me, it just keeps on falling.

"You can believe in anything you want," I say, "as long as

it feels right. Even seeing the things I grew up with, I wanted to pretend they weren't real. I have all the proof in the world, while some people go lifetimes hoping to see a miracle. It was easier to think I was living the wrong life. It's easier to want to be someone else."

"I would never want you to be someone else." She coils my hair around her finger. The ends have started to curl on their own. *Magic transforms you.* "I want you to be you. You're magic, Alex. I always thought so, even before I knew your secrets."

Her smile is full, and hearing these things, my heart feels so full it might burst. I exhale hard, look up at the circle of stones that surround us.

Then, a bright light explodes, like the flash of a camera. Nova stands just outside the temple. The worry mark on his brow is gone. His hands glow with light.

"Find anything interesting?" he asks.

"If you think ancient witch carvings are interesting, then sure," Rishi says. She walks toward him and leans on a stone pillar.

"Well?" Nova asks me. "Was Agosto pulling *our* chain?"

"Not funny," I say.

"Too soon?" He shrugs a shoulder.

I ignore him and continue tracing my fingers along the stone. The magic here is strange. It isn't the dull pulse of the earth I've felt during this journey. It's like a sigh of relief.

There's a carving above eye level of a crescent moon lying sideways. The symbol of El Papa. I touch the necklace my father gave me. The next pillar has the mark of El Terroz, a square stone. A feather for El Cielo, an eight-pointed star for La Estrella, an arrow for El Corazon. I walk in a full circle, looking at all thirteen pillars—each one is for the High Deos—until I reach the sun, for La Mama. Here, the grass is wild and overgrown. I try to imagine what this place would have looked like in its prime. The grass would be green, not yellow. The stones would be newly etched, not fading. Brujas and brujos would stand in this circle.

"It feels so forgotten," I say.

"I don't get it," Rishi says. "If the Devourer or Xena or whatever her name is was also a bruja like the tribes who built this, why would she kill them all?"

"What do you do with an obstacle?" Nova asks.

I don't like where he's going with this. "You go around it."

"What if it keeps moving in your way?"

"You get rid of it." If I shut my eyes, the wind sounds like the ghosts of brujas and brujos screaming for their lives. "My mom believes in the balance of all things. She says La Mama and El Papa are a symbol of that."

"The Deos don't create the balance," Nova says. "We do. Their power is in us."

"Maybe they should be more careful in giving power to people in the first place," Rishi says.

"Then why did they choose me?" I wonder aloud.

"Don't go down that rabbit hole, Alex," Nova says.

"I mean, no one should have this much power. No one. But here we are."

"It could be worse," Rishi says. "Your spell could have worked, and then who would be here to fight the Devourer?"

"I would."

"But you stand a better chance having this great bruja power."

I reach down for the earth and push my magic into it. The land's weak pulse answers back in greeting. *I remember you.* It doesn't speak it, but the thought pops up in my head. The land aches, as if waking from a deep slumber. I pull at the dead patches of grass. Right where my magic met the land, a tiny, green bulb appears.

I place my hands on another patch of earth. The dry, yellow grass comes away with a snap. It reminds me of Mama Juanita plucking the feathers off a chicken. It reminds me of pulling at my hair in an angry fit, alone in my bedroom with the lights turned off while I listened to my mother crying for my dad.

I remember you, says the earth.

Green sprouts twist from the ground like newborn fingers stretching. My heart races with the boost of my magic. Instinct, as old as this place, grips me. I take a step toward the center of the temple, pulling away the dead plants from the dirt. My fingers touch something hard. A worn stone tile buried and forgotten. I jolt as sparks burn my fingertips.

I need light. I raise my hands to the overcast sky.

"La Estrella," I say, "bless me with your light."

The air in my chest escapes in a gust. My magic pushes against the clouds, and they race away across the night sky until there is only the blazing light of a million stars. They shine down on the circle of stones.

One by one, the symbols etched at the top of the stone pillars glow, creating a circle of light that reaches down to the ground. The newborn grass bulbs spring up higher, alive and lush.

Something's missing. I can feel my magic, taut like a guitar string, urging me to take another step. I place both feet on the stone tile. It gives under my weight, sinking into the earth, snapping into place. The light bounces off each pillar, then funnels into a single beam, crashing over me.

"I remember you," I say as the light fills me. Every cell of my body snaps awake, and I wonder if this is what it feels like to be born once again. If this power is a good thing. If I can control it.

The skin at my throat burns where my necklace catches the light that shines down on the grass in front of me. Yellow grass breaks away, revealing another stone. The stones glow, and when I step on them, they sink. The dirt ahead clears, revealing the next step for me to take—then another and another, leading out of the circle and down a hill and then up another.

When I look up, I'm filled with so much color and joy and light. I walk ahead, lighting up the path for Rishi and Nova to follow. The path is dizzying, and just when I think I'm heading in the right direction, the stones change. I struggle for breath as the stones lead us up a new hill, then alongside patches of lavender, and then another stretch of dead earth.

After a while, I look over my shoulder. Nova's face is full of awe. His eyes are wide and looking only at me. Rishi, my little magpie, urges me to keep going.

So I do. I keep going until my muscles ache and my tongue is parched. Until the incline is too steep and we struggle to breathe. Until I see the ripple of the glamour, and I know we're closer. Until the clouds return, darker and stronger, and the light of my crescent moon disappears.

29

Take me to the glittering mountain
to find the riches of the world.
Take me to the glittering mountain
to mine its treasures untold.

—FOLK SONG,
BOOK OF CANTOS

hen I fall down, hands grab me instantly to pick me back up. Nova turns me over on my back.

"I'm fine." My body is screaming with pain, and my heart and mind are racing.

He holds my face in his hands. "You're not fine. We've walked for miles. You're exhausted."

"Don't tell me what I am."

A smile creeps on his face. "Stubborn."

"Jerk."

"Do you see that?" Rishi shouts, running ahead.

"Wait!" I call after her, but when we make it around a steep hill, I can see what has her so excited. There's a smattering of trees that grow so low to the ground they appear to be bowing. It's a tiny oasis in the middle of a barren land.

Despite the ache in my bones and the sight-splintering headache that comes from recoil, hunger, and general exhaustion, I sprint to the perfectly round pond nestled in a valley between two hills. I cup the water in my hands and drink greedily until my belly is full and my head spins.

"Sweet, sweet nectar of life," Rishi says.

I look up at the dark-purple sky, torn between the need to keep going and the toll the journey is taking on us.

"We need rest," Rishi says. "We're not going to be of much use if we crawl the rest of the way."

Nova holds his hand out to me. "Give me your dagger. I'm going to find us something to eat."

"Since when are you the hunting-and-gathering kind?" Rishi asks.

"Just thank your stars you've never been so hungry you hunted squirrels in Central Park at night."

I can't tell if he's joking or not, but the idea of Nova alone and hungry in the dark makes my heart hurt. Then he breaks into that sly smile of his, the kind that makes you forget about all the worries you might have.

"You collect wood," Nova tells Rishi. Then he turns to me. "You should get your rest. I don't like being out in the open like this."

When Rishi and Nova leave, I fill our empty water bottles. I look at my reflection in the pond. My skin is bruised, and I look like I went a few rounds with a heavyweight champion. I take off my clothes. With Rishi and Nova gone, I let myself cry out in pain instead of keeping it in. I wade into the water and submerge myself until my chest burns for air. I let myself float on the surface, and the tepid water washes away the dirt on my skin and more. It fills me with a pleasant warmth that pulls me beneath the surface. I feel myself sink. I *let* myself sink.

I know I'm dreaming when I'm standing on top of the pond. I jump when I fear I'll fall straight through the surface, but my feet only create small ripples. There's a woman standing in front of me. When I recognize her, I want to fall on my knees and weep.

"You always fell asleep during your bath time," Mama Juanita says. "Even as a baby. I told your mother she gave birth to a fish instead of a little girl."

Suddenly I'm six years old again, and my sisters and I are running around the yard, pretending we're part of our great-grandmother's Circle. Mama Juanita, our favorite person in the world. She had a mean face, but she baked the best sweets and told the best stories—the kind my mom said we were too young to listen to.

"Mama Juanita?"

The glow of her soul is so bright against the violet of the day. She looks just as she did before she died—skin dark as coffee, and the same gray eyes as my dad and Lula. Long, white dress. A ring of orchids around her neck. A prex made of onyx. A thin cigar hanging between her red lips. Mama Juanita was our matriarch before her heart attack at ninety. Mama Juanita has this way about her, like the world should tremble when she walks. She could speak to the dead like Rose. She could recite all the blessings to the Deos, every canto in our family book. This is the woman who named me. She died before my sisters and I could grow up. Before my father left. Before my mother started going crazy from missing him. Before the greatest Circle of brujas and brujos dwindled to handfuls.

She clicks her wooden cane on the water, then smacks my leg with it.

"What was that for?"

"Don't be such a drama queen, nena," she says. "It's only a tap."

"Is that what you told yourself all those years?" I rub the spot she hit. "Mama, why are you here?"

"Why do you think I'm here, eh?" She takes a puff of her cigarillo and blows at the sky like she's exhaling a cloud. Ghost secondhand smoke can't kill, but the scent reminds me of late mornings, watching her strain coffee through a sock and fry cheese on top of plantains. "I'm waiting for you to come and get us out."

"I'm trying."

"Try harder." She smacks my other leg with her cane.

I hiss, then bite my tongue.

"I didn't know what was going to happen! I just wanted—"

"Don't you yell at me, Alejandra." She points her finger at me. "You're not the first witch to make a selfish choice, and you won't be the last. I should've been there to teach you the ways. Your mother didn't want me starting on you three too young. I respect that. The first time I saw a dead body, I was five years old. Neighbor was murdered and the cops couldn't figure out how. So the family brought him to us. I had the Gift of the Veil, like Rose. Had to sit in a room with his dead body for three days and wake his soul, ask him how he died. I didn't talk for days after that."

I look up when she says that. She smiles like she knows the secrets of the world, and in my heart, I believe she does.

"I told you," she says, "you're not the only one. I couldn't be there for you, but I'm here now. Rose is a fine little bruja. Between her and me, we can project ourselves to you, but you're a hard one to reach."

"I've been told."

"Don't get fresh with me." She smacks her cane on my arm. "Who are the witches you're traveling with?"

For an apparition, it hurts like hell. Talking back will just get me another ghost slap, so I stay quiet.

"There's this boy. He's a brujo. He's got the gift of light."

She sucks her teeth. "Parlor trick. Human matchstick if you ask me."

"*Ma.*" I sigh. Why is it never easy to talk to your family, living or dead? "He was going to help me get to the Devourer. Then there's Rishi, but she's not exactly a witch."

"What do you mean 'not exactly'?"

So I tell her about Rishi and how she followed me here. How we started at the Selva of Ashes and met the avianas. How we faced the Devourer and found the Hidden Path.

I brace myself for another slap from the cane, but it never comes. I gnaw on the inside of my cheek.

"Do you know what the Devourer did when she saw me?"

Mama Juanita shakes her head solemnly.

"She *laughed.* She laughed because she thinks I can't beat her. I'm sorry I did this to you. Every step I take, I think about how everyone I love is going to die because I'm not enough."

"Listen here, nena." She clicks her cane on the water, sending a wave that spills onto the banks. "You listen good. I don't *ever* want to hear you say that. You are the blood of *my* blood, and you are more than enough. You think we don't know the burden of our power? I lived with it for ninety years. Believe me, I know."

"You're the first one who's actually called it a burden."

"I can say whatever I want. I'm dead. But burden or gift, this is who we are. Just think, nena, if you didn't fear your own power, then you wouldn't have respected it enough to rein it in. But you have to get past that. Magic is an extension of us. Imagine the things that we could do. Create. Destroy. This Devourer, she doesn't fear her power. She fears someone who could be stronger than her."

I think of the fear in the Devourer's face when I was able to cut her. I enjoyed that feeling. I wanted to see someone afraid of me.

"I'm not blaming your mother," Mama Juanita says in that passive-aggressive way of hers. "Bless her heart, but if I had been alive, this whole mess never would've happened. You would've known not to mess with cantos you had no business messing with. You would have memorized every herb and poison in the Book of Cantos."

"But you *weren't*," I shout. "Where was the magic when my dad left us, huh? Where was the magic when my mom had to take two jobs just to pay the mortgage? How was I supposed to see the good in magic when we've only had suffering? I don't live in the old days, Mama. I live in Brooklyn circa now. The only reason this happened is because of me. Not my mom. Not you. *Me*."

Something inside of me just snaps. The earth trembles. Boulders roll down the hill. Mama Juanita cocks her eyebrow and takes a puff. The winds around me have funneled into baby tornadoes. Mama Juanita reaches out her hand to touch one, and for the first time since I was five, the old woman smiles. Actually smiles with teeth biting on that cigar.

"That's my girl," she says. "You need your family blessing. You need to hurry and free us."

Then, her smile disappears. She looks over her shoulder and winces. It's only for a moment, and then her sassy, cranky self is back.

"What happened?"

"I'm sorry." She shuts her eyes and shakes her head. "I didn't come to make you feel guilty, nena."

"Could've fooled me."

She purses her lips but keeps talking. "I came to tell you that your magic isn't enough. You're an encantrix. You've been chosen. You have magic, but all brujas need a way to conduct it. That's why wands and charms became part of witchcraft. Our bodies, they're just flesh and bone. The Deos are not, but our powers come from them.

"Without your family blessing…" She lets it linger. "That's what the Deathday is for: to fortify you, so you can use your gift and not burn your body or mind so quickly. Have you started feeling it? The nightmares, the body aches? That's the recoil, but it'll get worse. At least I don't see any marks."

"Marks?"

"Without a Deathday, your power starts to consume your body. It eats away at you. It leaves behind black marks. When you're covered in it, well, that's when you know it's the end."

I shake my head. "No, that can't be right."

She leans in close, reaches for my face but grabs air. "Tell me you don't have marks, nena."

"I don't." *I* don't, but Nova does.

"Alejandra, you can't—" Mama Juanita drops her cigarillo from her lips. She chokes on black smoke.

"Mama!"

The shadows slither around her neck.

I reach for her, but this time I do grab air. She flickers away, and for the first time in my whole life, I see fear in her eyes.

"Alex!" Nova shouts. It's like I'm hearing him from the other end of a tunnel.

The water gives beneath my feet. My mouth fills with water. My dreams are of the dead. My family. My friends. Myself. We lie in a field of thorns and turned earth. Over us stands the Devourer. She licks her fingers. Every single one. Then settles her red stare, her face hidden behind that helmet of bone and steel. I feel her hunger. *My* hunger.

When she takes it off, she's wearing my face.

30

The oceans sparkle with your tears.

The land aches for your return.

—FOLK SONG,
BOOK OF CANTOS

I did not travel through a portal and across a strange land only to drown in a pond. I kick up and reach the water's edge.

"Alex!" Rishi and Nova both shout, running for me.

I'm too busy coughing my throat raw to answer. I brush water out of my eyes and wring my hair out.

"I'm fine," I say. "I had a vision of my great-grandmother."

When I look up, Rishi and Nova are staring at me. Nova's eyes are more green now, like sparkling jade crystals. His cheeks are bright red. He holds a bloody animal in one hand and a knife in the other. His lips move in a jumble of words that end up nonsensical, and then he turns his face to the side.

"Alex," Rishi says, her eyes wide with wonder. Whatever she's holding falls to the ground. She looks at me the way people usually look at Lula.

I look down to realize I'm naked and a golden light covers my skin. I hold up my hand and push a blinding light out so they have to look away. I grab my clothes and run behind a tree, their laugher tinkling in the wind.

"Not funny!" I shout at them.

I get dressed. My clothes cling to my wet skin. I could swear that Lula's apparition is nearby making fun of me. She'd say, "What's the big deal? That's how we were made." Why has it always been easier for Lula to be freer than I am? It's not like I'm covered in boils and puss. It's not like Rishi and I don't have the same parts. It's not like Nova doesn't know what a naked girl looks like.

I hit the back of my head against the tree trunk, and I can't help but smile at how nervous Nova was and the blush on Rishi's face. I'm not used to making people react to me that way because, for the most part, I'm not used to being seen. My heart races and I think this has to be a different kind of power.

I dust myself off and get ready to return to my friends when I realize the bruises on my arms are all gone. Then, my heartbeat spikes when I see a dark spot on my palm. Fear of Mama Juanita's words takes hold of me. My mouth goes dry and my fingers shake as I move to touch the mark.

It comes away easily—just a smudge of dirt. It didn't take long for my witchy hypochondria to start now that I know what happens to brujas who don't have their Deathdays.

I find Nova and Rishi sitting around a small fire. Nova is skinning a large, rabbit-looking creature and Rishi is sharpening sticks. We sit in complete silence with only the brush of the weeping willow making noise as it slaps the surface of the pond. Rishi hands over one of the sharpened sticks to Nova and he skewers the animal straight through. I'm trying to put together an image of Nova, but it's hard because there are missing pieces.

"Where'd you learn to skin?" I ask him.

His eyes, more blue now, flick to my forehead, then back to the animal. He smiles. "You wouldn't believe me if I told you."

"He worked in a butcher shop," Rishi says. "He's just trying to make you guess the worst."

"You have no chill, Rishi," Nova tells her.

She blows him a kiss, and he rolls his eyes.

"So," Nova says, "what was with all the glowing when you came out of the pond? You looked like the painting of that Greek lady surfing on a giant clam."

Rishi slugs him in the arm and he just laughs. "Classy."

"Oh come on," Nova says. "I'm just trying to make things a little less awkward. We could all go skinny-dipping and then we'd all be on an even playing field."

"Pass," Rishi says.

"First of all," I start, "that was probably one of my most embarrassing moments, so I'd appreciate it if you didn't make fun of me."

"Believe me," Nova says softly, "there's nothing to make fun of."

Heat spreads from my solar plexus across my skin. I push the feeling away and realize there is something I do want to know. "I have a better idea than skinny-dipping."

Nova's eyes light up. "Yeah?"

"I want a secret."

"*Psh.* That hardly seems like a fair exchange."

"You're a Neanderthal," Rishi mumbles.

"Mankind had to start somewhere," he says. "At least I can make a fire."

"You used your magic," Rishi counters.

Nova turns the rabbit. Juicy fat melts off and pops in the fire. "Magic makes the world go 'round."

"Why didn't you tell me that you never had your Deathday?" I blurt out, growing tired of Nova and Rishi's bickering.

Whatever he thought I was going to say, it wasn't that. He avoids my eyes and cleans my dagger on his pant leg. Rishi looks like she's about to speak, but I shake my head. I want to give Nova space. I know that's what I'd want. I'm torn between wanting to know more about him and wanting him to tell me on his own. We sit and watch the fire burn and wait for Nova to be ready. But what if he's not?

"How'd you know?" he finally says as a nonanswer.

"My great-grandmother appeared to me." I fill him in on the charm of Mama Juanita and the shadow smoke that attacked her the way it did Lula and my mom. "She told me that power burns our human bodies without the family blessing."

I look at Nova's hands. The black marks have spread farther up his biceps. One tendril flows from his stomach to his clavicle and then his shoulder.

"Why didn't you say anything?" Rishi asks.

He shrugs like it's no big deal.

"Nova, stop. You know I can't let you keep using your powers."

"No one *lets* me do anything."

"Well, maybe if someone did, you wouldn't get yourself in so much trouble."

He shuts his eyes and gives me his cheek. "You guys don't know squat about me."

"Then *tell* us something. Your answer is to act like the world is against you. Believe me, I know. I felt like that every single day. I felt like my magic was the worst thing that could ever happen to me. It broke my family. It breaks so many people."

"Now you've changed your mind?" He's being defensive.

"Something's changed—me, the magic, this place. I can't explain it. There are moments when the magic feels *right*. There are other moments when I'm afraid of what I could be capable of. There's this tiny voice that takes pleasure in doing bad things. I'm afraid I could become like the Devourer."

"Never," he tells me. He reaches for my face, but then he catches himself and instead rubs his hands over his face.

"You could never be like that," Rishi says.

Nova looks up at the sky and mouths a silent rezo. "I never had my Deathday because my parents died when I was a kid. Deadbeat dad, drunk mom, delinquent brothers and sisters. The only ones who got away were my eldest brother, Unico, who turned his back on us and became a cop. Then my sister, Cinqua. She ran away the first minute she got a chance and I haven't seen her since. I should have gone to my grandmother, but she already had too many kids in the house. Plus, she was still mad at my pops. Isn't that something? Only brujas can stay mad at someone who's dead. Besides, my old man would've been real disappointed if he knew I'm just a human matchstick."

"Don't say that," I tell him.

He smiles, but I can see the strain in his face. "Don't worry about me, Ladybird. The first time my magic appeared, I hurt someone. I didn't mean to. Let's just say my foster parents weren't exactly out of a fairy tale. My foster father deserved it. After that, I just kept running and hiding. When the marks started, I wasn't sure what was happening. I don't have a Book of Cantos like you, and I don't belong to no Circle. When my grandma finally took me in, she tried to give me the family blessing. But my family's so broken, even the dead have forgotten us."

"So you knew the consequences, but you use your powers anyway." Rishi licks her lip. She's hungry. We're all hungry, but it seems wrong to eat while Nova is talking about his past. "Why?"

"Survival of the illest," he says, but his laugh is forced. "I've never been much good at being anyone other than who I am. Even if it got me locked up. Even if it kills me in the end."

"What happened?"

He shrugs. I hate when he shrugs.

"Girl was in trouble. I tried to help her from getting mugged. Someone called the police. She couldn't really tell me apart from the people trying to hurt her."

He won't look at us. He's startled when Rishi is the one who takes his hand to give him comfort.

"The marks have only gotten worse recently." He holds up his hands. The black marks are as dark as ink. No wonder he has so many tattoos. What better way to cover up his magical ones?

"I told myself I'd figure out a way to reverse it." He holds his hands up to the flames. "While I was in juvie, these guys showed me there was a way."

"Is that why you need the money?"

LABYRINTH LOST

He looks down at his feet and nods.

"I promise I'll help you," I tell him. "After all of this, I'll do everything I can."

"I don't deserve that," he says. "Besides, if I burn up in Los Lagos, then you don't have to pay me at all."

And that does it. It hits me in the gut that he's not here for me. Not truly.

"I'm sorry, that was a stupid thing to say," he says.

I put on a smile and shake it off. "Well, you've made up for it by cooking dinner."

"Hold up," Nova says. "I confessed a secret. It's Rishi's turn."

"A nice Guyanese girl like me?" Rishi winks. "Alex already knows all my secrets."

"I doubt that," Nova mutters.

"I am sorry I didn't tell you sooner," I tell Rishi. "I was afraid you'd see me differently. You were the one person that made me forget about my magic."

"I love your magic." Rishi holds my stare. Her eyes flick to my lips, then back to my eyes. "I should tell you that you look different. Good different. You walk with your head up and your eyes are brighter. You wear the magic on your skin. It's the most beautiful thing I've ever seen."

I always used to say that magic transformed Lula. I didn't think it would do the same to me. But the more I use my power, the more I feel it changing me.

Nova clears this throat. He takes the rabbit off the fire and rests it between the three of us. "You guys ready to eat or what?"

"Wait. Give me your hands." I hold out my hands for them

to take. I do something my mother used to when I was younger. "Thank you, La Mama, for this meal and for lighting our path. El Terroz for the bounty of your rich, strong earth."

"And La Estrella," Nova adds, "for a new hope."

"And to Alex," Rishi says, "for this adventure."

We keep on going.

I find the stone path again easily. Or perhaps it finds me. The farther we walk, the more Los Lagos starts to feel familiar. The sky is violet, and there is not a skyscraper in sight. The grass is tall and yellow, and wild beasties scurry underground. It is unlike anywhere I've ever been, but somehow it reminds me of home.

You are the blood of my blood, Mama Juanita told me. She believes my power is enough.

Every now and then, I turn around to make sure Rishi and Nova are keeping up. Rishi's face is flushed, but if she's tired, then she doesn't complain. Nova is quieter than usual, his bipolar eyes searching the sky. I go to check my watch for the time and realize my watch is long gone. The moon and sun are inching closer as they pass each other in the sky. The eclipse is approaching, but so are we.

"I'm coming for you," I whisper, and hope the wind will carry that to my family.

We stop once more to drink water and eat the rest of our rabbit. But I can't sit still for too long. When the moon and sun set, I pull light from the stars and create three glowing, green orbs, so we don't have to walk in the dark. My skin tingles, and I know we're close. We rest again, so I can heal the blisters on Nova's and Rishi's feet. When I'm exhausted, my green orbs are extinguished like candle flames. I'm the only one who can't sleep, and so I try to make shapes out of the stars. I wonder if the Devourer can feel us approaching. I think of the one way she can hurt me—my family. I envision all the different ways I want to hurt her.

"I'm coming for you," I whisper before I fall asleep.

The very second the sun and moon rise again, I wake Rishi and Nova up and we keep going for another half cycle.

"It's up ahead," I say.

"I can feel it too," Nova says.

"I know I'm not a witch or anything," Rishi says, "but this place is making my skin crawl."

"Is something finally scaring you?" Nova asks her.

"It was bound to happen," she says.

I take her hand and squeeze, just to let her know that I'm here. I shut my eyes and let the mountain speak to me. Like the rest of this land, it has a voice. It calls to me, magic to magic.

La luna, the voice whispers in the Old Tongue.

"The moon," I say. I step away from my friends and line myself up with the moon. I step on the next stone, and when it sinks, a wave of energy crashes over me. A moonbeam connects to my necklace, shooting a prism of multicolored light into the glamour. The veil falls away, revealing a mountain range that glitters like stars and stretches higher than the Empire State building.

"The entrance!" Rishi says.

The prism of light that beams from my necklace illuminates a rift in the mountain that would be easy to miss in the dark. It looks as if El Terroz took his golden ax and created the gash himself.

When we stand at the entrance, the prism flickers and goes out. I struggle to bring back the light, exhaustion pulling at my life force.

"I've got it," Nova says. He releases a ball of light over his head and blows on it. It floats ahead of him.

"Ready?" I whisper to Rishi.

For the first time since we've journeyed together, she looks nervous. I hold her hand and walk with her, a promise that I won't let go.

In turn, she stays close and whispers, "I would follow you into the darkest dark."

31

They say El Corazón has two hearts:

the black thing in his chest and

the one he wears on his sleeve.

—TALES OF THE DEOS,
FELIPE THOMÁS SAN JUSTINIO

The path is full of whispers and loose stones tumbling from the highest peaks. Our footsteps echo all the way to the top.

"Was that you?" Nova asks.

"Me what?" I say.

"Touching me."

I scoff. "You wish."

"It's probably just a poisonous spider that's evolved to kill you," Rishi tells him.

"Just stop helping," he mutters.

I'm so thirsty, but without another source of water, the water we carry is precious. I wonder...

"Nova, if I can conjure fire, would I be able to conjure water as well?"

He makes a *hmmm* noise. "Depends. I've heard the recoil for elemental magic is pretty bad. Fire burns your skin. Lightning makes your heart stop."

"I conjured lightning at home to fight the maloscuro. I passed out. Would water just make you get wet? Like maybe a rain cloud following over your head?" My chuckle echoes to the top of the mountain and gets lost there.

"No," Nova says, like it's the silliest thing he's ever heard. "Maybe your lungs would fill up with water. La Ola isn't exactly known for being even tempered. I'd rather take my chances with El Fuego honestly."

"You talk about these gods like they're people," Rishi says. "They're not actually flesh-and-blood people are they?"

"You can field that one, Alto Brujo," I tell Nova.

He gives me a side eye over his shoulder. "No one I know has ever seen them. We create our gods to look like us, don't we? Only better. The god of the butterflies would look like a butterfly, right? So our gods have human qualities, but also the great power that makes them individuals."

"But *how* do you know?"

Nova sounds frustrated as he says, "I can't explain belief. I just have it. I know the power in me comes from somewhere. I know that the magic in my veins is real. No, I can't tell you that if I speak to the Deos, they answer back with words, but there are other ways. When was the last time *Zeus* came down for Olympus and hung out just to prove his existence? Besides, the Deos didn't create us to interact with us. We're just pawns moving across the board. There's a checkmate waiting at the end for all of us. At least, that's what my grandma says."

Rishi clears her throat. "The more you talk about her, the more charming she sounds."

"I'm not exactly easy to love," he says.

As he says that, stones clatter overhead.

"Watch out!" Nova turns and pushes Rishi and me against a wall.

"I might've been wrong about the spiders," Rishi whispers.

"Whatever it is," I say, "we're not alone. Come on."

I lead the way, our boots pounding down the narrow path. We've come too far to go back, and there's no climbing up something so high.

"Alex!" Rishi trips and falls on something.

Nova helps her to her feet before I can reach her. He holds a ball of light over them.

"Oh my Deos," I gasp. There's a skull at Rishi's feet. I hold up my hands and shoot flares of light down the path. For a moment, it lights up as bright as day. Bones litter the ground. Some are scattered. Some are entwined, as if they died together in an embrace.

I bend down and pick up the skull Rishi tripped on. I close my eyes as an imprint of memory latches onto me. I've seen it happen to Rose. When she touches an object at a garage sale or when we're walking in the historic parts of the city. She relives the scene the way I'm doing now.

There's a girl my age with dark skin and darker eyes. One minute, she's running through the Forest of Lights with a beautiful boy. The next moment, the sky turns dark and he's dead in her arms. The girl is filled with anger and hate, and she runs into battle with her people. The leader is a wild-haired woman with a crescent moon inked into her forehead and hands that spark like lightning.

The girl is ready to fight the shadow creatures. The girl is ready to take back Los Lagos.

But when they reach the mountain pass, they are betrayed. The Shadow Bruja knows they are coming. She has red eyes and a face as white as the moon. Alta Bruja Kristiñe blasts the Shadow Bruja with lightning, but the Shadow Bruja keeps going, striking down everyone in her path. She rides a saberskin onto the path, the creature scaling the walls. She leaves a trail of death behind her. Her pack of beasts rips people apart with their claws.

The girl has one chance. She has a weapon of her own design—a glove with a palm covered in metal spikes. The girl's fist hits the Shadow Bruja's face. There is blood. A terrible laugh. The Shadow Bruja in turn, rips out the girl's heart. The Shadow Bruja devours it. She devours every heart around her.

Kristiñe is wounded. She's bleeding out. She's lost everything. She uses the last of her power to punish her traitors. She gouges out their eyes and then curses them—for their outsides to reflect their monstrous hearts...

The Shadow Bruja resurrects the blind men. She gives them power. She binds them to the roots of the earth. She binds them to her.

I jump out of the memory and scream. I scream until I'm out of breath. I scream until Nova has to shake me.

"Alex, what did you see?" Rishi asks.

But I can't answer her. Shadows move around us and stones fall to the ground as the mountain shakes.

"Go!" Nova shouts. We run down the path, but a hulking figure jumps from somewhere above and slams into the ground, rattling the earth.

We have to retreat. I grab Nova's and Rishi's hands and start to run back the way we came from, but a second figure appears. They now block our path in and out. One of them walks closer to us, and as it steps into the light, I can see it. The creatures Kristiñe punished and the Devourer saved.

His skin is the green of aging leaves, and his body is covered in thorny vines that move like extended limbs. He raises his hand, and a vine slithers out of the center of his palm. I can see the remnants of the man it once was. Its face is distorted and black veins are visible beneath its skin. In its open mouth are black gums and pieces of broken teeth. Gouged eyes are a mess of torn flesh. *They don't need eyes to see.* The blind giants.

The giants charge at us from both sides, and the earth trembles under their feet. They shoot vines from their palms to trap us. I create a shield to stop them. I grit my teeth and reach for more power. My arms tremble; my blood rushes to my head. Their vines are laced with the Devourer's dark power. It burns right through my shield. I direct all my magic into an arrow of lightning. I aim it at the nearest giant. It rips through its chest and electrocutes him.

"Now! *Run*," I tell Rishi and Nova. "I'll be right behind you."

Two giants replace the one I killed. They land feet from me and close in. I dodge vines that want to pierce my heart.

Fire, the voice tells me.

Heat blisters my skin as I conjure flame. I close my eyes and hiss at the air as I say the words of El Fuego, Bringer of Flame. "Rain of fire! Birth of ash!"

I grind my teeth against the searing pain in my hands. I hold balls of white-and-red flames in my palm. I blast them at two giants that attack me. Their blistering screams become echoes as my fire burns them to a crisp.

Vines snap around my wrists and pull me back. Another giant appears from the shadows and takes hold of me. My muscles and bones strain against the force. A six-inch thorn hits my shoulder. The pain slices through me, and for a moment, all I see is red. Then, the pressure is gone and I fall forward.

"I got you," Nova says, coughing and wheezing the smoke from his lungs. "I got you, Alex."

He pulls me up.

"Rishi! Where is she?"

One of the giants is still alive. It crawls toward me, tripping on the bones. Since it's on its knees, I can look into its decrepit face. My hands are wet and soft with blood pouring from my blistered palms. I find the anger, the fear in my belly, and I scream it out into the giant's face. I'm a siren, a banshee, howling in the wind. All I have are my hands and my power. So as the giant reaches me, I throw a punch straight into its torso. My hand breaks through its meaty skin, scraping against bone until I wrap my hand around its heart. I squeeze and twist, but it won't come free. The creature groans, then falls lifeless to the ground, pulling me with it.

"Let go," Nova shouts. His hands are on my shoulders.

I don't understand what he means until I realize the reason I can't break free is because I'm still holding on to its heart.

My body shakes from head to toe, the recoil crippling me to the ground. Nova grunts as something knocks him to the side. But Nova is fast and jumps on the creature's back. He grips the giant by the throat and struggles to choke it.

There's a shadow, another creature coming for me. I push myself up. Face the giant. I conjure a ball of flame and hurl it at him. Its skin catches on fire, but the giant keeps advancing. It growls as it pulls back its arms, ready to shoot me down with its vines. I crawl over bones and jagged stones, shielding my face with my arm, but then there's Rishi, jumping from the ledge above. She cracks the giant's head open with a whack of the mace. Her dark hair is matted to her cheeks with sweat and blood. I force myself to get up.

"It's not over, Ladybird," Nova says, panting.

"Alex," Rishi says.

The three of us stand back to back to back. More of them climb down from the mountain walls. There are so many blind giants I can't keep count, and they close in.

The sky trembles above us, matching the rhythm of my heart. I see lightning break across the sky, and I know what I have to do. The power inside of me urges me to reach for it. Every cell in my body wakes up with electricity.

I grab hold of the lightning with a tight fist, feel its current hit my heart. I am an element. I am the storm. The lightning is a whip, and I lash it at the giants. Suddenly, the world is vibrant, over-exposed. When my lightning hits the giants, they break apart, all burned limbs and shattered bone.

The explosion blows me back. My ears ring and my skull throbs. I land on top of Rishi and Nova. I call for my mother. Pain sears from my skin down to the core of my bones. I try to push myself up but can't. I am dead.

No, I am *death*.

The inside of my eyelids is red. Hands, warm and strong, hold me and carry me. I don't even have to look. I've already memo-rized the way his heart beats against mine.

Nova buries his face in my hair and then something settles over us. I can feel shadows and fear fill his heart, though the darkness has surrounded him from the moment I met him. I cling to him because I can't seem to move. It's the worst recoil yet. How does anyone live with this pain?

"We made it to the other side of the mountain. We've made it out," he whispers, but I know there's something wrong.

The wind is cold and carries the scent of cinder. My senses are so sensitive, I can hear the spike of Rishi's heart, the way her lungs expand for air, the way she struggles as something takes hold of her.

"Rishi?" I reach for her in the dark, but Nova holds me tighter.

"Now, Alejandra," the Devourer says, "let me see how easily you are broken."

32

Liar's tongue and feathers fair,

take this path, if lovers dare.

—THE FORBIDDEN CANTO,
A.K.A. THE ROMEO DEATH,
FROM THE ART OF POISON,
ANGELA AURORA SANTIAGO

The Devourer appears out of the dark, a creature of the shadows. She stands feet away from Rishi. My eyes begin to clear, but I wish I couldn't see anything. I pull myself out of Nova's hold. When he sets me down, my knees want to give out under me. I fight the urge to cry and scream because the recoil is making it impossible to think clearly. All I see is Rishi, bound and gagged. She shakes her head.

The Devourer's dress of metal and bone clings to her like darkness. Her red eyes are bright behind the helmet of bone. She traces her long, pointed nails along Rishi's cheek. Vines rope around Rishi's feet, keeping her locked to the ground. A thorny rope winds around her arms, torso, neck, and mouth. Blood drips where the thorns pierce her lips shut.

"So tender," the Devourer says in her smoky voice. "Tell me, Alejandra Mortiz. Did you begin to hope that you three would make it out of here alive?"

"Don't move," I tell Rishi. Every time she moves, the vines wrap tighter, the thorns dig deeper. "Let her go," I say through gritted teeth.

The Devourer walks on the gray earth. For the first time, I notice the dark hill in the background, a great structure erected at the top like a crown. The labyrinth. She stops inches from me. My power is a weak pulse, struggling to come to my aid. I have a dagger, but my mace is on the ground beside Rishi's feet. How quickly would the Devourer break my neck if I move?

She conjures a glass vial on the palm of her hand. It glows red like lava and has tiny gold flecks inside.

"Nova," she says, "be a dear, won't you?"

"I'm sorry," he whispers. I can hear the regret in his voice.

Nova won't look at me. He stares at the ground. Then at the Devourer's hand. He takes the vial and goes to Rishi's side.

"Nova?" I hate the way I sound. *Hurt. Childish.* The Devourer watches every movement of my face. She grins wide, taking pleasure in all of this.

"My dear, Nova," she says. "You chose her well."

I hate the way she says his name. Hate the way he moves when she tells him to. Hate the way he doesn't put up a fight. Mostly, I hate that I didn't see.

I didn't want to.

Look twice.

Nova stands at the Devourer's right-hand side. She rests her

hand around his throat, like she'll snap it in two. Then, all she does
is rake her fingernails softly down his neck.

"You remember this potion, Alejandra, don't you?" the Devourer
asks.

"No."

"Liar's tongue, feathers of a golden bird," the Devourer sing-
songs. "I have to thank you. You've helped my boy so much. It's a
pity you didn't fall in love with him like the others. You're losing
your touch, Nova."

Nova won't look at me. *Look at me*, I will him with my mind.
My power whimpers in response, and so Nova just stands there.

"No matter." The Devourer walks around us like she's corral-
ling her prey. "I have this sweet, sweet girl. Her love for you is so
strong she threw herself into another galaxy to be with you. That's
the kind of magic I can't fabricate anymore. Surrender, Alejandra
Mortiz, or Rishi dies. I will open her mouth and empty this vial
down her throat. Do you know what the Forbidden Canto does?"

Rishi's eyes are shut. Fat tears carve their way through the dirt
on her face. She shakes her head. When she squeezes her lips, the
vines get tighter and blood drips from every puncture wound.

"What?" I growl.

"You really should study your cantos, dear," the Devourer
chides me. "The Forbidden Canto breaks the heart. It's meant as
a form of poetic suicide. It'll attack all her tender human organs,
saving the heart for next to last. In those moments, she will endure
lifetimes of agony. You see, she will stay alive long enough to
watch you watch her die. Then, her brain will give out, and that is
the last thing Rishi will ever see.

"Nova's grandmother wrote this particular canto and created the draught. Your world is full of so many possibilities. I can't wait to rip a hole through it. Now, surrender your power, or I will pour this down Rishi's throat."

With a wave of the Devourer's hand, the vines around Rishi's face come undone. Blood drips from the holes around her lips. She cries out once.

"Don't," Rishi tells me. Her midnight eyes are locked on mine. "Don't."

Nova uncorks the vial. He brings the glass to Rishi's lips. She tries to keep them closed, but the Devourer forces them open.

"Nova," I say his name. "You don't have to do this."

His voice is hard, and when he looks at me, he says, "Yes I do."

The red liquid slides down the glass, a red bead pools at the tip. I stop breathing. It's as if El Corazón has ripped my heart right out of my chest. How can I watch Rishi die?

"I surrender," I scream.

Nova drops the vial on the ground. It spills into the dirt.

The Devourer raises her hands, and I feel her magic seize me. My chest burns as I struggle to breathe. I kick the air, try to pry the force from around my neck until I feel a terrible pain stab at my heart. Warm liquid drips from my ears, my nose; blurry, dark tears sting my eyes. I'm choking. I'm dying. My heart flutters like the wings of a hummingbird. My mind is heavy as the sea. I feel like I've aged a hundred years and now I'm brittle and broken.

I stop struggling.

My arms drop to my sides. The force around my neck releases, then drops me on the ground. A light floods from me and into the

Devourer's palm. My power pulses like a star in her hand. She blows on it, and the orb travels directly to the labyrinth, to the Tree of Souls.

The realization hits me like a gunshot to the heart. Tears spill down my face. She took my light. She took my magic.

Sometimes, the Deos choose wrong.

There was an encantrix who broke the laws of nature.

She claimed herself a god. So the Deos

banished her to a land forgotten.

They should have known, wild magic can't be tamed.

—THE WRITINGS OF ALTA BRUJA KRISTIÑE

Noveno Santiago," the Devourer says. She takes her nail and drags it across her palm. Scarlet blood bubbles from the wound. "I free you from our contract. From my blood to yours. I bless you with the lives of the banished. Rise, no longer servant, but child of my darkness."

He stands taller, tilting his face up to the heavens. She squeezes her palm over his head. The blood drips down his forehead, over his closed eyes, down his lips.

The black marks on his chest and arms light up. His chest expands, then shudders. His light is blinding. I force myself to watch. To remember the way this feels, so I can never feel this way again.

When the light fades, Nova stands still. The boy who crossed my path on the street, the boy who found me, the boy who lit up the dark for me is dead to me. I realize he never existed, and I'm just a fool for thinking he did.

You chose well this time, the Devourer said. *You're losing your touch.*

How many others has he led down here? Does he think of them now as he looks down at his hands? There is no recognition in his eyes, only awe. They're unmarked. Perfect. New. He touches his chest where the marks were spreading around the sacred heart of his tattoo. They're all gone.

As if noticing I'm still standing here, he jumps.

A bit of metal glints in the black grass. My dagger.

"Don't do anything stupid," he warns me.

"Like think I could trust someone like you?"

Hurt flashes across his face briefly.

I try to stand tall and defiant, but I can't. My muscles cramp and burn until I double over.

"What you're feeling is going to get worse, Alejandra. If you try to fight me without your powers," the Devourer tells me, "you will die with the rest of your family. You're only human now. If you'd like to go home, Nova will create a portal." She glances at the moon and sun, and a broad smile fills her face. They're nearly lined up perfectly. Today. The eclipse happens today. "Though I suspect I'll be seeing you on the other side soon."

The Devourer presses her hand on her chest. Something is wrong with her. A thin line of blood trickles from her nostril. She wipes the blood away. Licks it off her finger. She starts to glide across the field covered in fog, back into the labyrinth. Then she stops. She turns to look over her shoulder. "Nova." She says his name the way a mother would, urging her child to come along, to follow.

"If you stay here, I will kill you with my bare hands," I tell him.

He nods and disappears with her.

When she's gone, I sink to the ground. I curl into fetal position. I spent so many days and nights in my room like this, begging La Mama to take the power from me. Now that it's gone, I feel a void. A cold sweat bubbles on my skin. I shiver uncontrollably and dig my fingers into the earth. I can't hear the pulse of the land or hear the words in the wind. I can't feel my family anymore.

"I'm sorry," I whisper.

"Alex," Rishi cries. "Alex, please get up."

Rishi needs me, I tell myself. The vines are still squeezing her. I hear the crack of a rib, followed by Rishi's scream. I push myself up and find my dagger. I slice the vines, but it's a hydra. Everywhere I cut, the vines multiply and grow. I start digging around Rishi's feet until I find the root. I stab the core of the plant over and over until it lets go of Rishi and dries up.

I catch Rishi as she falls. She wraps her arms around my neck and we cling to each other. The land here is gray and bleak, cast in the shadow of the labyrinth. I search for the magic inside of me but it's gone.

"I failed them," I say.

Rishi shakes her head into my shoulder. "You're still alive."

"Sh." I brush her hair out of her face. She's covered in her own blood. I reach for my power to heal her and come up empty. The void inside me grows bigger by the second. I try to conjure a spark between my fingers, and when I can't, I pound my fists against the ground. "You know when you want something so badly, but when you get it, it's not what you expected?"

She nods, stroking her thumb over my cheekbone.

"That's what it felt like when I gave her my power. Only a thousand times worse. When we were back home, I thought it was the magic that made me do terrible things. I've always blamed the magic. I hid behind it. But here, magic was the only thing that made sense. Now it's gone."

Alejandra, a voice whispers to me.

Rishi turns to the labyrinth. She heard it too. It's different from the voice I was hearing in my head. That was the voice of my power guiding me. This voice is different. It sounds like my aunt Rosaria.

"I want you to take the mace," I tell Rishi. "Find a place to hide."

She makes a very loud noise that lets me know she's not going to listen. "I heard that too."

"I don't have my power to protect us, but if the Devourer thinks I'm going to turn around and go home, she's wrong."

"She can't feed from the tree until the eclipse," Rishi says. Her lips are swelling, but she refuses to stay quiet. "You heard her. She'll have your family's power. She'll come into our world."

I think of what Agosto said. She's nearly drained Los Lagos dry. She needs somewhere else to go. With our combined power, she could break free of Los Lagos and into my world.

"You were right before when you said the answer is in the Tree of Souls. Nova was just trying to make you second-guess yourself because he was working for her."

That stings more than it should. I'll deal with Nova later on.

The tree. The answers lie in the tree.

"We have to get through the labyrinth. What would Lula do? Without my powers, they can't reach me. I wish I could ask them."

"Do you know what I ask myself sometimes?" Rishi takes my hand in hers. "What would Alex do?"

I press my forehead to hers. The thing that drew me to Rishi was her happiness, the way she wore it on her sleeve, the way it lit her up like the stroke of midnight on New Year's Eve. Now, in the most hopeless of places, she gives me that light.

We pull each other up. We face the labyrinth. There's a swirl of black-and-gray clouds directly above it. I take a deep breath and stretch my aching muscles. No power, no recoil.

Rishi takes my dagger, and I sling the mace over my shoulder.

I'm not the encantrix everyone thought I would be. Right now, I'm just a girl, and there is also magic in that.

PART III

THE
ONE

34

I search for you in lost fields.

Hear me, my dear. Your loved ones wait here.

—Canto of Spirits,
Book of Cantos

We run into the Campo de Almas.

There is no life, only dirt where nothing grows and rain doesn't fall. The sky is a fiery burst of red, like the top of the sky is on fire while the rest of it sleeps.

The campo is a field of wandering souls. These souls are different than the ones in the river. They're thin as fog and move slowly, like they've forgotten where they're going. I wonder what's worse than roaming aimlessly without knowing you're dead.

A cold hand grabs at me, and I instinctively pull on my magic. Nothing comes. The hand on my shoulder is cold and soft. As soon as it touches my skin, it passes through me. They're less than ghosts—they're shells of memory. The soul repeats a word I don't understand. I realize it's a girl's name. He says it over and over in a gruff voice, like it's the only word he remembers, the only word that matters beyond years and life and death.

"What's wrong with them?" Rishi asks.

Directly above us is the labyrinth. It hits me. "This is where she throws them away after she drains their energy."

Rishi takes my hand, and we run through the wandering souls. Their essences make my skin pucker, my heart ache. I can't let his happen to my family. Rishi squeezes my hand tighter. We're chain links of desperation attached to one another.

We reach the twisting black arches that mark the entrance of the labyrinth.

"Stay close," I tell her.

We step inside. The deep-blue darkness surrounds us, and I prick myself on the twisting vines that wrap around the laby-rinth wall. The path is narrow and littered with stones. Above me, the sky is a sea of storm clouds. My eyes adjust to the dark. The hedges tremble as they shift. A deep rumble shakes the ground. My heart is in my throat as I tell myself to run. Pick a path. Neither is going to be safe. Leaves and branches change shape.

"The entrance is closing!" Rishi tries to run for it, but the arch-way disappears and she hits a wall.

There's no way out.

"You should've gone home," Nova says, appearing in front of us.

"You're moving on up," Rishi tells him. "The Devourer got you a new wardrobe and everything. Tell me, who are you wearing?"

"Shut up," he snaps. His broad torso is covered in a black

material that looks as slick as oil but as hard as metal. It's trim and simple and makes his eyes that much brighter. He says my name.

I pull my arm back and punch him. His head snaps back and blood gushes from his nose. My knuckles throb and my arm hurts like hell, but I want to do it again.

"Don't," he tells me.

"Why are you here?" I ask him. "You got what you wanted. You've got a power boost and it only took how many sacrifices?"

Nova wipes the blood from his nose. "You act like you're so much better than me. At the end of the day, you made the same choice I did. You chose yourself. You have no idea what my life has been like."

"I'm not like you at all, Nova." I squeeze the mace handle, daring him to make me use it. "I came here to fix my mistakes. You played me. From the very *beginning* you played me. Did you jump in front of Maks's car on purpose? Or did it start at Lady's shop?"

Nova rubs his hands across his head. It's strange to see them without the marks, but his brown skin is beautiful just the same.

"You don't want to know," he tells me.

"I need to know."

"As you wish," he says, unable to meet my eyes. "I could hear this energy everywhere I went in the city. It was like a sigh that wanted to be a scream. I thought I could find it. I needed more power to get out of my contract."

"Contract?" Rishi asks. Her eyes are so dark, I fear she's going to lunge at Nova with that dagger.

"Sinmagos like to joke that they make deals with the devil. In my case, I really did. The Devourer promised she'd save me. All

271

I had to do was find brujos and brujas. It was the only thing I got from my mother: the ability to charm my way into people's hearts."

"I hate you," I tell him.

"I didn't want to die, Alex," Nova says. "The marks started spreading, and I could feel it wrapping around my heart. Haven't you?"

I hold out my palms, sucking in a breath. Thin, inky marks zigzag around my wrists, up the meaty base of my palm, and finally pool at the center, like two blazing, black stars.

"It happened after you conjured the elements. You were just too"—he looks at Rishi—"preoccupied to see."

I rub my palms on my pants as if that's going to get rid of the marks. "Why are you here?"

Nova takes a step toward me, but Rishi gets in the way. Nova smirks, and for a second, I see the boy who traveled alongside us, the boy who shared his magic with me and helped me fly a boat across a river of souls.

"I'm here to tell you to turn back. I'll make you a portal. I'll get you home."

I step around Rishi and get up in Nova's face. "My home is trapped in that tree. Now, either sound the alarms, or get out of my way."

I watch his features turn hard. Maybe the marks are gone, but he's still the same lost boy that wandered the streets of New York.

"If I walk away from you," he says, "I'm as good as dead."

But he holds out his hand and disappears into the open path. The hedges change. They ripple, then form into a solid wall that blocks our way.

"Why would he do that?" I ask.

"It's another trick," Rishi says.

Maybe Nova is trying to trick me again, or maybe a part of him regrets what he did. I focus on looking for a way out. I need to find the voice again. I close my eyes and listen. The wind stirs and carries with it a whisper.

"Follow the light," Aunt Rosaria's voice says.

"I'm not crazy," I say. "You heard that too?"

Rishi nods. "I heard it."

The wind whistles as a ball of light appears out of thin air. It bounces in place, then races to the right.

Follow the light.

I follow the ball of light as it travels down the pitch-black path. Creatures hiss and hoot and caw from the shadows, between the leaves, and everywhere, unseen. Something tries to grab my arms. Its flesh is cold. I bash it with my mace and keep running. The earth curves slightly, then becomes a ninety-degree angle that leads left.

The ground beneath me undulates, like a great serpent is traveling beneath it. I lose my footing and fall forward. When I press my hands to the ground here, all I see is black. It wraps around my heart, whispering my deepest nightmares back to me. It is unlike the rest of the earth I've touched in Los Lagos. It wants me out.

No, it wants to eat me alive. The dark is moving. I roll over to the side as the ground opens up in a red, red mouth. A black, forked tongue comes up and licks at the air.

The dark has teeth, I think. *The dark has teeth.*

I roll again and push through the ache in my legs. When I turn around, Rishi is gone. I head back the way I came, but it's all the same: black hedges and dark earth.

"Rishi!"

The light we were following has disappeared. The labyrinth walls change around me. They retract like curtains to reveal Rishi. She's on the ground with her hands around her knees.

She whispers, "It isn't real. It isn't real. It isn't real."

I run to her. Push her head back. Her face is dirty with sweat and tears.

"Rishi, it's me."

"No, it's not!" She pushes me to the ground.

I get up and reach for her, hold her by her shoulders. "Look at me. Remember what Madra said? Look twice. So look at me. What do you see?"

She hiccups with every breath. Her fingers reach out for my face. "There's something in here. It showed me—I don't want to say."

"You don't have to."

I pull her into my arms to stop her from shaking. I get that feeling again, that dread that crept along my skin before the ground opened up to swallow me whole. I let my embrace warm her cold skin. She presses her forehead against mine.

"Whatever was in here showed me you," Rishi says. "You were dead, Alex! You were dead in my arms."

"I'm right here. You have to know that."

Rishi presses her hands on my face. "I do know. You gave up your magic for me. I couldn't stand it if I lost you."

"You won't."

"Please don't break my heart, Alex."

I feel like my heart will beat right through my rib cage. "I have all these feelings that I can't sort out. I think I've felt it since the day you found me. But when this is all over, we'll figure it out, okay?"

Even in the dark, she finds my lips. They're warm despite the air around us. I press my lips against hers, softly and slowly, like stepping into a wide, unknown ocean one foot at a time.

The labyrinth rumbles around us. A slithering shadow undulates beneath the ground. The ball of light returns. It pulses weakly, and we follow it to another dead end.

"This isn't right," Rishi says, pressing her weight against the hedge.

"Alejandra!" Aunt Ro's voice is clear as a summer's day. "The moon!"

I look up at the clouded sky. The mammoth clouds part for a moment to reveal the crescent moon. It is inches away from eclipsing the sun, but for now, its moonlight shines down on my necklace. The prism of light returns, revealing a hidden door on the hedge.

Then the clouds gather with more force, and the light is gone.

"There," I say, and swing my mace. The hedge twists and writhes, but I bash my way through.

Rishi has to hold me up because I feel like I'm falling.

It's Aunt Ro. I reach out for her smiling face. Her black corkscrew curls billow around her head in a wild halo. She's really real.

"You're alive."

Once, the brujas fought the shadows and won.

Twice, the shadows pushed back.

—FROM THE JOURNAL OF
JUANA LUZ SARTRE DE MORTIZ

Mostly alive," Aunt Ro says. The hedge shuts behind us, and the ball of light pulses weakly in our circle.

"You mean you're like a zombie?" Rishi asks.

Aunt Rosaria smiles at her, and in that moment, my whole world makes sense. "I died in our world. There is no going back. But the Deos, they can make mistakes."

I know she died. Her dead body fell on me. We mourned her for days. Then, I see something my seven-year-old self wouldn't have noticed: the thick, red scar across her neck. I touch the keloid.

"You were—" The word is so ugly I can't even say it. *Murdered.*

"It's not something I ever wanted you to know."

"My mom said that it was a canto that went wrong."

"Oh, it did," she says, laughing darkly. "When they found me, no one was more surprised than me."

"Who found you?"

She frowns. "That is a story for another day. What matters is that it wasn't my time. That's what everyone says, don't they? Everyone thinks they have another day, month, year to keep going. As if all of this world and the others were designed for them alone."

"Maybe," I say. "But you were the world to a lot of people. To me."

"That's why we mourn." A sad smile appears on her face. "Death is the most sure but unexpected part about life. It's almost up there with love. It's bound to happen, but how and when—now that's the tricky part."

"Tricky isn't the word I'd use."

She brushes my hair from my face.

"Who broke your heart, nena? That boy you were with? I wish I could have been there to tell you to never trust a boy with star eyes. They blind you like a deer in headlights."

I make a face and motion to where Rishi is standing with her arms crossed. "It's more than that." Then I realize something. "Why can I talk to you now?"

She settles into a cross-legged position. That's when I see her feet are shackled to the ground. "Because your magic is gone. I've been trying to contact you for a long time. I'm your godmother, after all. I should have been there to guide your powers when they came. I should have been there to stop you from doing what you did."

I swallow the bitter guilt in my mouth. My body craves water. Rain. My veins itch. She puts a hand on my arm where I'm scratching.

"Withdrawal."

"So soon?"

"You're never the same without it."

"So now that I'm not a bruja, you can talk to me?"

"Don't sass me." She slaps the back of my head and Rishi snorts. "The reason I couldn't talk to you was *you*. You kept your ears closed."

"Me?"

"You didn't want to listen. That's why our bond was broken."

"It didn't help that every time you materialized, you looked like a corpse."

"That was your fear making you see me that way." She brushes her fingers through my hair, which is caked in blood and mud and La Mama knows what else.

"I didn't want to think about you dead."

"That's the thing, my love. Even if you don't think of the dead, the dead are thinking of you."

"Sorry, but why are you trapped here?" Rishi asks.

"And what do you mean the Deos made a mistake?" I add.

Aunt Ro throws her arms up in mock surrender. The gesture is so familiar that I could cry. "You ignore me for years and now you want all the answers. Listen here, girl, the Deos gave me this chance. Even they believe I was meant for something great. Perhaps not in our world, but there's still hope in this one."

"You live in a literal prison inside the labyrinth of a demon witch who is about to kill our entire family. How can there be any hope?"

"We found each other, didn't we?" She smiles, and it makes my heart break. I've missed her so much. This whole time, all I did was push her away. "Your godmother is supposed to guide you through your magical journey."

"As in the fairy variety?" Rishi asks, and it feels so good to hear her voice twinkle with happiness.

"I could see glimpses of Alejandra throughout the years," Aunt Ro says. "But Los Lagos isn't like the realm of the dead or the paradise fields where the Deos live. It's harder, almost impossible, to break out of here. I always wondered why they chose this land for me. The moment I woke here, I was in chains. I was furious. After everything they put me through. After everything I saw you go through. When I realized the Devourer was targeting you, I knew I had to act. The Deos act through us. They want us to save this land."

"That was you I heard calling out to me when we were in the River Luxaria, wasn't it?"

"You needed a push. Now that we're together, we'll set things right."

I scratch at the inside of my wrist. I can't stop shaking. "When the Devourer took my power, I wanted to die. I felt like there was no place for me anymore. And there won't be—not without the others. I wish I'd told my mother the day my powers arrived, but I was too scared."

"I should've been there to teach you."

"It wasn't your job. I had a mother."

Have, I correct myself. I have a mother.

"You can't be mad at her. She had a hard time. I watched you guys every day. You're an amazing girl, Alejandra. Your mom did the best she could even if it didn't feel like it was enough. *She did the best she could.*"

"I get it, okay? I'm afraid to face her now. She'll know what I did. She'll know about dad—"

"What happened with Miluna, with your father—that was *not your fault*! I'm going to tell you something about your mother, but you can't tell her."

"She's being held captive by an evil witch," Rishi says. "Alex couldn't tell her even if she wanted to."

"You certainly have a mouth, don't you?" Aunt Ro winks at her.

"What about my mom?"

"You know, Alejandra, you're just like your mother when she was your age. Impatient and bossy. Magic was different then. It was the eighties. Brujas were coming over from the islands to practice freely. We were wild back then. Careless. A lot of people we knew died from using too much or getting into nasty business. We were hunted. We went underground. Your mother wanted nothing to do with her gift after our dad was killed by hunters."

"I didn't know that. I thought Papa Renaldo died of a heart attack."

"Caused by a hunter," she says bitterly. "It was a different time. There's a truce, a treaty now. The Thorne Hill Alliance they call themselves. But back then, your mom told me we were going to run away to the middle of nowhere. We could hide and never use our powers again. It was the day before my Deathday, and I was scared. Treaty or not, my powers were wild. The elements called to me. She feared for my life. Rightfully so, I suppose."

"What made you stay?" I ask.

"Your father." She looks pleased with the shock on my face. "That same night, we were at a social circle. We had to make the rounds, so our mom wouldn't suspect anything. You always had to be one step ahead of her. She had the Sight, like Rose.

"So at the circle, there's this handsome guy with big, gray eyes and creamy, light skin. Real fresh, you know? He spoke about all these hopes for all magical kind. How we needed to come together with not just brujos and brujas, but with the half-beings. I thought he was cute."

"Gross."

"But your mom, man. She loved him even before he started speaking. She loved him even more when he walked up to her and introduced himself. I knew I couldn't leave. If I left, Carmen would have come with me, and I just couldn't do that to her."

"Do you think you made the right choice?"

She looks at my face for a long time. "I don't regret staying. I regret a lot of things, but staying, being part of your lives, I never regretted that. I want you to know that we could have left. The thought was there. You weren't the only one who felt like the magic was too much."

"I wish she'd told me. Maybe I wouldn't have been so weak."

She grabs my face in her palms. "Never, ever could you be weak. We all *think* about leaving, Alejandra. We all get scared and want to turn away, but it isn't always strength that makes you stay. Strength is also making the decision to change your destiny."

"But look at what I did! My powers are gone."

"That's where you're wrong." She stands and dusts off her white dress. She holds out her hands for me to take.

"What do you mean I'm wrong?" I ask.

"The Deos act through us. Only my own blood can free me, and here you are. You were born a bruja, Alejandra." She looks at the big sky. "Your powers are at the Tree of Souls, but your body is still a conduit. Your body is made to hold your personal brand of magic. It'll always be yours. That's why the Devourer constantly needs to feed to accumulate power. With every bit she consumes, it takes a toll on her physical body because the power is stolen. What happens when you don't feed a fire?"

"It burns out," Rishi says.

"What do I do in the meantime?" I ask.

Aunt Rosaria grips my hands tighter. I jump with the shock of power. "You're going to borrow some of mine."

She ate the stars and swallowed the earth.

She is the girl with all the power.

—WITCHSONG #5,
BOOK OF CANTOS

Aunt Ro's power floods my body. It's familiar but foreign all at once, like listening to my grandparents speak in the Old Tongue and understanding what they say even if I can't pronounce the words myself.

Every time I look at her, I'm filled with more wonder. *She's alive.* I don't know if I'll ever be okay. I'm not sure if this will work, but Aunt Ro says to trust her, and I do. The first step is breaking her free. I pull the borrowed magic and rip the chains from the ground. I think of Agosto and the Meadowkin. I whisper a prayer to El Guardia for their safety. The chains break apart and melt into the ground. I hiss as the recoil hits me harder, and my hands glow as black marks burn farther along my skin.

The labyrinth shudders around us. For a long time, I wanted nothing more than to be ordinary. As we run through the changing paths of this maze, I realize I was never ordinary to begin with. We are built a certain way, and the only thing I regret is that it took me so long to see that. The Devour tried to take that from me when she took my family. I'm going to get it back.

"Has the Devourer seen you here?" I ask. "I mean, the Deos put both of you here."

"The Devourer was put here by her crimes in her realm, your human realm," Aunt Ro says. "I have a different path. When Xara discovered she could make herself stronger by feeding off the Tree, she thought she could become so great, no Deo could imprison her here. She recruits vulnerable creatures in other realms and uses them to bring others she feeds off here."

Nova. An unblessed brujo. A marked brujo. A boy who wanted more, to never be powerless. A boy who didn't want to die.

"So if she has enough power, she can break out of Los Lagos?"

"I believe so," Aunt Ro says. "Power is addictive. She needs it to survive, just as much as she needs it to destroy. The only way for her to break free from her punishment, to rule with unlimited strength, is to become a god herself."

"Is that even possible?"

"By definition of immortality, yes. With the right amount of powers, she could. Our family is among the oldest lines of brujas in the world. She'd get pretty damn close."

No, I think. *She won't.*

We stop at a fork in the labyrinth.

"Remember what I said," Aunt Ro tells me. "Don't stand in one place for too long. If you get taken by the vines, stab the thickest part closest to the ground. Even plants have feelings, after all.

"Get to the tree, Alejandra," she tells me.

"Keep Rishi safe," I tell her.

Rishi kisses my cheek, and then they're gone. A hedge separates us. I run. With Aunt Ro's magic, my strength is renewed. I skid on the ground as a wall appears in front of me. The labyrinth blocks my way, creating a perfect square around me.

"Alejandra," he says.

The ground swims beneath me as I look at his face.

He hasn't aged a day. It's like looking into a mirror when he smiles—same teeth, same smile, same shape of our eyes. His are gray like Lula's. His hair is combed back. I can smell the gel he used every morning, the spice in the aftershave he used after making his face silky smooth and trimming his mustache. I remember the way his mustache tickled my skin when he'd kiss me good night.

"It's all right," my father says.

"It is *not* all right."

He looks around him. "I can take you to the others. I know how to get us back home."

I find myself breathing hard. I can't stop my heart from racing in my chest. Can't stop the questions from racing through my head. *Why did you leave?*

"You're not real," I whisper.

I can feel the shadows surround us.

Look twice. Look twice. Look twice.

"Listen to me, Alejandra," he says.

It sounds just like him, I think. It even has the scars on his hands. The laugh lines around his eyes. It looks *just* like him.

"Listen to me, nena," my father says. "I had to leave. Leaving was the only way your power would become as great as it is now. From the moment Rose was born, I knew my children would have a bigger destiny than I ever did. Me? I thought I'd change the world. But I couldn't. I was never good enough for you, for your mother. You made me feel…inadequate. I couldn't look at you without remembering my own failure. I tried to make the world better for you, and I couldn't."

"Stop it." I shut my eyes and stumble back.

"I left because I could never love you," he says. His body becomes straighter. The smile fades. "No one can."

A shudder passes over me. I've wanted to believe this for so long—that there is something inside of me that is so wretched, no one can love me. But that can't be true. My whole family, living and dead, protected me from the Devourer. Rishi followed me into a black hole. I touch the moon pendant between my clavicles. I feel a weight lifting off my chest, a truth I didn't want to see in my own heart.

"My father loved me."

I see his eyes flash dark. He advances on me.

Then, the winds change, wrapping around me like wings. I can *feel* them—my family. All of them. The Tree of Souls is so close. I can feel their love brushing against my skin. It banishes the shadows that crawl all over me. Even if they'll never forget what I did to them, I know in my heart that they still love me.

"I *am* loved." I push against the shadow and fear that surround me.

He staggers, snarling. The dark moves around us. Shadows gather, taking the shape of a person. The gray skin of the dead.

One human leg, the other a stump, replaced by gold. Like Oros, the duende of the Luxaria. A swollen belly marked with bites and bruises. Bony arms with sagging flesh. Its face, misshapen and contorted. Teeth covered in black and green decay. It looks at me, and there is no looking away from eyes so black it's like staring into the terror of the unknown.

"You are the one with all the power," it tells me, limping around me.

"You're a duende," I say, turning to keep him in my sights. "What do you want? Gold? This?" I touch the crescent moon around my neck.

The duende grins, tapping his long, thin fingers against each other. He's missing two on each hand. He deeply inhales the air around me.

"I want to hear you scream," the duende says.

It waves a hand, and for a moment, I feel like the space around us spins. The hedges turn over. The sky is beneath me, then above me again.

I blast the duende with my magic, but it goes right through him. He *tsk tsks* at me.

"You're supposed to be the chosen girl. You should know that wouldn't work on me. I am fear. I am the shadow of your mind. I have no name. I am everything you hide, and I cannot be defeated." Then slowly, the missing fingers of his hands start to grow back.

The duende snaps his teeth in my direction, hungry for more. Then it sees something behind me.

"Be gone," Nova commands him. "The Devourer sent me for her."

"I am never gone, girl," the fear duende says, bowing to Nova. "Remember that."

Nova walks around me like a hawk. He presses his palms to his temples and screams. "Why are you doing this, Alex?"

"If it bothers you so much," I shout, "then stop following me. Go back to your master."

"I can't!" He takes a step toward me, and I blast out a shield. He presses his hands on it. His perfectly healed hands. "I can't watch you die."

I let my shield down. "But you can watch my whole family die, right? You're so noble."

"I'm trying to make this right."

"Try harder!" I shove him to the ground.

When I turn around to run, there's a snarling shadow beast at the end of the path. The maloscuro's snarling teeth are wide open and coming for me.

"Get down!" Nova shouts, blasting his light. The labyrinth starts to change again. He grabs my hand. "Come with me."

"I'd rather take my chances with the maloscuros." I pull my hand out of his.

Nova shoots a blast of burning light at the maloscuros running toward us. I swing the mace like a baseball bat and slam it into the shadow creature's face. Blood sprays my skin. My hands tremble as I pull my weapon back just in time to swing at the next one.

We're surrounded in seconds. The blind giants turn a corner, their feet shaking the earth. Nova creates spears of light in his hands. He slings them at the giants, piercing the tender, unprotected skin of their eyes. When the giants scream, it echoes all through the labyrinth.

I look up just in time to see a saberskin ready to pounce on me. I push my borrowed magic into a shield. It's weak and it flickers, but it keeps the beast away long enough for me to get a better grip on my mace. I conjure flame in my hand and light the head of my weapon. Then, I bash it into the creature. Its oily skin catches fire. I blast a horde of bat-like creatures that attack overhead. Nova burns them to a crisp.

There are too many of them.

I can hear the Devourer cackle. It sounds like it's coming from all directions. I concentrate on singling it out, then take the open path to my right when a light blinds me. I don't have time to scream. His hand clamps down over my mouth. Nova pulls me into a pitch-black corner.

"Sh," he whispers in my ear. He's holding me around my waist. The hands of a stranger. They seem empty without the black marks covering his skin. The Devourer is on the other side of the wall. She's speaking to herself nonsensically. Every now and then, she stops and laughs, then screams and cries out for blood. She curses at the moon and the sun and tells them to hurry up.

"Withdrawal," Nova whispers.

"No, I had withdrawal," I whisper back. "That's something else."

"She gets this way toward the end, when she hasn't fed since the last eclipse."

We're boxed in my black, trimmed hedges. I remind myself of Nova's betrayal. I remind myself I can't trust him. I throw my elbow back and dig it as hard as I can into his gut. Slam my boot against his foot. He grunts and falls, and I lift my hands into the air to—kill him? Can I?

"Take me to the *tree*," I tell him.

"Wait, Alex, please."

"Don't say my name."

"Fine," he snaps. He gets back on his feet. "*Encantrix*, let me explain."

I call my borrowed power to the surface. I'm not going to kill him. I'm going to make him hurt the way he hurt me.

He meets my power with his own. I fall back on my ass. "Alex, don't."

"*Don't* say my name."

He makes a frustrated gesture at the air. "We don't have a lot of time. I'm trying to help you."

"Then get me to the Tree of Souls."

"I'm trying. You just—you have to know. I was just doing my job. I wasn't trying to hurt you."

"You didn't have to try." I take a step away from him. "You just did. You made me think you were on my side. You made me think I could trust you."

"It wasn't supposed to go down this way. There's more I wanted to tell you. I just couldn't do it in front of Rishi."

"Why?"

He's quiet. I can see the indecision in his face. He takes several steps away from me, hugging his body. He looks up to where the moon is touching the outline of the sun. When he turns around, he moves so quickly, I don't have a chance to react—my hands are still raised in the air, and he stops inches from me. I can feel the hum of his heartbeat. Like the time I stole his life force, like the time he carried me in the mountain pass.

"The job was to gather power for the Devourer. I scouted you for weeks."

I shut my eyes. I see him walking in front of the car that day. I see him crossing the street while looking back at me.

"It wasn't hard to find you. There aren't many of us left, you know? Everyone knows someone, but none of them had your potential. A score that big, I could get the Devourer to keep up her end of our bargain. To set me free. All I had to do was swap out your Deathday ingredients with mine, and your power would get sent here. It was easy to do when I dropped off my delivery. I didn't expect your whole family to get in the way to protect you. I didn't know what would happen, Alex. The Devourer still wanted you. Without you, none of this would work."

"You created the portal. You made me think *I* banished them." I shut my eyes for a moment, and tears run down my face. He starts to touch my hand. "*Don't.*"

"There's more."

I turn to run through the hedge, but something grips me from behind. White-hot pain sears my skin. Magic floods my veins, and then we're on the ground together. Pure magic flares through me so quickly that my head spins. His memories flood into my mind. I see my face the way he sees me, hear his heart slamming against his ears like fists against the wall.

There's Nova as a kid, beating his knuckles bloody on a wall of exposed brick. His tortured back cut up in cruel, bloody gashes.

There's a little boy hiding in a closet while guns go off in the next room.

There's a police officer throwing him into a bus like a criminal.

291

There's home after home. Monstrous hands that come out of the shadows. His heart beating and beating until it creates a spark. The magic finds him and burns a woman's face.

There's Nova, older, bolder.

There's a boy who never got the chance to be a child. He roams the streets all night and sleeps in the nooks and crannies of the subway, the park, the construction site of a million-dollar high-rise. He's so hungry he steals and steals until he's just another shadow in the city.

The black marks start to spread every time he uses his magic. At first, he measures the progress, but soon enough he stops caring. He calls them tattoos.

People look at him a certain way. Fear. Awe. It's the same thing, I guess. He's older still, pulling his hood over his face so people won't ask him what he is. Brown skin and light eyes, like the world's biggest mystery.

He finds friends on the streets. Lost boys and girls surviving by any means necessary. There's an accident. A girl screaming. A man with a gun. Nova uses his magic to scare away an attack. The girl runs in fear, not of the attacker but of him. There are blue and red and white lights, and accusations.

There's juvenile detention. There are men there with magic too. They smell like steel and blood and fire. They whisper of a creature who can help. They call her the Devourer. She appears like a succubus in his dreams, all red lips and promises.

There's hope. For the first time in so long, there's hope.

He's a pied piper of souls. He leads power to the woman with the mask of death. He hears their screams as she consumes. He wants to break away, but he's bound to her. He longs for her promise to make him strong. He searches for more. He's walking to a job. He almost gets hit by a car. There's a girl. He sees her fear. Her power. He knows her from around the way. He loves her anger and her fight. He loves the way she holds her fears close to her heart. The Devourer sees her too. That's the girl. Watch her. Wait. She's the One.

He leads her down the dark. He holds her. She saves him. He saves her. He wants her. He loves her. But the human girl loves her too.

He betrays them. He doesn't want to die.

The sound of rushing blood roars in my ears. Our connection breaks.

I sit up, shaking in his arms.

"There's nothing I can do to make things right with you," he tells me. "But that doesn't mean I'm not going to try."

He holds out his hand.

It's a stranger's hand, a traitor's hand.

"This doesn't change a thing," I tell him.

As the sky breaks above us with pouring rain, Nova creates a long passage through the hedge. There, at the end of the narrow path, is the Tree of Souls.

37

Find me where the sun meets the moon.

Past the wicked trees,

past the desert dunes.

—WITCHSONG #2,
BOOK OF CANTOS

Nova and I run through the maze. The hedges try to shift, try to trick me, but I barrel forward. I smash at the dead hands that reach from the black leaves with my mace. I can smell fire and smoke. It starts on the outer rings of the labyrinth and races toward the center.

"How did you do this?" Nova asks me.

"I have a few tricks up my sleeve." I hope Aunt Ro and Rishi are safe out there.

I stop at the base of the Tree of Souls and land on my knees. I feel dwarfed by its grandeur. Its long, thick branches reach for the sky, barren of any foliage. Instead of leaves, the branches are filled with hundreds of cocoons. The cocoons pulse with white light, and when I touch the tree trunk, I get impressions of the powers trapped in there.

Alex! I hear Lula shout.

She made it, another voice.

Encantrix, a united whisper.

"I'm here," I say, then a sharp pain digs into my side. The blast sends me flying back, away from the tree and crashing into Nova.

Black, sinewy smoke surrounds us, toys with us. I pick myself up and get ready for another attack. The smoke settles in front of me and materializes into the Devourer. Her eyes are a deeper red now, almost black. Dry, red lips smirk. Her neck twitches, as if something inside of her is fighting to get out.

"Nova. I'm surprised," she says. "I thought human self-preservation was better than that. I suppose not."

"I'm used to being a disappointment," he says without a trace of irony.

"I'm taking my family back," I tell her.

"How?" she asks. "Kill me? You can't. You're alone. You'll always be alone. I have your power, your family. Now, I'm going to take your life."

"Enough, Xara!"

I turn around at the sound of his voice. Agosto, the Faun King, is flanked by his people. They wear armor made of tree bark and metal, their weapons are ready to charge. Madra stands beside the faun and bows her head in my direction. The avianas flap their wings and caw a warning. There are so many of them, even creatures I don't recognize.

The Devourer takes a step back. It's a single step, but it's enough to show she didn't expect this.

"The tribes of Los Lagos," she says, recovering easily. "We've been down this road before. It never ends well for any of you."

"Maybe this time it will," I tell her.

"Look at you," she says. "I love it. A few days ago, you were scared of your own shadow. Now, you're ready to lead a rebellion."

I'm still not ready, I think. My heart pounds. My legs shake. *But I have to be.*

"How noble of you," the Devourer says, turning her face to the sky. The perfect circle of the sun and the crescent of the moon eclipse each other. The symbol of La Mama and El Papa. "But I'm afraid you're too late."

The Devourer raises her face to the sky. The rain clears and the clouds part to reveal the coming eclipse. The crescent moon crowns the white sphere of the sun, and together they're lined up above the tree. The cocoons of stolen power pulse faster and faster, changing from white to black.

"No!" I shout. "Keep her away from the tree!"

Madra attacks first, swooping down from the sky. Her war cry fills the air. Her talons scratch the Devourer's face, ripping her eyes from their sockets. The witch's scream is a terrible thing that cuts through my eardrums. Her trembling fingers touch the blood streaming down her face.

The avianas swoop down and scratch her hands, peck at her hair, her skin.

The Devourer blasts the air with crackling energy. It strikes four birds down. They land, broken and twisted, at our feet.

It's not enough. Her power isn't weakening.

Your magic is your anchor. I used to believe it was my burden.

I used to believe it was the reason everything terrible happened to my family. But what if we were ordinary people, without this darkness surrounding us? Terrible things could happen still. That's just the way of the worlds. Here, in Los Lagos, my magic has done good. *Can* do good—if I let it.

Wild magic can't be tamed, I think, and for the first time in forever, I don't want to hold back. This magic is mine. I can feel it calling to me.

I understand now. Magic is a living thing. It's part of me. I summon it, call it like a snake charmer calls a snake out of its slumber. The magic answers back. It slithers from the tree. The Devourer's face contorts when she feels what I'm doing. My power, all of it, is expelled from the cocoon and back into me. This time, I don't fight it. This is what Mama Juanita meant. *I accept you.*

I remember you.

The Devourer grabs my hand, and I get a flash of something.

A young woman alone on a hill, cursing the Deos.

I don't want to see her impression. I don't want to know, so I pull away, leaving her staggering to the ground. I want to ask her, *How does it feel?*

Instead I turn to the voices of the trapped souls in the tree. They're waiting for me. I just need blood, and I need it fast. The eclipse is happening.

Blood of my blood.

I climb the roots of the tree to get to the center of the trunk. The answer is the tree. I can't help but think of Nova. It has to be blood. Blood is life. I cut from my wrist up, blood flowing down the trunk. I bite back the pain that burns as I cut. The tree becomes soft as human flesh.

Free us, the voices whisper.

Release me, the land screams.

I raise my dagger and drive it deep into the bark.

38

Given the gifts of the Deos, the encantrix has a choice in the worlds.

To heal it.

Or destroy it.

—THE CREATION OF WITCHES,
ANTONIETTA MORTIZ DE LA PAZ

The world falls apart.

It's the only explanation for the way fire falls from the sky. Gashes rip fresh wounds into the earth. The roots of the Tree of Souls rise up from the ground like they're waking up from a long, long sleep. The black cocoons shatter into fractures of multicolored light.

My magic hums against my skin. Every part of me is glowing. Even my necklace. The light beams at the tree, illuminating the people that emerge. The sight of them brings me to my knees.

My mother, Lula, Rose, Mama Juanita. Tio Guacho and cousin Betsey. Hundreds of generations of my brujas and brujos stand before me. There's a woman who looks like she walked out of a Renaissance portrait. Her ruffled collar is almost as tall as her curls. She looks at me with a haughty face that tells me she's not pleased, that there is no better place for me than this—on my knees asking for forgiveness.

"There is nothing I can say that would change what I've done," I tell them.

"You got that right," Lula mutters. I could kiss her beautiful face.

The lady with the collar speaks in Castilian. I don't understand it, but I don't expect what she says is forgiving. Beside her is a woman I've only seen in a black-and-white photo. My great-aunt Santa Orchidia who lived to a hundred and twenty. Her skin is black as coal. Her silver hair is wrapped in a white scarf that matches her mourning dress. White. We mourn death in white. She speaks in a language that rattles my bones.

Mama Juanita steps forward. She puts her hand on my cheek. "I'm proud of you, nena."

I lower my head. They surround me now, the way they tried to do on my Deathday.

An old man steps forward. In his withered old face, I see my father's eyes. Lula's eyes.

"Alejandra Mortiz," Papa Philomeno says. "You have my blessing now, then, and always. Do you accept?"

"I accept." I hold out my bleeding wrist. He touches the blood and uses it to trace our symbol—the crescent crowning the sun—on my forehead.

I can feel their hands, all of the Old Ones, encircling me, repeating, "You have my blessing, now, then, and always."

I didn't expect a being as old as the Devourer to go out without a fight.

And she doesn't.

She shakes with magic, blasting away the ring of avianas and Meadowkin. When she turns to me, I don't recognize her.

Her skin is aged like cracked desert. Her body is doubled over like a question mark. Talons and nails have bloodied her arms and face. But still, she's a fighter. She pulls at the magic of the earth, the roots of the tree. My family has escaped, and so are other souls, floating away into the air in silver wisps. She tries to draw them back, but they fight like fish swimming upstream. Those who were captured alive stand ready to fight.

"We're not finished, Alejandra," she says.

"No, we're not, Xara."

"Don't you dare use my mortal name. Xara was weak and afraid, just like you will always be."

But I'm not afraid anymore. "The Deos don't take kindly to false names."

An unusual sense of calm settles in my body. I can feel them, all of them, the lines of my family crisscrossing, not just living beside my magic but merging together to create something more. I know why everyone was so excited when they found out what I was.

Encantrix. The one chosen by the Deos.

"I will destroy you," she tells me. "I will drink the magic from your bones and then spit them out."

"You should be careful who you threaten," Mama Juanita says, clicking her cane at my side.

One by one, they come forward. I can see Xara counting. Her eyes grow wider with each person she sees.

"This is over four hundred years of my family," I say. "And these witches are pissed."

I thought I was ready, but I'm not. My family channels their power through me all at once. I can see our lifelines twisting like sinew, like DNA, like roots in the earth. When I can breathe again, I direct the flow of magic. It floods in prisms of color that can only exist in between the realms. It is pure, undiluted power, and I fire it at the Devourer.

She lashes out with everything she's got. It feels like she's throwing stones while I wear Kevlar. Together, our magic fills the skies with blinding lightning. I hold it in my hands and throw. It cuts through the Devourer until there is nothing left but the ghost of her scream and a shower of ashes.

39

'Round the twisting paths of eternity,
o'er the bridge of forgetting.
There, you'll find the Kingdom of Deos.
—BOOK OF DEOS

T he gash on the tree spreads, sucking up anything and everything around it. Creating a portal through the tree was the only way to free it from the Devourer.

"We have to go!" I shout.

One by one, the spirits of my deceased family members disappear into the ether, back to rest until the next time they're called upon. The ones that are still alive wait for me. Then there are the others, strangers, who were trapped against their will. Their souls fly around me, they touch me, thank me, and then they vanish.

"Alex!" My mom's voice cuts through the howling wind. I run into her open arms and hold on tight. "We have to go. The portal is going to seal itself."

"Wait!" I pull out of her embrace. I run to where Agosto and

Madra are weary from the battle. Black clouds circle and twist, ready to form a tornado at the center of the labyrinth.

"You must go, encantrix," Agosto says.

"I'm making sure everyone gets back."

There's so much to say. It's too much to convey with a simple embrace. Madra gives me one of her feathers; Agosto, one of the throwing knives from his belt.

Aunt Ro pulls me back to the tree. "Go, Alejandra."

She's different too. The symbols of the sun and crescent moon are marked on her forehead. She glows with a light that comes from deep within.

"What happened to you?" I ask.

"The Deos have a plan. They always have a plan!"

When my mom sees my aunt, she nearly faints. "Rosaria?"

Aunt Ro's dark skin glows with a different kind of blessing. A balance. The Devourer is gone and someone needs to take her place. This is why the Deos gave her a second chance. The sisters embrace. My mother shudders in her little sister's arms. Aunt Ro kisses my mother's wet cheeks, then forces herself to let go.

"Okay, head count," Lula says.

One by one, they jump in—Lady, Rose, my mom, and so on.

I watch the labyrinth crumble as the fire dies and leaves the skeleton of branches. Funnels of clouds swirl across the hills and carry the ashes away. The Meadowkin and the avianas wave from a distance. Rishi takes my hand and squeezes.

"Ready?" I ask.

"Don't stand me up again." She kisses me and jumps into the portal.

Then there's Nova, standing alone.

"I'm staying," he shouts.

My heart, the treacherous, bloody mess, betrays me. It squeezes with unexpected hurt.

"If you stay," Madra says, cold as ice, "I'll make sure you pay for your betrayal. The Devourer may be gone, but this still isn't paradise."

Nova nods an understanding.

I look at Madra and Agosto once more. I commit them to memory. I never want to forget this moment.

The force of the gateway pulls at me, but so does a part of me I didn't know was there. A part that wants to stay. How easy would it be to stay? What version of myself is going to come out of the other side of that portal?

Aunt Ro takes my hand. She kisses the inside of my palm where my cut stings. "Don't shut me out again, nena. I'll be watching over you always."

"I'll be waiting."

The first time we went through a portal, Nova pushed me. I see the hesitation in his eyes and the fear of not belonging. Before I can change my mind, I wrap my arms around him and pull us into the portal.

40

La Mama gave her heart to El Papa.

They lived in the Kingdom of Deos for all their days,

chasing each other across the skies.

—HISTORY OF THE DEOS,
BOOK OF CANTOS

Falling a second time isn't the same as the first.

This time, I wade through time and space. My magic is linked to everything—the infinity of time, the rapid snuff of death, the sprinkle of stardust, and the released sigh of freedom.

I don't remember landing in the backyard. Only blurry red and blue lights. Sirens replace the rush of the wind. Strong hands pick me up from the grass. A stranger's face belongs to someone who puts me in an ambulance that takes me away.

I sleep for days.

We all do.

There is no official story except that a family on our quiet Brooklyn street was attacked. The house robbed, even though I know nothing was taken. There is no explanation for the singed earth in the backyard or the tree cut down and burned to a stump. While I know it was the portal sealing itself for good, the police decide it was lightning. It felt like we were gone for weeks, but when we returned, only moments had passed.

For days, I dream of Los Lagos. I see Aunt Rosaria and Madra and Agosto burying the dead. I see Aunt Ro conjure rain to hydrate the parched earth of Bone Valle. It'll be a slow change, but they've got nothing but time. There's the start of new trees and fields of green and purple and gold. The Tree of Souls, now free, replenishes the land. It grows taller than before, and there's a white scar where my knife ripped into the bark. Leaves replace the cocoons of stolen energy. The Wastelands show signs of growth, new buds that bloom like starflowers. Tall creatures with long, silver hair plow the earth and breathe light into the forests.

Madra lets the avianas roam free. Their feathers grow full and silky and bright. Inside of the Caves of Night is a small nest and on the wall hangs a set of black wings. And at night, under the cloak of stars, they tell the fledglings stories of the Thief, the Magpie, and the Bruja that destroyed the Devourer.

· ❧ ·

When we all finally wake up, my mom takes us home.

There are no police follow-ups. No suspects, no leads. I think the police have had their fill of my family for long enough. They wash their hands of us, and I think they're relieved that we want to be left alone.

At home, my mom kisses my forehead as we watch the news.

They stopped reporting on our freaky "attack" after we refused to comment. Still, we watch for signs of other strange things. Mom wants to make sure nothing else came through the portal with us.

There is no sign of Nova. He wasn't at the hospital, and I don't know what happened to him after we fell.

"Don't worry, nena," my mom says. I look at her face. The smattering of gray hair that she's named after each of us, the crow's-feet at the corner of her eyes. Other brujas get glamours to hide them, but my mom never does. "These things work out on their own way."

Rishi takes longer to recover, so my mom and I visit her in the hospital.

I bring her a sprig of lavender. I look over my shoulder and pull the drapes. My mother decides to distract Rishi's parents while I visit. I fish out a crystal from my pocket, break the spring of lavender, and place them on her chest.

I lean in closer to her, whispering the prayer of the Deos. I hold her hands and find the root of her malady. I press healing waves into her skin, let them travel through her system until my mother knocks on the door. I'm dizzy, but I don't want to leave.

"You ready, honey?" my mom asks, standing with her hands on my shoulders. Ever since we got back, she's had separation anxiety. Whether it's dropping us off at school or even going to get groceries. I fear she's a step away from regressing to baby leashes.

"Not really."

"Do you love her?" my mom asks.

"I think so. I mean, I've never felt this way before, so I'm not sure what it's supposed to feel like to begin with. Rishi was the one who always believed in me, even when I was powerless. I'm just afraid of what it means. Look at you and Dad."

My mom holds my chin gently in her hand. "I'm going to tell you something, nena. Even after everything you told me, even if I knew one day I'd wake up and never see him again, I would still love that man."

I look at Rishi. Her breath is steady and her machine lights up with all sorts of colors. Somehow she's the brightest part of my day. My little magpie.

"Then, yeah," I say. "I do. I love her."

"You know," Rishi says, sitting up to stretch. "If you'd have said you loved me like ten minutes ago, I would've probably woken up sooner."

My mom bursts out laughing. I feel myself turning red, but still I go to her. I pull her into a hug and hold on tight.

"We're back," I say.

She brushes my hair. "I see that. Now there's no getting rid of me. I know all your secrets."

"Good," my mother says, "because you're invited to Alex's Deathday."

41

She is the light in the hopeless places.

She is the sky when the night blazes.

—REZO DE LA ESTRELLA,
LADY OF HOPE AND
ALL THE WORLD'S BRIGHTNESS

Not everyone gets second chances. I'm grateful for mine.

Rishi helps me find a dress. It's a splash of different purples and makes a *swish, swish* sound when I spin in my room.

"You look like the Los Lagos sky," Rishi tells me.

Lula rolls her eyes and scrapes the bobby pins too hard against my skull. "Will you guys stop with your Los Lagos bonding? You got to have all the adventure while were tortured by an evil old bruja."

"You're just jealous," Rishi says.

"She is jealous," Rose says, lighting a new candle on my altar beside Madra's feather and Agosto's throwing knife.

"Don't tell me you're on their side, Rosie," Lula mutters.

"I don't choose sides. I just know things."

"So how come Alex has to do another party? Didn't she accept the blessing when she freed you guys?" Rishi flips through *The Creation of Witches*. After everything that happened, Lady apprenticed me at her shop. I don't mind the extra work.

"Sure, Alex got a blessing," Lula says, pinning the rose on my head. "But we didn't get a party. Plus, everyone is clamoring to meet the encantrix. We're getting free stuff every day."

"Not to mention all the people coming to our door searching for miracles," Rose says.

"Wow," Rishi says. "You're like a celebrity."

I wouldn't call myself a celebrity. But all over town, brujas talk. They talk about the girl who destroyed the Devourer of the Los Lagos. They don't mention that I was partly responsible for banishing my family there or that four hundred generations of both ghosts and the living helped right my wrong.

"We can't turn anyone away," I say. "Our spare room is like a magical infirmary. My mom had to quit her receptionist job to take care of our patients. We take care of people with demonic possessions, wounds that can't be treated by a regular doctor, and irregular births."

"We had our first *vampire*," Lula says. "My heart nearly fell out of my chest when he came in with an arrow sticking out of his shoulder. He was so hot."

"His shapeshifter friend was cuter," Rose says quietly.

"Aw, Rosie has her first crush."

And then we all fall into fits of laughter.

The second party is better than the first. Everyone sings and dances and drinks copious amounts of Lady's rose punch because we're alive and it's a beautiful thing.

I shake the hands of friends, family, and strangers. It's still overwhelming. Everyone seems to want a piece of me. They want to look at my hands, at the marks that refuse to heal. I've grown rather fond of them. A reminder in case I ever lose my way again.

An old bruja brings her child to me so I could bless her. I don't think I'm quite there yet, but it seemed to make her happy. No matter what I say, people think I'm more than what I am. That's the difference between Xara and me. I'm quite happy with my slice of power, doing what good I can.

Rishi quickly becomes everyone's favorite, retelling our adventure with details I seem to leave out—the way the sun shone, the way the water tasted, the beings we met. Rishi even seems to make sense of Crazy Uncle Julio's ramblings, and his prediction of a zombie invasion this summer.

"Let's dance," Rishi tells me, pulling me onto the dance floor. "Is it weird that I miss the Meadow del Sol? And that you could see so many stars. Sometimes I dream of it."

"I'll give you stars," I tell her.

I conjure the Los Lagos night sky on the ceiling, and I thank the Deos for making me who I am. An encantrix, a bruja, a girl.

EPILOGUE

Grita al sol! Grita a la luna!

If the Deos hear, they'll answer.

—THE CREATION OF WITCHES,
ANTONIETTA MORTIZ DE LA PAZ

There is a hard knock at the door. My mother is on the couch, resting her dancing feet. The house is in shambles after the party. It's well after three in the morning. Lula fell asleep on the couch still wearing her dress, and Rose is reading an anatomy textbook. My senses are wide-awake.

Knock knock knock.

"I got it," I say, drawing on my power in case it's a threat.

"Hey," he answers.

"Hey," I say.

Nova stands in a blue hoodie and jeans. It doesn't look very warm, but he doesn't shiver. I instinctively look at his hands. His fingertips have started to turn black with marks again.

I go to close the door in his face, but he puts his hand on it.

"I know you'll never forgive me," he says.

"That's right." I don't look at him. I can't because I know that a sick, twisted part of me cares for him. I'll just never be able to look at him the same way.

"But you have to know that I wasn't lying about the way I felt for you. That was real. Every little bit."

"I believe you," I say.

I have so many questions, like: Where have you been? Where did you go while we were all in the hospital? If you love me so much, then why did you vanish? If you love me so much, then why did you still hurt me?

Not all loves are meant to last forever. Some burn like fire until there is nothing left but ash and black ink on skin. Others, like the love I feel for Rishi, stay close to the heart so I'll never forget.

"What are you doing here, Nova?"

He looks to the side, like he's being watched. "There is nothing I can do to make you forgive me. But this is a start."

He turns and runs down the front steps and back onto the street, leaving his footprints on the snow. I run after him, but he's quick and vanishes around the corner.

"Wait!"

I realize there's more than one set of prints in the snow.

There's Nova's and mine—and a third.

I whip around. Inhale so much cold air I think my insides are frozen. On the porch is a face I thought I'd never see again. It's like looking through a foggy window.

From the house, my mom yells, "Shut that door! You're letting out the heat!"

But I can't move. Every part of my body is locked. I think my heart has stopped beating.

"Alex, what—?"

Lula and Rose run out to see what's happened, but they scream too. Lula rubs her eyes as they adjust to the dim porch light, and she clamps her mouth shut in disbelief.

He looks older, that's for sure. There's recognition in his eyes but also confusion. It's like he's trying so hard to remember our faces, like he's one of the lost souls in Campo de Almas.

I say the word carefully, like it's made of glass. "Dad?"

AUTHOR'S NOTE

Alex's story has been in my heart and mind for a long time. *Labyrinth Lost* has taken different shapes and titles, and undergone many revisions, but the one thing that hasn't changed is the idea of family as identity. Alex struggles with who she is, who she should be, and who she wants to be. I think that everyone, no matter where they come from, can relate to that. In order for me to create this matriarchy of brujas, I took inspiration from some Latin American religions and cultures.

BRUJAS

Bruja is the Spanish word for "witch." In my Ecuadorian family, we call each other brujas as a joke. When you wake up with your hair messy, your aunt will say, "Oh, mira esa bruja!" The word itself has both negative and empowering connotations. In Latin

American countries, like Ecuador, the neighborhood "bruja" might be someone to be feared. One of my most vivid memories is watching a neighborhood bruja rub an egg over a baby's body to determine whether or not he had the Evil Eye. Since all of these countries have a large Catholic population, it's easy to place a bruja, or witch, in a negative light. In the last couple of years in the U.S., I've seen Latin women all over the Internet take back the word "bruja" with pride, from the Latina skate crew in the Bronx (The Brujas) to the contemporary young women who practice nondenominational brujeria.

Brujeria is a faith for many, but it is not the faith in my book. In *Labyrinth Lost*, I chose to call Alex and her family "brujas" and "brujos" because their origins do not come from Europe or Salem. Alex's ancestors come from Ecuador, Spain, Africa, Mexico, and the Caribbean. Her magic is like Latin America—a combination of the old world and new.

DEATHDAY

The Deathday is a magical coming-of-age of my own creation. Like a bat mitzvah or a sweet sixteen, but for brujas and brujos. It is a time when a family gets together and wakes the dead spirits of their ancestors. The ancestors then give their blessing to the bruja/o. With the blessing, the magic can grow and reach its full potential. Without the blessing, well, bad things can happen. Like many traditions, they grow and become modernized. In Alex's time, Brooklyn circa now, Deathdays are lined up with birthdays for extra festivities. Even though the Deathday ceremony was created for the world of *Labyrinth Lost*, aspects of it are inspired by the Day of the Dead and Santeria.

318

El Día de los Muertos, or the Day of the Dead, is a Mexican holiday that celebrates and honors deceased family members through food and festivities. Altars are filled with photographs, flowers, food, and candles. The celebrations are then taken to the cemeteries, where people play games, sing, and even leave shots of mezcal for the adult spirits. The unity of death and family is what drew me to it and one of the things I wanted to include in Alex's life. One of the best books I've read on the subject was *The Skeleton at the Feast: The Day of the Dead in Mexico* by Elizabeth Carmichael.

Santeria is an Afro-Caribbean religion that syncretizes Yoruba beliefs and aspects of Catholicism. It developed when slaves from Western Africa were taken to Cuba and other Caribbean Islands against their will. Slaves were forced to convert but held on to their religion in secret, and used Catholic saints as parallels to their orishas. Those who don't understand it often see Santeria as a secretive and underground religion. Like some Santeros, the brujas of *Labyrinth Lost* use animal sacrifice and possession, and connect directly to their gods. The Santeria orishas, however, are not gods but *parts* of the Supreme God. For further information, a popular starting point is *Santeria: The Religion: Faith, Rites, Magic* by Migene González-Wippler.

DEATH MASK

The matriarch of the family paints a death mask on the bruja receiving her Deathday. The Deathday ceremony was originated by Mexican brujas in *Labyrinth Lost*. The death mask is white clay that covers the face. Then a black paint or charcoal powder is used for the eyes, nose, and lips. Thousands of years ago, Alta Brujas realized that the dead weren't appearing at the Deathday ceremonies. They decided they needed to dress up like the dead to make them feel at home. Death became an intricate part of day to day bruja ceremonies and festivities.

The death mask itself is, of course, influenced by the sugar skulls of the Day of the Dead. In real life, sugar skulls are used to represent the dead and decorate the wonderful feasts of Día de los Muertos. They're colorful and smiling and are sometimes meant as social commentary. In the early 1900s, an artist named José Guadalupe Posada created the Catrinas. They were skeletons dressed in upper-class Spanish clothes and meant as satire of the Mexican Indians, who were trying to copy the European aristocracy.

THE DEOS

The Deos in *Labyrinth Lost* are the pantheon of gods worshipped by brujas and brujos. The Deos represent all aspects of nature, creation, and everyday life, similar to the orishas of Santeria and the gods of Greek mythology. When I was creating the Deos, I chose to name them using the Spanish and Spanish-like words that corresponded to their physical attributes and powers. El Fuego = fire. El Viento = wind. La Ola = water. The highest of the Deos are La Mama, the mother of all gods. Her sacred symbol is the sun. Her counterpart is El Papa, the father of all gods. His symbol is the crescent moon. Brujas and brujos often choose a Deo the way Catholics choose a patron saint to pray to. Alex knows magic is real, but she has a hard time putting her faith and belief in something that has caused her family so much pain. Even though the Deos rarely present themselves to mortals, they make their presence known. It is believed that the Deos act through the mortals they created—the brujas and brujos.

For more information about the world of *Labyrinth Lost*, email me at zoraidawrites@gmail.com.

ACKNOWLEDGMENTS

This is a book I've always wanted to write. It wouldn't be possible without my agent, Adrienne Rosado, and my wonderful editors, Aubrey Poole and Kate Prosswimmer. Thank you, ladies, for enduring every draft and revision, and staying with Alex to the very end. To the fantastic team at Sourcebooks Fire, including Alex Yeadon, Amelia Narigon, Elizabeth Boyer, Nicole Hower, and my publisher, Dominique Raccah.

My incredible beta readers: Natalie Horbachevsky, Hannah Gómez, Anne Greenwood Brown, Ellen Goodlett, and Rebecca Enzor. Elisabeth Wilhelm, for your thoughtful notes and for cheering me on as I revised on our train to Berlin. David Collett, for that medical torture advice. Cat Scully, for the most amazing world map. Gretchen Stelter for correcting my terrible grammar—and sorry about all the commas.

For Lauren McCall. Thank you for reading this book in its earliest stages. Thank you for bringing my words to life. To everyone who worked on the short film/book trailer: Brenda Salazar, Brenda Cespedes, Danielle McAllister, Erin Gross, Sam Rojas, Sara Ott, Varyana Galmadez, Daniel Waynick and lovely Lula, Jessica Naftaly, Madison Pflug, Emily Simpkins, Jasmine Carruthers, Macs Dawson, Jennifer Westburgh, Judith Parades, Gabby Wales, and Amanda DiMartino.

My bruja cast: Amanda Villanova, Adriana Medina, Aimee Alburquerque, Raiane Cantisano, Shari Abdul, Agustina Bernguer, and Nicole Coiscou.

To my witches, harpies, and badass writer ladies who keep me inspired. My friends who cheer me on and believe in me, especially Gretchen McNeil, Dhonielle Clayton, and Melissa Grey. Amy Plum, for Paris and for giving me a place to finish this book. My fellow traveling author buds, Adi Alsaid and Eric Smith.

To my parents, Liliana and Joe Vescuso; my incredible grandmother, Alejandrina Guerrero; my best roommate and brother Danny; Caco and Robert; Tio Danny and Ne; and the rest of my Ecuadorian tribe.

Finally, for all the girls and boys: you are enough.

Read on for an excerpt from Book 2
in the Brooklyn Brujas series

BRUJA BORN

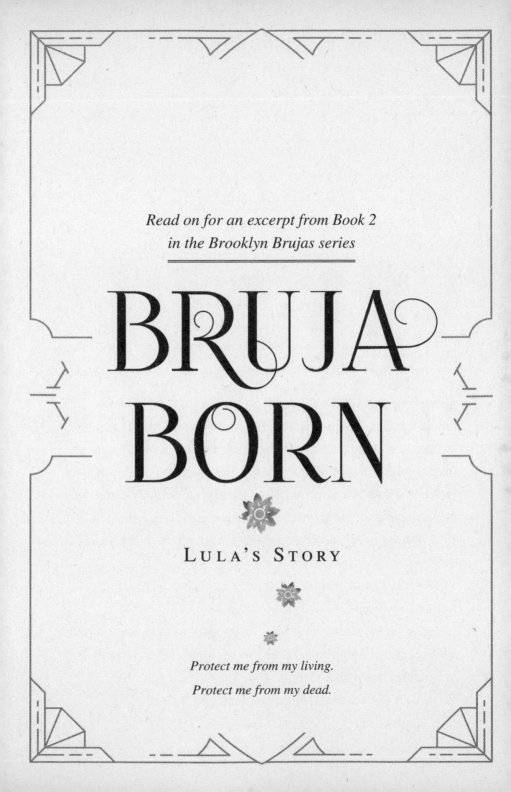

LULA'S STORY

Protect me from my living.
Protect me from my dead.

They say El Corazón has two hearts:

the black thing in his chest

and the one he wears on his sleeve.

—TALES OF THE DEOS,
FELIPE THOMÁS SAN JUSTINIO

This is a love story.

At least, it was, before my sister sent me to hell. Though technically, Los Lagos isn't hell or the underworld. It's another realm inhabited by creatures, spirits, and wonders I'd only read about in my family's Book of Cantos. The place where I was kept—where my whole family was imprisoned by a power-hungry witch—*that* was as close to hell as I hope I'll ever get.

But that's another story.

"Lula, you ready?" my sister Alex asks.

I stare at my open closet and can't find the socks that go with my step team uniform. I riffle through bins of underwear and mismatched socks and costume jewelry.

"Lula?" Alex repeats, softly this time.

For the past seven or so months, Alex has been extra everything—extra patient, extra loving, extra willing to do my chores. She means well, but she doesn't understand how suffocating her attention is, how the quiet in her eyes drives a sick feeling in my gut because I'm trying to be okay for her, for our family and friends. I think I've gotten pretty good at faking it. But sometimes, like now, I snap.

"Give me a minute!"

I don't mean to snap. Honestly. But everything that's come out of my mouth lately has been hard and angry, and I don't know how to make it stop. That's not who I am. That's not who I was before—

Rose, our younger sister, walks into my room wearing long sleeves and jeans even though there's a heat wave and it's mid-June. Rose has the Gift of the Veil. She can see and speak to the dead. Spirt magic runs on a different wavelength than the rest of our powers, and being so tuned-in to that realm means she's always cold. Rose takes a seat on my bed and picks at a tear in the blanket.

"Can I go to the pregame with you and Maks?" she asks me. "I've never been to one before."

"No," I say.

"Why not?" When she frowns, her round face gets flushed. Sometimes I forget that underneath all her power, she's just a fourteen-year-old kid trying to fit in.

"Because," I say, digging through my dirty laundry. "It's just for the team. You can drive to the game with Ma and Alex."

"And Dad." Rose's voice is a quiet addendum.

Right. Dad. After seven years of being missing and presumed dead, he's in our lives again. It's an odd feeling having him back, one we all share but haven't talked about. He has no memory of where he's been, and even if we can't say it out loud, maybe we've moved on without him. Alex was always the one who said he was gone for good, and perhaps deep down inside, I thought that too. But I always corrected her. I was the one who *believed* he'd return, because sometimes false hope is better than being completely hopeless. I believed in lots of things once.

"And Dad," I say.

The three of us exchange a look of unease. There are too many things that are unsaid between us. I wish we could go back to being loud and rowdy and something like happy. But it's taking longer than I thought.

So here are the things we leave unsaid:

One, we're brujas. Witches. Magical BAMFs with powers gifted by the Deos, our gods. A house full of magic is bound to cause some friction, and after what Alex did, there is plenty of friction.

Two, my sister Alex cast a canto that banished our entire family to a realm called Los Lagos. She got to traipse across its magical hills and meadows with Nova, the hot brujo we never talk about, and her now-girlfriend, Rishi.

Meanwhile, I was trapped in a freaking tree. A big, evil tree. I was surrounded by all-consuming darkness, and even though we're home and safe, I still feel that pull, like something is sucking at my soul and my light, and this house is too small and crowded, and I don't know how to make this fear stop. I don't know how to get over it.

Three, I can't stand looking at my own reflection anymore.

I took all the mirrors in my bedroom down, even the one that was on my altar to keep away malicious spirits. They don't need it. One look at my face, and they'll be scared off.

"Ready when you are," Alex says again, her guilt radioactive.

Technically, *technically*, the attack that left my face hideously disfigured with scars was Alex's fault. I'm a terrible sister for thinking it. Forgive and forget and all that. But the maloscuros that came looking for her attacked *me*. Their vicious claws raked across my face. Sometimes, when I'm alone, I can smell the rot of their skin, see the glow of their yellow eyes, feel their presence even though they're long gone and banished.

To be fair, Alex has scars from the maloscuros too. Right across her heart. But she can cover them up. I can't.

Not naturally, anyway.

Having a sister who is an all-powerful encantrix has its benefits. There are a million problems going on in the world, and here I am, worrying about scars. But deep down, I know it's more than the scars. I've been called beautiful my whole life. I've been aware of the way men's eyes trailed my legs since I was far too young. The way boys in school stuttered when they spoke to me. The way they offered me gifts—bodega-bought candies and stolen flowers and handwritten notes with *yes/no* scribbled in pencil. My aunt Maria Azul told me beauty was power. My mother told me beauty was a gift. If they're right, then what am I now? All I know is I left fragments of myself in Los Lagos and I don't know how to get them back.

So I turn to my sister, because she owes me one. But before we can get started, my mother knocks on my open door, Dad trailing behind her like a wraith.

"Good, you're all together. Can I borrow you guys for a minute?" Ma asks. She rests a white laundry basket against one hip and waves a sage bundle like a white flag. "I want to try the memory canto on your father before we leave. The sun's in the right—"

"We're busy," I say, too angry again. I don't like talking to my mother like this. Hell, any other time I'd catch hands for speaking to her like that. But we're all a mess—guilt, anger, love, plus a lot of magic is a potent mix. Something's got to give, and I don't know if I want to be here when it does.

Mom throws the sage stick on top of the clean laundry, scratches her head with a long, red nail. Her black-lined eyes look skyward, as if begging the Deos for patience. She makes to speak, but Dad places his hand on her arm. She tenses at his touch, and he withdraws the hand.

"We all have to pull our weight around here," Ma tells me, a challenge in her deep, coffee-brown eyes that I don't dare look away from.

"Dad doesn't," I say, and feel Rose and Alex retreat two paces away from me. Traitors.

"He's trying. You haven't healed so much as a paper cut since—"

I widen my eyes, waiting for the her to *say* it. *Since Los Lagos. Since the attack.* But she can't.

"You have Alex," I say, turning my thumb toward my sister. "She's an encantrix. Healing comes with the package."

"Lula…" Ma pinches the bridge of her nose, then trails off as my father tries to be the voice of reason.

"Carmen," he whispers, "let them be. It's okay."

But my mother doesn't fully let up. "How much longer will you keep having your sister glamour you?"

Alex looks at her toes. All that power in her veins and she can't escape being shamed by our mother. I might be *just* a healer, but I match my mom's gaze. We share more than our light-brown skin and wild, black curls. We share the same fire in our hearts.

"Until it stops hurting," I say, and I don't let my voice waver.

We share a sadness too. I see it in her, woven into the wrinkles around her eyes. So she just hands me a black bundle—my uniform socks—and says, "We'll see you at the game."

· ❦ ·

"Close the door," I tell Rose after our parents head downstairs.

I sit cross-legged on my faded flower-pattern rug as Alex prepares for the canto. Since she embraced her power, her brown eyes have tiny gold flecks, and her hair falls in thick, lustrous waves. She even wears it loose around her shoulders, and I think it's because Rishi likes to twirl it around her finger when they think we're not looking. There's a light inside of her. The light of an encantrix and a girl in love. I hate to say *I told you so*, but I did tell her so. Magic transforms you. Magic changes you. Magic saves you.

I want to still believe in all those things.

Rose cleans up my altar, sneezing when she breathes in layers of dust. She lights a candle for El Amor, Deo of Love and Fervor. Beside it, she lights a candle for La Mama, Ruler of the Sun and Mother of all the Deos.

"*Gross*, Lula. When was the last time you cleaned your altar?" Rose asks, wiping her fingers on the front of her jeans.

I only shrug and lie back on the floor. She sits at my feet and holds my ankles. This isn't for magic. I think she's just trying to comfort me in the only way she knows how. Alex kneels right over my head. A year ago, Alex kept her power bottled up. Now, she calls on it easily. She pulls the smoke from the candles, elongating it between her fingertips like a cat's cradle until it encircles the three of us like a dome.

Next, Alex rips the head off a long-stemmed, white rose and sets the petals in a bowl. Our magic, our brujeria, isn't only about putting herbs together and chanting rhymes. Anyone could do that. This canto has no words, just the sweet hum my sister makes as she sifts through the rose petals. The rise of her magic fills the room, settles along my skin like silk.

One by one, she places each petal on my face. She hums until she's covered every inch of pearlescent scar tissue and I'm wearing a mask made of roses. She pushes her power into the rose mask, and slowly, it takes on her magic. The petals heat up and soften, melting into my scars like second skin.

I'm never ready for the next part, but I grab the carpet and brace myself. Glamour magic requires pain. I hiss when it stings like hot needles jabbing into my flesh.

"Maybe we should stop," Rose tells Alex.

I shake my head once. "I'm okay. I swear."

Alex keeps going, holding her hands over my face, waves of heat emanating from her palms. I breathe and grind my teeth through the discomfort.

"There," Alex says.

The earthy sweetness of roses in bloom fills my bedroom.

Nothing coats the senses quite like roses do. Alex and I lock eyes, and there is so much I want to say. *Thank you. I'm sorry. Are you okay?* Her face, right where my scars should be, darkens with red splotches. I recognize the recoil of glamour magic— bruises and redness that match the person being worked on. All magic comes with a cost. The cyclical give-and-take of the universe to keep us balanced.

She never complains though. She smiles. Stands. Busies herself with her phone.

I go to my dresser and I pull out a round hand mirror that I got at a garage sale for a dollar. It's a dull metal but makes me feel like the Evil Queen from Snow White. When I was little, I used to root for Snow, but lately, I feel the queen was way misunderstood. Women with power always get a bad rep.

My mood changes instantly when I look at myself in the mirror. I feel like I'm bound to this bit of magic that gives me back a part of myself, even if it's superficial. The scars are gone. The Bellaza Canto is a stronger form of glamour. When I touch the area where the four claw marks are supposed to be, there is nothing there but flawless, sun-kissed skin.

"Mirror, mirror," I whisper to my reflection, tilting my face from side to side.

I grab my favorite pink lipstick and apply it. It's a coral shade that brings out the honey brown of my skin and make my gray eyes stormier. I fluff my mane of black curls and rub my lips together to make sure my lipstick is even. I wish I could make this feeling last. For now, I'm going to enjoy it until the next time.

"Thank you," I tell Alex, and press a sticky kiss on her cheek.

"Gross," she mutters, wiping it off. Then she picks up the decapitated rose stem and bowl of unused petals. "Let's go, Rosie."

My phone chimes and my heart flutters when I see Maks's name on the screen. I'm outside.

I analyze the message as I put on my socks. His texts get shorter and shorter every day. Part of it is my fault for being so distant. Ever since Los Lagos, shadows seem to leap around every corner and crowds make me feel as if I'm sinking, my head barely above water. Nothing puts a big, fat hex on a social life like the fear of monsters only I can see.

"Today will be better," I tell my reflection, slipping into Maks's letterman jacket before I run down the stairs.

"See you at the game!" my mom shouts.

I wave as I zoom out the door and into Maks's car parked out front. The minute I'm outside the house, I can breathe again. When I'm around Maks, I don't have to think about magic, and I'm ready to sink into the comfort of his humanity.

"Hey," Maks says, not looking up.

He fiddles with the radio stations, but they're all staticky. He ends up plugging in his phone. His personal coach doesn't believe in kissing, or anything else exciting, on game day. I want to believe that's why his voice is distant and that's why he isn't reaching for my hand. But seeing him fills me with a sense of need—the need to be my old self. The need to be happy. So I press my lips on his cheek and leave the pink imprint of my mouth.

"You're in a good mood," he says, thick, black brows knitting in confusion, and I'm bothered that he sounds so surprised. His knee shakes a little, and I place my hand on it to try to comfort him.

He always gets nervous before games. But he's the best goalie the school has seen in years. Nothing gets past him.

"Last game of the year. It's a big deal." I smile when he looks at me before putting the car in drive. Relief washes over me when he takes my hand in his and kisses my knuckles, then speeds down the empty Brooklyn street.

"We've beaten Van Buren like six hundred times, but they're still a solid team." He squeezes my hand once, then lets it go.

"You okay?" I ask. As a healer, I can sense the tension knotting his aura. He's always nervous before a game, but today it's worse than usual. Maybe I'm feeling the residual magic from Alex's canto. My magic *has* been way off.

At the red light, he turns to me. His hair is combed back at the top and his edges are freshly buzzed. I brush my fingers at his nape, where the barber didn't brush off all the stray hairs.

"Lula," he says my name like a sigh.

He turns to me again. I can't tell what he's searching for, but when I look at him, really look at him, I remember why I fell for him. The sweet, caring boy whose smile made me dizzy. I always keep a sprig of hydrangeas on my altar because they remind me of his eyes.

We both start when someone honks behind us, and he faces the road again.

"I was thinking," I say, trying to make my voice low and playful, but I end up feeling silly, "we could do something after the game. Just the two of us."

"I already told the team they could party at my house. My parents are on a business trip, and my sister's already at Uki camp for the summer."

I shouldn't be annoyed, but I am. I tell myself he's just tired. He's been practicing extra hard. He's going to Boston College on a soccer scholarship and wants to be at the top of his game.

"We haven't really been alone in a while," I say.

"That's not my fault."

"It's not my fault either. Look, I don't want to fight."

Another red light. He shakes his head, like he's dispersing the thought he just had.

"What?"

"I'm just saying"—he sighs and flicks on his turn signal—"we haven't been *alone* because you never feel like being alone. You've been so off, and I don't know what to do anymore."

"I told you about my dad coming back. And the break-in."

I watch the red light, the people at the crosswalk. We're a few blocks away from school. I recognize a couple of girls from my team by their black-and-red uniforms. A woman dressed in all black trails behind them. She holds a cane that glints in the sunlight, and with every step, her jewelry swings from side to side. She wears dozens of necklaces made of glittering gems and wooden beads. She glances at us in the car, and I swear I've seen her before. For a flash, the dark stare takes me to a place of my nightmares. My skin is hot, and when I close my eyes, I picture the shadows reaching for me with their claws. I grip the car seat so my hands will stop shaking.

"I know you have family stuff," Maks says, thankfully unaware of my tiny freak-out. "I just—I'm not sure how to say it. You're not the same person you were two years ago."

Two years.

Maks and I have been dating for two years. That's two years of dates. Two years of *I love yous* and *I want you forevers*. Two years of going to sleep reading his messages, of hearing his voice just before I drifted off and dreaming about us together. Maks wasn't the first boy to tell me I was beautiful. But when he said it, when he kissed the inside of my wrist and wrote it over and over again, *You're beautiful. I love you*, I believed him.

I roll down the window. My scars burn and I flip down the sun visor and double check that Alex's canto is holding up. There I am. I look like the old me even if I don't feel like her.

Maks pulls into the school parking lot behind the gym and puts the car in park. He taught me how to parallel park even though I don't have my license. It's a weird memory, but it pops into my head as he unbuckles his seat belt and holds the steering wheel with a white-knuckle grip.

"Maks." My voice is small because I know what comes next.

He breathes in long and deep, as if to steady himself. "I think we should break up."

ABOUT THE AUTHOR

Zoraida Córdova is the author of The Vicious Deep trilogy, the On the Verge series, and *Labyrinth Lost*. She loves black coffee, snark, and still believes in magic. She is a New Yorker at heart and is currently plotting her next novel. Send her a tweet @Zlikeinzorro.